Shot Through the Book

Also available by Eva Gates

The Lighthouse Library Mysteries

The Stranger in the Library
Death Knells and Wedding Bells
Death by Beach Read
Deadly Ever After
A Death Long Overdue
Read and Buried
Something Read Something Dead
The Spook in the Stacks
Reading Up a Storm
Booked for Trouble
By Book or by Crook

Writing as Vicki Delany
Sherlock Holmes Bookshop Mysteries

The Incident of the Book in the Nighttime
The Sign of Four Spirits
The Game Is a Footnote
A Three Book Problem
A Curious Incident
There's a Murder Afoot
A Scandal in Scarlet
The Cat of Baskervilles
Body on Baker Street
Elementary, She Read

Year-Round Christmas Mysteries

A Slay Ride Together With You
Have Yourself a Deadly Little Christmas
Dying in a Winter Wonderland
Silent Night, Deadly Night
Hark the Herald Angels Slay
We Wish You a Murderous Christmas
Rest Ye Murdered Gentlemen

Ashley Grant Mysteries

Coral Reef Views
Blue Water Hues
White Sand Blues

Constable Molly Smith Mysteries

Unreasonable Doubt
Under Cold Stone
A Cold White Sun
Among the Departed
Negative Image
Winter of Secrets
Valley of the Lost
In the Shadow of the Glacier

Klondike Gold Rush Mysteries

Gold Web
Gold Mountain
Gold Fever
Gold Digger

Ray Robertson Mysteries

Blood and Belonging
Haitian Graves
Juba Good

Tea by the Sea Mysteries

Steeped in Malice
Trouble Is Brewing
Murder Spills the Tea
Murder in a Teacup
Tea & Treachery

Catskill Summer Resort Mysteries
Deadly Director's Cut
Deadly Summer Nights

Also Available by Vicki Delany

More Than Sorrow
Murder at Lost Dog Lake
Burden of Memory
Scare the Light Away
Whiteout

Shot Through the Book

A LIGHTHOUSE LIBRARY MYSTERY

Eva Gates

NEW YORK

This is a work of fiction. All of the names, characters, organizations, places and events portrayed in this novel are either products of the author's imagination or are used fictitiously. Any resemblance to real or actual events, locales, or persons, living or dead, is entirely coincidental.

Published in the United States by Crooked Lane Books, an imprint of The Quick Brown Fox & Company LLC.

Crooked Lane Books and its logo are trademarks of The Quick Brown Fox & Company LLC.

Library of Congress Catalog-in-Publication data available upon request.

ISBN (hardcover): 979-8-89242-044-0
ISBN (ebook): 979-8-89242-045-7

Cover design by Joe Burleson

Printed in the United States.

www.crookedlanebooks.com

Crooked Lane Books
34 West 27th St., 10th Floor
New York, NY 10001

First Edition: May 2025

10 9 8 7 6 5 4 3 2 1

To Mom

Chapter One

As a librarian, I rarely get work-related visitors calling at my home. As a member of the modern world, I rarely get drop-in visitors either.

Thus my surprise when I peered through the frosted glass window in the front hall, in response to the doorbell on a Tuesday evening in July, to see Todd Harrison standing on the step. I'd last seen Todd only a few hours ago, at a meeting at the library.

He saw my face in the window and gave me a slight wave and an apologetic smile.

I threw the lock and opened the door. "Todd, what are you doing here? How did you know where I live?"

"Everyone knows where you and the mayor live, Lucy." My cat, Charles, sniffed the man's shoes, but Todd paid him no attention. "I'm sorry for dropping in unannounced like this, but . . ." He shifted his feet and avoided my eyes. "But I was hoping to talk to you, privately I mean. When the meeting broke up, you were immediately called away, and then Rick wanted to talk to me about book numbers, so I didn't get the chance. Do you have a couple of minutes for me? I know it's late, and I promise not to take up much of your time."

I hesitated. I was home alone this evening as my husband, Connor, was at a dinner meeting in his role as mayor of our town, Nags Head, North Carolina. I'd met Todd for the first time earlier today, when he came to the library to discuss plans for the upcoming Lighthouse Library Young Adult Authors Festival sponsored by the Bodie Island Lighthouse Library, where I work, the town of Nags Head, and Outer Banks Books.

As I headed for the meeting room earlier, I'd been waylaid by an elderly patron simply wanting someone to chat with. Providing community support is an important but unadvertised part of a public library's function, so I stayed to talk, making me late for the meeting. When I did come in, all apologies, I'd been hastily introduced to the only person in the room I didn't know, Todd Harrison. He gave me a broad smile, shook my hand, and told me he was pleased to get the chance to help promote literature in the community and hopefully reach a new audience of eager youthful readers. Todd was a bestselling YA author, recently moved to the Outer Banks. His books were popular with our younger patrons, but I'd never read one.

Surely, I thought now, *no one who writes books that have such an appeal to our teenage readers, could be a killer.*

I stepped back and said, "My husband is on his way home," which was a lie, but never mind that. "I'm not doing anything important."

Todd came into my house. He was in his early forties, short at about five foot six, thin to the point of verging on scrawny. Brown hair cut short, long narrow face with sunken cheeks, and dark eyes under round, frameless eyeglasses. He wore jeans that didn't show signs of much wear, and a buttoned pink shirt tucked into a thin brown belt. He nervously scraped his clean shoes on the rug by the door and stepped further inside. "Nice house," he said. "This is one of the Unpainted Aristocracy, isn't it?"

"It is." I was hugely proud of our house, a true piece of Nags Head history, restored and renovated by my husband, his father, and me. Although my part had been severely limited by the fact that what I know about ripping up flooring and installing dry wall and rewiring an old house is so little as to be dangerous. My part mostly consisted of making lunch and tea and running to the hardware store for emergency supplies.

"Do you know when it was built?" Todd asked.

"1923."

"Nice."

We stood in the front hall for a moment in an awkward silence. Finally, I said, "It's a pleasant evening. Would you like to sit outside on the deck? I always enjoy watching the beach settle down at the end of the day."

"Yes, yes, that would be nice. Thank you. I promise not to take up much of your time," he repeated.

Charles lifted his fluffy tail and led the way down the hallway, past the kitchen, and through the living room. He was a Himalayan, masses of brown and tan fur, intelligent blue eyes in a black face, pert black ears; a hefty eight pounds of fur and attitude.

"Very nice, very nice," Todd said again. "I'd love to talk to you at some length about this house and the others like it. I'm fascinated by OBX history, and I'm trying to find a way to incorporate it into one of my books someday. But considering the sort of stuff I write, that won't be easy." An awkward laugh.

"I'd be happy to chat with you," I said. "When we first bought the house and began making plans for the renovations, I read up on the history. It's fascinating."

The Unpainted Aristocracy is a collection of early twentieth-century houses, once mostly used as summer retreats for people fleeing the heat of the inland cities. So called because the cedar shingle siding has never been painted; the wood allowed to mellow with the effects of time and sea air. The design is traditional: two stories, wrap-around covered porch on three sides, hinged shutters to keep the harsh sunlight out but admit cooling sea breezes, vitally important in those pre–air conditioning days. This house had not been lived in for a number of years before we bought it, and it was falling into disrepair. Connor and I spent a lot of time talking about what we wanted to do to the house before work began, and we'd achieved exactly what we wanted: keeping as much of the traditional design as possible while making badly needed modern updates, such as to the kitchen.

I didn't think this nervous man had come to my home in the evening to talk about my house. But, for lack of anything else to talk about until he told me why he was here, I chattered on. We reached the door leading from the living room to the deck overlooking the wide beach and the open ocean beyond. I bent over, scooped up Charles with one hand, and slid open the sliding door with the other. Fresh, salty sea air drifted in, propelled by a light breeze coming off the waters.

"Would you like a glass of tea?" I asked. "I have some in the fridge." I'm from Boston originally, although I spent many of my childhood summers on the Outer Banks, visiting my mother's sister and her family. I married into a true Banker (what residents of the Outer Banks call themselves) family, and I was trying hard to fit into my new life. Offering a guest a glass of icy tea on a warm and humid summer's evening seemed to be the proper thing to do.

"That would be nice," Todd said. "Thank you." His accent was from North Carolina, but slightly toned down, as though he'd spent a lot of years away.

"Be right back," I said as my guest went out onto the deck. I flicked the light switch to the deck and carried the big cat into the kitchen. Charles would want to come outside with me, and that meant struggling to get the harness and leash on him. We'd been living in this house for almost two years, and Charles still refused to accept that he couldn't run wild across the sand dunes in pursuit of seagulls and sandpipers.

I plopped him onto the top of his cat tree and foolishly said, "Stay." Charles isn't the only one who refuses to accept that some things are not worth arguing about.

While I got the pitcher of tea out of the fridge, ice out of the freezer, two glasses down from the cupboard, and a tray out of a drawer, I tried to guess why Todd would want to talk to me privately. I was the assistant director at the library, in charge of arranging special events, such as the Young Adult Authors Festival, but if anything needed to be said about that in private, I didn't want to know.

Besides, I wasn't the one responsible for arranging guest authors, artists, and musicians for the festival; most of those details were being handled by our children's librarian, Ronald Burkowski.

This afternoon's meeting had gone well. Everything seemed to be under control. Todd would be the headliner, with two lesser-known YA authors also speaking and reading. A local band, who mostly played at weddings and had a good handle on popular pop songs, would provide the music. The local bookstore would sell the guest authors' works. As it was intended to be a family event, and we hoped younger children would come also, we'd arranged for a face painter and a clown who made fanciful animals out of balloons. A bakery booth would be on hand to offer refreshments to eager festivalgoers. And equally eager library staff and festival volunteers.

The only reason Todd might want to speak to me in private would be if he'd decided to drop out. Which seemed not only to be rather a dramatic change after his enthusiasm this afternoon but also something that could be done by phone or email.

If that was the case, no reason for him to be nervous about telling me. People's schedules change all the time, as I well know from hosting numerous other events. As long as they didn't wait to tell us they wouldn't make it as we were throwing the doors open, we could adapt on the fly.

I picked up the laden tray. Charles's tail twitched as he watched me. "Stay!" I ordered again.

He jumped down and followed me out of the kitchen.

The lamp over the door to the deck threw a circle of bright yellow light onto Todd, who'd taken a seat at the glass-topped patio table. His back was to the house, so he faced the sea. Our house sits next to the public beach. It's just a couple of steps down the deck stairs to the soft sand. In the east, over the ocean, it was full dark now, stars beginning to appear in the sky and lights from small charter boats moving slowly as they headed for the safety of harbor. The sun was setting in the west, and the shadows thrown by the houses along the beach were long. The surf murmured softly as it rushed toward land. Only a handful of people strolled along the shoreline; no one splashed about in the water, and the day's fishermen had folded up their chairs, pulled in their lines, collected their empty coolers, and headed for home.

I hoped Todd would hear me coming and hold the door for me, but he didn't move. I wasn't entirely surprised. The view from our deck of a summer's evening is mesmerizing.

I kicked at the door, but Todd didn't move.

I looked down at Charles. His wicked little face looked up at me.

"Aren't you going to open that door," he seemed to say.

I put the tray on a side table, picked up the cat, and slid open the door while Charles tried to free himself from my grip. "Can you give me a hand here, please, Todd."

He didn't move.

"Please?" I repeated.

Instead of getting to his feet, Todd began to slowly topple to one side. His chair tipped, spilling him out. He fell to the wooden planks of the deck without making a sound, and there he lay, staring up into the dark sky, unmoving.

I forgot Charles and I forgot the tea. I ran onto the deck and fell to my knees next to Todd. I reached for him, assuming he'd simply lost his balance, and the chair had been unsteady.

Instead, I jerked back, shocked to my core.

His eyes were open wide, a dark red stain spreading rapidly across the front of his pink shirt.

A long metal shaft was firmly implanted into the center of his chest.

Chapter Two

I stared at Todd's unseeing eyes. I stared at the shaft buried deep into his chest. I didn't know what to do: Should I try to pull it out or leave it where it was?

I dropped to my knees next to him. Blood continued to leak onto his shirt, but the pace was already slowing. I touched the side of his neck. Nothing moved beneath my fingers.

My attention elsewhere, Charles came onto the deck after me. Rather than leaping off the railings in search of birds to play with, he rubbed his face into my arm. I stroked the soft fur, grateful for the support of his small but sturdy body.

Was whoever had done this still here? Were they watching me?

I scrambled to my feet, heart pounding, still clinging to Charles. I looked around us, but I could see no one hiding in the shadows of the house, waiting to leap out at me. The deck offered no place for anyone larger than a cat to conceal themself. The table was glass; no one was hiding beneath it. I held my breath and peered into the shadows, listening for the settling of a board on the covered porches running down either side of the house or movement beneath the pilings. All was quiet.

Then I saw it: an arrow stuck into the boards near the door frame, still quivering. The shaft was silver-colored metal, at least twenty-four inches long, the fletching red and green. The point must be deadly sharp to imbed itself so deeply. The fletching and shaft appeared to be the same as on the arrow that struck Todd.

Other than a scattering of people by the water, no one was on the beach. No one seemed to be paying me any attention. No trees or large shrubs were planted on this side of the house. Nowhere for an attacker to find concealment.

I saw no one running away, no one tossing a bow to one side. A couple of cars drove slowly down the road on the other side of the house. Nothing unusual about that at this time of night. In the house immediately to my left, all the lights were off. Our house was the last one on this stretch of the road; to the right, nothing but sand dunes and beach grasses for miles.

I'd been reading in the living room, waiting up for Connor, when the doorbell rang. I grabbed my phone off the side table before answering the bell, likely just through sheer habit.

I pulled it out of my skirt pocket now and dialed 911 with shaking fingers. It rang once and was answered. As I spoke, I took Charles into the house. As much as the big cat would enjoy watching all the activity when the first responders arrived, he would be seriously in their way.

* * *

"I heard nothing. I saw nothing. I know nothing." I was sitting on a stool in my thoroughly modern kitchen, a mug of hot, heavily sugared tea at my elbow. I've found that in a crisis, iced tea doesn't cut it.

My poor husband arrived home to see police cars and an ambulance parked in front of our house. Blue and red lights breaking the night, doors slamming, people shouting out orders or asking what was going on, neighbors gathered on their porches and balconies or standing on the sidewalk. He couldn't even park in our driveway, but left his car half in the middle of the road, with the engine running, and ran. "What's happening?" he yelled at the officer guarding the door.

"Don't know, Mr. Mayor," the cop said. "Mrs. McNeil called 911 to say someone was dead."

Connor almost fainted in relief. If I'd called 911, then I couldn't be the dead one.

I learned all that much later, when at last everyone had packed up their equipment; Todd Harrison had been taken away; and we'd been allowed to collapse gratefully into our own bed.

But before that happened, we had a long night ahead of us.

I'd put Charles, protesting loudly, into the bedroom, met the police and medics at the front door, and showed them to the deck. I stood in the living room, watching through the wide windows while first the police and then the paramedics checked on Todd.

"Lucy," said a deep voice behind me, "come away from the window."

I turned to see Officer Butch Greenblatt, a good friend of Connor and mine, standing behind me. He was in uniform, and the radio at his shoulder emitted a stream of incomprehensible static. His handsome face was, as always, kind and concerned; his six-foot-five, two-hundred-pound-plus bulk, reassuring. "Why don't you wait in the kitchen? The detective's been called and he's on his way."

I nodded and pointed behind me. "Is he—?"

"Looks like it," Butch said. "Can I get you a glass of water or some tea?"

I glanced at the tea tray I'd prepared for my guest, still sitting on the side table, and swallowed heavily. "No. I mean, no thank you."

And then Connor was there, his arms around me, murmuring soft words into my always-out-of-control curly black hair. I'm five foot three, and Connor's around six feet; it is nice being held by him. He's in his mid-thirties, a year older than I am, and strikingly handsome, with thick dark hair inclined to curl slightly in the damp air, sharp cheekbones, gorgeous blue eyes, and an infectious smile.

I reluctantly pulled myself out of his arms and looked up at him. He was not smiling now. "I don't know what happened. I was getting us tea. I was worried that Charles would—"

"Later," Connor said. "Let's get out of these people's way."

Detective Sam Watson found Connor, Butch, and me in the kitchen. He looked between Connor and me, and then he said, "You okay, Lucy? Do you need to go to the hospital?"

"I'm fine. Nothing happened to me. I don't know—"

"Let me have a quick look outside," Watson said. "Then I'll be back to hear what you have to say."

Connor got up and followed him out, but Butch stayed. I'd seen Watson give him a small nod, clearly telling him to remain with me. Had he been ordering Butch to comfort me or to guard me?

To guard me from being attacked or to keep me from fleeing the scene?

From the hallway came the sounds of men and women streaming into our house, carrying equipment, issuing orders, talking among themselves. I didn't hear the wheels of an ambulance stretcher. If Todd hadn't been rushed to the hospital, that could only be because . . . I swallowed.

Butch gave me what he probably thought was an encouraging grin. "We haven't seen you guys for a while," he said, making polite, friendly conversation. "Steph wants to have you around for dinner, but you know how things get."

"Busy, busy," I said. Stephanie Stanton was Butch's girlfriend, and also a close friend of mine.

Watson and Connor returned. Connor went to the fridge and got himself a bottle of beer. He didn't offer anything to our "guests."

"Connor says he doesn't recognize that man," Watson said. "Do you know who he is, Lucy?"

I nodded. "His name—" I cleared my throat and tried again. "His name is Todd Harrison. He's an author of YA—young adult—books who recently moved to OBX. He was at the library this afternoon for a meeting about the YA authors festival we're putting on next month."

"And?" Connor prompted. He stood behind my stool, his strong warm hands resting on my shoulders.

"And nothing. I don't know anything more about him. I was late for the meeting, so I missed the opening round of introductions. He was briefly introduced to me when I got there, and then we went on to discuss details of the event. And that's it."

"Why was he here tonight?" Watson asked.

I shook my head. "I don't know. I was surprised to see him at the door. He said he was hoping to get the chance to talk to me privately, but he didn't say what about. I told him to take a seat on the deck while I went to get the drinks. When I came out—when Charles and I came out, I found him . . . I mean, I found Todd, not Charles."

"Take your time, Lucy," Watson said.

Connor pressed his fingers harder into my shoulders. I leaned back against them. I closed my eyes. I tried to remember exactly what had happened. But that was rather the point: from my perspective, nothing had happened. "When I came out with the drinks, he was in a chair, not moving. Then he just sort of . . . fell over. I ran to him, thinking he'd fainted or had a spell or something. Instead . . ."

"Instead, indeed," Watson said.

I looked up in time to see Watson and Butch exchange looks.

From the bedroom, Charles informed us that he appeared to have been accidentally locked in.

"I know it's hard, Lucy, but tell me what you saw when you reached the body."

"Like I said, he just fell over, taking the chair with him. He didn't move again. Something was stuck in his chest, and he was bleeding—a lot—from that spot. I didn't see anyone. No one on the beach, not nearby, anyway. No one on the deck or hiding in the shadows or running away. Another arrow, which looked the same, was stuck into the house by the door. Did you see it?"

"I did."

"It looked . . . unused? Not that I know precisely what an arrow looks like, other than from movies like Robin Hood. It's a hot night, so he was naturally just wearing a light shirt."

"One arrow hit him?" Watson asked.

"I only saw the one point of injury."

"Another was embedded in the wall."

I sucked in a breath, and the men all turned to look at me. "You don't think the other arrow . . . was intended for me?"

"You say you weren't on the deck at the time, Lucy." Watson gave me a reassuring smile. "So, no, I'd say it's highly unlikely it was meant for you. I'm inclined to think either a warning shot or a miss."

"Guy was a good shot, then," Connor said. "If he only needed two tries to hit what was presumably his target."

"Or a lucky one," Butch said. "Or an unlucky one, if it wasn't intended. What was the light like out there, Lucy?"

"Good question," Watson said. "The deck light is on now. Did you turn it on when you called 911?"

I thought for a moment. "No. I switched it on when I showed Todd outside and told him to take a seat while I got the drinks. It was almost full dark out then, so we needed the light. It's nice out there at this time of night. Darkness setting, beach going quiet."

"He would have made a good target," Connor said. "Sitting out there, lit up by the light above him as though he was on stage."

"You didn't see anyone carrying a bow and arrow walking past the house?" Watson asked me. "Either earlier tonight or when you found this man on the deck?"

"No," I said. "I would have mentioned that."

"Such a thing would be rather obvious, wouldn't you think?" Connor said.

"As Lucy said, it was almost full dark on the beach at that time," Watson said. "Not many folks around. Everyone minding their own business. Have you ever seen anyone practicing archery out on the beach? Kids maybe?"

"No," Connor said.

"Me neither," I said.

"If someone did see someone carrying an archery kit, depending on how bulky it was, they might have thought it was a kite rolled up," Butch said. "Or a kid's game. Fishing gear even, if they didn't look closely."

"I've got officers searching the beach," Watson said, "and checking with your neighbors."

"The people next door aren't home," Connor said. "They mostly only come down on the weekends."

"The victim's wallet was in his pocket—driver's license, credit cards, and all the rest," Watson said. "His phone. Plus, the keys to a car parked out front. Was he married, do you know?"

"I don't know. Like I said, I don't know anything at all about him other than what I told you. Ronald suggested him as a guest speaker at the festival, so he likely will have more information for you. Someone would have invited him to the meeting this afternoon, probably Ronald. It wasn't me."

"Who else was at this meeting?"

"You can't think his death had anything to do with a teenage book festival?" I asked.

"Until I know way more than I do now, I have to consider that anything and everything might have something to do with what happened here. You know how this works, Lucy."

Unfortunately, I did. I've been involved in police cases before, although never willingly. "Ronald Burkowski, Louise Jane McKaughnan, and me, representing the library. Shannon McKinnah and Ruth Vivac, local YA writers; Lorraine Kittleman, who will be providing music with her band. They played at our wedding—do you remember her?"

"I do," Watson said.

"Rick Black from the bookstore in town. The purpose of the meeting was to finalize the agenda for the day."

"I don't suppose," Connor said, "you know if any of the people who attended this meeting are archers?"

"Not that I know of," I said. "The subject didn't come up. I'm sure I would have remembered if it had."

"You have no idea as to what this Harrison wanted to talk to you about?" Watson asked. "Privately? With such urgency he couldn't wait to phone you in the morning?"

"I've not the slightest idea, Sam. He gave me no hint."

Chapter Three

"Not the slightest idea," I said to my colleagues the following morning.

"Weird," Louise Jane said.

"Very weird," Ronald agreed.

"An arrow, like the sort fired from a bow?" Louise Jane said. "Robin Hood and all that?"

"I don't know what sort of implement was used. Presumably a bow, but what I saw looked like an arrow, yes."

"Are Shannon and Ruth capable of being our festival headliners, Ronald?" my boss, the ever-practical Bertie James asked.

"They're both competent writers, but they're not the sort of draw Todd Harrison was," Ronald said. "He's a big name in that world. *Was*, I suppose I should say. Weird."

The morning news on the radio reported the death of the "*New York Times* bestselling author and local resident," and mentioned the police were regarding the death as "suspicious." Nothing specifically had been said about where it happened, but that wasn't any sort of a secret, as ambulances, police cruisers, and forensic vans had been parked outside our house last night, with all the attention that means. The police hadn't kept it under wraps that Todd Harrison had been shot with an arrow likely fired from an archery bow. Instead, they were asking anyone who'd seen someone with archery equipment in the general area of the southern Nags Head beaches to come forward.

I arrived at work, about fifteen minutes before the library opened for the day, to find Louise Jane, Ronald, and Bertie gathered in the main room, already discussing the situation, and I reluctantly told them what I knew. The lights were all on, the computers booted up, the welcome scent of fresh-brewed coffee drifting down the hallway.

As usual, I'd brought Charles to work with me. I put the cat carrier on the desk and opened the door. A ball of tan and white fur soared across the desk, tumbled to the floor, and Charles began sniffing under the shelves and in the corners, presumably checking for signs of overnight rodent activity.

Charles takes his library duties seriously.

Ronald is our children's librarian, and today he wore a bright yellow tie featuring a cartoon drawing of Bugs Bunny. He's a short man in his forties, with a mane of wild gray locks that almost put my curls to shame. His life's passion is books and helping children read. Ronald's been called the best children's librarian in the state, and that is not an exaggeration.

Louise Jane is just about Ronald's opposite. Tall, thin, almost bony, with huge brown eyes above sharp cheekbones and a pointed chin. She wore her regular work clothes of dark pants and a dark blouse with practical sneakers. Today she had on a pair of silver earnings and the thin sliver bracelet she'd worn every day since returning from her most recent trip to France.

Louise Jane's passion in life is the history of the Outer Banks, and that passion sometimes veers into the not-entirely-historically-accurate, as she considers herself to be one of a long line of women particularly sensitive to the supernatural.

Bertie's passions are libraries and yoga. Today she wore a swirling, multicolored summer dress that reached her calves. Her long gray hair was loosely piled at the back of her head. This early in the day, it hadn't yet started coming out of its pins.

"The meeting about the festival wrapped up shortly before five," I said. "I didn't linger to say goodbye, as a patron was wanting to talk to me, but Todd left at the same time as the others, didn't he?"

"I walked them to the door," Ronald said. "I didn't wait to see if they immediately got in their cars and drove away."

"Lorriane left early, as I recall," Louise Jane said. "Around quarter of five. Something about a doctor's appointment."

"Todd showed up at my house at nine. Might he have come back here after hours? Louise Jane did you see him or his car?"

"I left right after closing to have dinner with my grandmother at her residence. Doing my weekly duty. We played a couple of hands of gin after dinner, and I got back here about eight. I didn't see any signs of Todd Harrison having been here after he left, or anyone trying to get in." Louise Jane lives in the lighthouse tower itself, in a tiny but comfortable apartment I've always called the Lighthouse Aerie. "I might mention that the sum total of what I owe Grandma from our weekly gin games so far this year currently stands at seven hundred and eighty dollars. And sixty-five cents. You're not paying me enough, Bertie."

"I'll mention that to the board," our boss said.

"Todd didn't try to contact me," Ronald said. "He had my phone number, if he'd wanted to."

"I wonder what could possibly have happened in those four hours that made him decide he needed to talk to you," Bertie said. "Privately. Something that couldn't wait until morning."

"Not necessarily over those four hours," I said. "I've been racking my brains trying to remember everything that happened, or was said, in the short time he was at my house, and I believe he said something about wanting to talk to me after the meeting, but he didn't get the chance."

"Weird," Louise Jane said.

"Did anything seem to be bothering him when he was here?" Bertie asked. "Did he have any issues or express any concerns at the meeting?"

Three heads shook. "Not at all," Ronald said. "It was a highly congenial meeting. Everyone got on well and everyone left happy. I thought so, anyway. I mean, I didn't know the man, so I can't say what something on his mind would have looked like."

"It seemed to me he wasn't paying all that much attention," Louise Jane said, "particularly not when we got to matters other than him. But that seemed normal to me. He must have been to plenty of these things over the years he's been writing. He knows the drill."

Ronald nodded. "Mildly distracted sometimes, perhaps. But nothing I can put my finger on and all natural enough when we talked over some of the finer details of the event."

"You approached the writers with the invitation to be part of the festival," I said. "Did you get the feeling Shannon or Ruth resented Todd being the main draw?"

"More the opposite. They're lesser-known authors, almost complexly unknown outside of this part of the state, so they were pleased with the chance to reach readers new to them who would come specifically to meet a major name like Todd."

"Anyone not invited who might now be in the running?" Louise Jane asked. "Considering the position is now available, so to speak."

"You don't think someone killed him for a chance to be in our literary festival?" I asked.

"People have killed for all sorts of strange reasons," Louise Jane said.

"I have thought of one thing," Ronald said. "Might mean something or not. I told them we were waiting for you to join us before getting the meeting started, and Todd asked what your position is here. And—"

"And," Louise Jane said, "Ruth said you're the library's resident amateur sleuth. We all laughed politely, but Todd seemed to take her seriously. He asked what that meant."

"Ruth told him you've been of help to the police on occasion," Ronald said. "Todd and Shannon write fantasy, but Ruth's books are amateur sleuth mysteries: teenagers solving crimes in their high school. She made a comment about how she shouldn't bother trying to come up with ideas, she should just follow you around."

I groaned. "You don't think he wanted to consult with me? I hope one of you told him, I am not the Outer Banks version of Miss Marple or Sherlock Holmes."

"'Fraid we didn't get the chance," Louise Jane said. "At that moment you came in, introductions were made, and the meeting got started."

"Any further speculation will have to wait," Bertie said, "It's almost nine thirty. Time to throw open the doors once again to eager literary enthusiasts."

"What are we going to do about the festival?" Louise Jane asked. "Should we cancel?"

"I wouldn't like to do that," Ronald said. "Some of the kids, and their parents, are looking forward to it."

"You three talk it over," Bertie said. "I'll leave it up to you to decide. Personally, I think we should go ahead." She headed down the hall to her office.

Ronald, Louise Jane, and I looked at one another. "We need to talk," I said.

"We do." Ronald pointed to the windows. "But not now. I see a car heading our way, and I have a parent and baby group arriving in half an hour. I don't have any programs scheduled between noon and three today."

"Denise will be in at noon," Louise Jane said, referring to her direct boss, our academic librarian. "So, I can get away."

"Lunch meeting at one then," I said, and we went our separate ways.

Chapter Four

Shortly before noon, Detective Sam Watson came into the library. He gave me a smile, but I could tell by the heaviness in his eyes, the stubble on his chin, and the weakness of that smile that he hadn't had much, if any, sleep last night. Watson was no longer a young cop, and the long hours were wearing on him. Whispers of pending retirement were in the air, but I'd heard nothing concrete about that. "Got a minute, Lucy?" he asked me.

High-pitched voices drifted down the stairs from the children's library on the second floor. Toddlers' story hour was about to get out. A few patrons browsed the stacks, but otherwise, on a sunny Wednesday in July, the library wasn't at all busy. But at the sound of the detective's voice at least one head popped around the shelves, and I noticed the woman sitting in the comfortable wing-back chair in the magazine nook shift in her seat, positioning her ear so it was pointing in our direction.

"Sure," I said. "Let me get someone to watch the desk. Maureen!"

Today's volunteer from our Friends of the Library group was shelving returns, and she came at my call.

"Can you take the desk for a while, please?" I asked her.

Maureen Peterson was one of our most dedicated patrons. She'd haunted, figurately speaking, the children's library for years, determined to use Ronald as the personal librarian for her five daughters. She could be difficult, demanding, and opinionated, but I always forgave her because at heart all she wanted was to nurture a love of reading and of literature in those daughters, although sometimes, her pushiness threatened to have the opposite effect.

The girls were getting older now, the eldest having finished her first year of college. They were branching out in their friendship circles and in their reading and sports interests and activities, less dependent on their parents to bring them to library events or story time, so Maureen joined the library volunteers' group in order to remain involved. She was an enthusiastic and eager volunteer, although she did tend to have some strongly expressed ideas about how we could improve things. Ideas that usually involved spending money we didn't have.

"Happy to." She straightened her eyeglasses and tucked a piece of unruly black and gray hair into the clip at the back of her head. "Good morning, Detective Watson. I heard about that awful business last night. Such a tragedy. Primrose—you know Primrose of course—my second girl, she's simply beside herself. She was so looking forward to the festival and hearing Todd speak. I offered to introduce her to Todd myself, personally. Wouldn't want to take advantage of my position here at the library—oh no, I'd never do that—but in this case I thought no harm. Of course, at sixteen, Primrose is always beside herself about one thing or another. And then, by lunchtime it's the another. Do you . . . have any knowledge of what happened?"

"The investigation is underway," Watson said as by rote. "An arrest is expected imminently."

"That's good to hear. I hate to think people of the stature and importance of Todd Harrison can be . . . uh . . ." She floundered around for a suitable word. "Felled on our beaches," she concluded.

"I won't be long," I said. "Call me if any problems come up."

"I'm sure they won't." I felt Mrs. Peterson's curious eyes on my back as Watson and I crossed the floor of the main library and turned into the hallway leading to the restrooms, offices, and staff break room.

"Is an arrest imminent? I asked Watson.

"We'll get there. Eventually, if not imminently," he said.

"I have no doubt about that. Have a seat. Can I get you a glass of water or tea? There might be some coffee still in the pot, although I can't testify as to how long it's been there."

"A glass of tea would be nice—thanks, Lucy." He sat down while I poured his drink, and then I took the seat across the table from him and waited for him to speak.

"About last night," he said after taking a long drink.

"I assumed that's why you're here."

He rubbed his tired face. "Do you have anything to add to the statement you gave us last night? Remember anything new?"

"I would have called you if I had. I didn't see anything, didn't hear anything, and I still have absolutely no idea why Todd Harrison came to see me, never mind why someone would . . . do what they did. I asked Ronald and Louise Jane if they knew what he wanted to talk to me about, and they didn't. He didn't, far as they know, try to contact either of them after the meeting. Did you find what was used to kill him?"

"We did. Searchers located an archery bow in a patch of seagrass not far from your house, just off the path that circles back around the dunes to the road. It's been identified to me as a compound bow. Often used for hunting. No prints on it. No identifiable marks. We're trying to determine where it might have been purchased, but it's not an uncommon item, and it's readily available, even online. Serial numbers on bows of that sort are easily removed, and that seems to have been done to this one. I have officers contacting archery clubs all over this part of the state, but there are more of those than I would have guessed. I don't know much about archery. I don't suppose you do, Lucy?"

"Only from watching Robin Hood movies or *the Lord of the Rings.* Did this person have to be an accomplished and experienced archer? They hit what was likely their target with their second shot. Unless you found other arrows scattered about?"

"We didn't, no. I'll be asking the people who know about these things as to the amount of skill required. At a guess, if the person was standing not too far from Harrison, they might not have needed to be Olympic class. We found a patch of scuffed footprints indicating they might not have been more than twenty or so yards away from your deck when they took the shot."

I shuddered. "Can you tell anything from the footprints?"

"Hard to take definitive prints off dry sand as it's always shifting, particularly if there's a wind, and there was a light one last night. Standard sneakers. Average size for a man. A bit on the large size for a woman, but nothing out of the ordinary. Larger than yours, if it matters."

"I'm glad to hear it." Instinctively I crossed my feet under the table.

"What remained of the treads was indistinct, likely worn down by regular use. As a lot of people's sneakers are."

I thought of my own shoes. I kept meaning to get new ones, but never seemed to find the time to go shopping.

"I called Ronald this morning, asking how he heard about this Todd Harrison and if they'd met before. Ronald says no. He only knows the man through his work—his books are stocked in the library. He'd heard Harrison and his wife had recently moved to Nags Head, so he had the idea of inviting him to the festival. Harrison's appearance was arranged through the publicist at his publishers."

"His wife. Have you spoken to her?"

Watson sipped his tea. He nodded. "I paid a call on her last night. Name of Heather. Heather Harrison. Do you recognize the name?"

"Not offhand, no. How did she seem?"

"Distraught. Not accepting what I had to say at first. Those calls are never easy, Lucy. She told me Todd grew up around here, went to Raleigh for college, which is where they met. After graduation, they moved to New York City when he got a job as a technical writer for an insurance company. Last year, Todd started talking about moving back to his roots, and she agreed. They've been here about nine months."

"What does she do?"

Watson hesitated.

"Sam?"

"She's a journalist. Temporarily unemployed, so she tells me, as a result of the move."

"Plenty of unemployed journalists around these days," I said. "Does Todd have other family here?"

"She says no. He has one sibling in Phoenix, but he's had little to no contact with him, and his parents also live in Arizona now." He finished his drink and put down the glass. His eyes slid to one side, making me wonder why he was acting so uncharacteristically hesitant in talking to me. More than once Detective Sam Watson has tossed around theories regarding his cases with me. I'm not usually much help, but I get the feeling he likes using me as a sounding board.

"I should tell you, Lucy," he said at last, "it has been pointed out to me that what we know of the exact timing of last night's events is only what was related by you. No one that we can locate so far saw Todd Harrison in the hours preceding his death, and no one noticed what time he parked his car outside your house. You would have been able to"—he cleared his throat and looked slightly embarrassed, if that were possible—"lure Todd Harrison onto your deck, go inside under the pretext of getting the drinks, grab a bow and a couple of arrows, run out the kitchen door and around the house to the beach, fire, dash across the dunes to throw away the bow, get back to the house through the kitchen door, and then walk out bringing the drinks."

"Huh?"

"Such a possibility was mentioned."

"Mentioned by who? By *whom*, I should say."

"I can't tell you that, but I can tell you I am not seriously considering it as being likely."

"In my own defense, if I need one, I've never picked up a bow and arrow in all my life."

"That's good to know," he said. I looked for humor in his eyes, but I didn't find it.

"Is that why you pointed out my feet are too small to have made those prints?" I asked. He didn't reply.

I've been involved in police cases before, and I like to think Sam Watson and I have a good relationship. I like to think he likes and even respects me and my judgment. But I was well aware that if he had reason to suspect me, he wouldn't hesitate to investigate fully.

Fortunately, the scenario he'd so reluctantly outlined was preposterous.

Wasn't it?

"We found your personal cell phone number in Harrison's contact list. Do you know why he had it?"

"Nothing mysterious about that. At the meeting we all exchanged phone numbers. Standard practice when planning an event, in case someone has a last-minute emergency."

"He didn't call you? Maybe to arrange a time to come to the house? You didn't miss a call from him?"

"No and no."

He pushed his chair back and stood up. "Thank you for the tea."

"I don't suppose there's any possibility this was a random thing? Someone out to make trouble just because they could, and they saw a man sitting alone under a bright light, otherwise surrounded by darkness, and acted on impulse?"

"I'm not eliminating the idea. Harrison was a good and clear target to anyone on that beach. I've heard of nothing similar happening recently, so at this time I'm not considering such to be a strong possibly. It might have even been an accident, someone out fooling around who fired at a shape and then ran off in panic when they realized they'd hit a person. Again, unlikely. Hard to mistake a grown man for a seagull, no matter what the light."

I stood up. Watson headed for the door, and then he stopped and turned around. "I'm puzzled by why he came to your house at that time of night in the first place."

"As am I."

"His wife, Heather. Was she a patron here at the library?"

"I'll check our files, but the name isn't familiar. Not at the library or anywhere else I can think of."

"He specifically said he wanted to talk to you, Lucy? Not to Connor?"

"People do occasionally show up at the house to see Connor. Usually, they have some gripe or another that they have to get off their chest *right now*. More than once they've been on their way home from the bar. But not in this case. Todd didn't even mention Connor. He said he wanted to talk to me in the library after the meeting, but I was busy, so he left."

Chapter Five

The festival planning committee reconvened in the staff breakroom at one. I'd brought my lunch from home today, and I spent a good part of the morning looking forward to the thick sandwich made with leftovers from the weekend's roast chicken slathered with a serious amount of mayonnaise. Ronald brought a salad packed in colorful layers in a glass jar. Louise Jane unwrapped a quarter of a baguette and a selection of creamy white cheeses and thinly sliced meats to create an impromptu charcuterie board.

"I can smell that cheese from here," Ronald said, helping himself to a jug of cold water from the fridge.

"All the best cheeses are stinky." Louise Jane cut herself a thick slice.

"Is that what they taught you in France?" I asked.

"Mais oui," she said.

"Speaking of France," Ronald asked as he took the top off his jar, "any more trips coming up?"

"Not on my part." Louise Jane gave me a broad wink. "I'm taking a few vacation days the week after the festival. Nothing in particular in mind. I'm thinking of going down the coast a bit. Maybe rent a small house on the beach. Have myself some alone time, you know."

"Last minute rentals in July on the beach cost a heck of a lot," Ronald said.

"Do they? I'm sure I can get something I can afford." She gave me another wink, which Ronald missed as he poured dressing from a small plastic bottle onto his salad.

Louise Jane had recently fallen madly in love with a man with a somewhat shady past. And a very shady present. He was American, but he spent most of his time in France, and she'd visited him there twice. If he was coming to the United States to see her, he'd be traveling under a fake name and passport and not showing his face, disguised or not, in Nags Head. Sam Watson still had questions for the man he knew as Tom Reilly. I owed Tom an enormous debt, so I certainly wasn't going to tell on him.

When Louise Jane came back from France after her first trip, full of the glow of new and requited love and a marvelous vacation, I wondered if she might be thinking of moving there permanently. But she told me late one night, when we were alone in the library, that her home and her family were in Nags Head. For now, a long-distance relationship would have to suffice.

I munched my sandwich. As good as expected. "The festival," I said, bringing us back to the matter at hand. "First question: Do we want to continue with it?"

"Yes," Ronald said.

"Yes." Louise Jane added a swipe of creamy blue and white cheese to a hunk of bread and popped a slice of sausage on top.

"Okay," I said. "To the matter at hand. Do we need to find a replacement for Todd Harrison?"

"Let's step back a moment," Louise Jane said. "What exactly happened last night at your place? Is there anything you didn't tell us earlier?"

"Nothing to tell. I don't know why he came to see me, and I don't know why someone killed him. We didn't even have much of a chance to talk about what was on his mind." Instead, I'd chattered on about the history of the Unpainted Aristocracy in general and our house in particular. I refused to blame myself for taking up the man's last few minutes with trivialities. He had come to me, unannounced, but he hadn't been forthcoming about what he wanted with me.

"Shot by an arrow. Weird way of getting rid of someone," Louise Jane said.

"Weird, but effective. No need to get close to the victim, as with a knife, and risk getting blood on you. No noise that would attract attention, as with a gun."

"Detective Watson phoned me this morning," Ronald said. "He wanted to know why and how I'd invited Todd to the festival. The man was a bestselling YA author, now living near here, so he was an obvious choice for our festival. All the arrangements were made through his publisher. I met him in person for the first time yesterday."

"First and last time," Louise Jane said. "Do you know anyone who practices archery?"

"No. Do you?"

"I've been thinking about that all morning, and I can't come up with anyone. I've been trying to recall if any previous incidents in these parts were committed by bow and arrow, but I'm blanking on that too. I'll keep investigating."

I said nothing to that. By "investigating," Louise Jane meant she was going to troll through centuries of Outer Banks history, hoping to find a paranormal presence who might be skilled in archery who might have had a grudge against Todd Harrison for some unknown reason.

"To continue," Ronald said. "I'd like to invite another author, yes. But Todd's going to be hard to replace. I didn't realize the size of his fan base until we started promoting the festival. Teenagers are planning to come from all over the state, and far beyond. *Were* planning, I should say. I doubt we can get another author of that popularity at the last minute."

"Why's he so popular?" Louise Jane asked. "Is he that good? I've never read anything by him."

Ronald shrugged. "His books are nothing special, as far as I'm concerned, anyway. Good enough, but not great. Definitely not outstanding. Who knows why some authors take off and some, just as good, don't? When it comes to YA fiction, the fan base just grows, like Topsy, and from there on it takes on a life of its own."

"Mrs. Peterson told me Primrose is distraught," I said. "Her word."

"I can believe that. Primrose in particular was beyond excited when she heard Todd Harrison was coming. Apparently, she's the president of his OBX fan club."

"If we can't find someone else of Todd's importance, what about just going with Shannon and Ruth?" I asked.

"I'd prefer not to. They're both competent writers, but they're with small publishers who have limited distribution, and not known outside of the Outer Banks. They won't be any kind of a draw around here. They do book launches at the bookstore whenever they have new books out, and everyone knows them."

"Everyone who lives around here," I said. "But that's not the only people we're aiming our festival at. We're hoping to get tourists and summer residents to come out, not just Bankers."

Ronald nodded in agreement.

"I could tell two stories," Louise Jane said. As a major component of her love of Outer Banks history, Louise Jane had developed some considerable skill as a storyteller and was widely recognized as such. For the festival, she was researching the tale of a Civil War era fourteen-year-old-girl who took control of the family fishing business when her father and older brothers went to war.

"Even with that, we'll need a recognized author," Ronald said. "Let me take care of finding someone. I'll start making calls this afternoon. Maybe I'm being overly pessimistic. It shouldn't be too hard to find an author who wouldn't mind spending a summer weekend in the Outer Banks, even at the last minute. I'll check with Rick at the bookstore, ask if has any ideas."

A knock sounded on the door, and without waiting to be invited, Shannon McKinnah came in. "Hi, there. Looks like I'm just in time. The woman at the desk told me you guys were back here. I heard what happened to Todd. About him dying, I mean. How awful was that? You never know, do you?"

"Nope," Louise Jane agreed.

"Anyway, I wanted to check whether the festival's still on. You are going ahead, right? I'm excited about it, and I've told absolutely everyone I know."

"We plan to continue with it, yes," Ronald said.

She clapped her hands. "Great. Who's going to replace Todd?" Shannon was in her early fifties, short and round, with makeup-free plump pink cheeks; cheerful blue eyes; and overly dyed blond hair, fastened at the back of her head with a big, sparkling clip. She wore navy-blue capris, a pink T-shirt, and flat white sandals.

"Still to be determined," Ronald said. "We have some options."

"Good. Good. Obviously, you need a major bestseller. You wouldn't want anyone who doesn't have the reach Todd Harrison did."

"Like I said," Ronald said, "we have options."

I glanced at him. His voice had turned uncharacteristically chilly.

Louise Jane gathered together her empty lunch wrappings and stood up. "Back to work time. Have you decided what book you're going to read from, Shannon?"

"Gosh, no. I keep changing my mind. Should I read the first in my series, to introduce it to new readers, or what I'm working on now, for my long-time fans, who want to hear what's coming next?" The author followed Louise Jane out the door.

I looked at Ronald. "What was that about? I detected an undercurrent there. Shannon doesn't think she should be the main attraction, does she?"

"She doesn't expect to be, no, and she's sensibly content to bask in the overflow from a big name. I'm guessing she came in because she's worried we'd decided to make Ruth the headliner."

"Would that be a problem?"

"For Shannon, yes. Those two positively hate each other. I once made the mistake of having both of them in for a summer preteen program. I'm surprised the kids weren't traumatized for life, the way those two just about knocked each other aside, never mind the constant stream of catty comments. Unfortunately, these days even preteens are alert to catty comments, and they knew what was going on. On the other hand, maybe that wasn't such a bad thing. It sure livened up the afternoon. The kids loved it, and most of them thought it was all an act. When drawing up the schedule for the day, I know better than to have them near the stage at the same time. They'll be separated by music from the band."

"Okay, I get it now. I thought they were unnaturally formal yesterday, considering they should know each other well, but they weren't out and out nasty."

"No need to be—as long as someone else is our festival headliner. But if we put Ruth or Shannon in the role, the other might get murder on her mind." Ronald's eyes opened wide when he realized what he'd said.

"But," I said, "neither of them were killed last night. Our bestselling author was."

And with that, the meeting was over.

* * *

I couldn't stop wondering why Todd Harrison wanted to talk to me so urgently he'd come to my home at night. I'd never met the man before yesterday. At the meeting he'd given no indication of having any particular interest in me, and I don't think he even addressed me directly after the initial greetings.

Before relieving Maureen Peterson of circulation desk duties, I went outside to make a phone call. I was boiling hot the minute I stepped out of the cool of the library. The big yellow sun resembled one found in children's drawings all over the world. Scarcely a breath of air stirred the tall reeds poking up from the marsh. The lighthouse in which our library is situated is located on a patch of marsh near Roanoke Sound and Blossie Creek, about ten miles from Nags Head. The highway runs between us and Cape Hatteras National Seashore, with the ocean beyond. The views from the top of the lighthouse tower are spectacular. The marsh is a popular place for birdwatchers and walkers, and a well-maintained boardwalk wends from the parking lot to the water. That lot was full of cars today, and I could see people slowly walking along the path or studying the treetops and the sky with binoculars. A couple of children burst out of a car, to run screaming with delight toward the boardwalk, as a flock of Canada geese flew overhead, the leaders calling to the sluggards to keep up.

I went around the building to find a patch of shade in which to make my calls. As I'd told Sam, at the festival planning meeting we exchanged phone numbers, and I called up Ruth Vivac first. She answered almost immediately.

"Hi, Ruth. It's Lucy from the library. Did you hear about Todd?"

"Oh, Lucy. Yes. I am absolutely beside myself. Hard to believe I was sitting directly opposite him yesterday, having such a lovely chat, and now . . . I was going to call Ronald later. Is the festival still on?"

"We hope so. Ronald's looking for someone to replace Todd."

"Not that anyone can replace Todd. I don't suppose Ronald gave you any idea of what he might do if a suitable candidate doesn't come up? Time's running out; we might have to go with what we have. You might not know this, Lucy, but I have extensive experience in public speaking, and I can easily speak and read for considerably longer than the time slot I was initially allotted. I was a teacher before taking early retirement to pursue my writing career, and I'm more than comfortable in front of an audience, particularly an audience of young people. Of course, that's if—"

"Ronald's handling the authors and the schedule. I'm leaving those decisions up to him."

"Of course. Just mentioning it. In case he asks for your opinion, that is."

"I'll bear all that in mind. I'm calling with a specific question. Yesterday, you, Shannon, and Rick left the library at the same time as Todd."

"That's right."

"Did you all get in your cars and drive away at the same time? I guess I'm asking if Todd lingered."

"You're investigating, Lucy! How marvelous. I told Todd you did that. He said it was interesting. Like something from a book."

"I'm not investigating. I'm just curious."

"In my books, I make the point that it's the natural curiosity of Tamerlane—she's my protagonist—which causes her to—"

"Tamerlane? Never mind. Todd?"

"We said goodbye, got in our cars, and drove away. I'm trying to remember exactly how it all happened, and I think Todd was first down the laneway. That's right. I was immediately behind him. He turned left, toward Nags Head, as did I. I didn't see where he went or where he turned off. Traffic was heavy with people returning to town after their day at the park or at the southern beaches."

"Did he say anything as you walked to your cars? Anything at all out of the ordinary, shall we say?"

"No, not to me, no. He walked with Rick. They talked about the number of Todd's books Rick should get in for the festival. I tried to tell Rick he's not ordering nearly enough of mine for the expected crowds but—"

"Thanks, Ruth," I said.

Shannon had been in the library only a short while ago, but I gave her a call next. I asked the same questions, and she gave me the same answers. She didn't know where Todd went once he drove away. She didn't talk to him on the short walk to their cars, except to say goodbye.

I was about to phone Rick at the bookstore, when a van drove up. I recognized it as one from a retirement home, bringing residents for their weekly supply of books and some assisted computer time, if they needed it. I put my phone away and went to greet them.

* * *

Outer Banks Books isn't far out of my way, so I decided to pop into the store on my way home rather than find the time to make a phone call during the busy afternoon.

It's a small but cheerful store located in a strip mall not far from my cousin Josie's bakery and café, between a nail salon and a tattoo parlor.

At yesterday's meeting Rick talked about the in-store and front window displays they planned to put up to promote the festival. I'd drawn up some posters and other publicity material to spread around town and use online, but I hadn't distributed them yet. I'd have to redo them; obviously, I couldn't use them now that Todd would no longer be appearing.

The big front windows of Outer Banks Books were normally bright and cheerful, full of books with colorful covers, a collection of puzzles or children's toys, maybe a backdrop showing people reading at the beach or kicking a ball around the sand. But today it had been changed into a tribute to Todd Harrison. The window was largely empty, with a plain white sheet serving as the backdrop, and nothing on display other than a small selection of books and a framed publicity photograph of the author on a side table next to a copy of his biggest book, his one *New York Times* bestseller. The picture was a good one, likely professionally taken, and recent. The photo had been taken from the waist up, showing the author in a black leather jacket standing against a background of an age-darkened brick wall. His arms were crossed over his chest, his unsmiling face dark and serious. I studied the photo for a while, looking for clues in his face, wondering why he'd sought me out. Finding no messages hidden there, I went inside the store.

The chimes over the door tinkled cheerily, and I stood still for a moment, breathing in the gorgeous scent of fresh paper and new books. I love bookstores almost as much as I love libraries. As well as a good selection of novels and nonfiction for all ages and tastes, Outer Banks Books sells puzzles and games, toys, stationery and greeting cards, magazines, and coloring books. Even book-related items, like Sherlock Holmes–themed socks, help to keep small, independent bookstores alive in these difficult times.

Rick Black himself was behind the counter while his assistant helped a customer in the children's section. Several people browsed the shelves. A stack of Todd Harrison books was piled on the main display table in the center of the store.

"Lucy, hi." Rick nodded to the books. "Terrible what happened."

"It is."

"I heard he was killed at your house. What was he doing calling on you at that time of night?"

"I have no idea, and that's what brought me here."

"I don't know how I can help with that, but regarding the festival, Ronald called me a short while ago and said you intend to go ahead. I'm good with that. He asked if I knew of an author who might be able to come at short notice, and I gave him a couple of names I think will work."

"Did Todd sell well here?" I indicated the display of his novels.

"Yeah, he did. Even better once he moved to Nags Head and word got around. He hadn't had a book out for more than two years, though, and popularity wanes, particularly in that world. YA fantasy, I mean."

I picked up the topmost book. The cover illustration was of a young woman with striking green eyes and dark hair tumbling almost to her waist. She wore a midnight-blue velvet gown adorned with jewels, and was sitting on an elaborate chair upholstered in red and gold, an unsheathed sword across her lap and a watchful, blue-eyed wolf at her side.

"That's the latest in his Frighteners series," Rick said. "Todd gave a talk here a couple of months ago. Later, when he was signing books for store stock, he told me he was finished with that series and was writing something he called groundbreaking and original."

"Did he finish it?"

"I don't know."

Chimes over the door tinkled again as more customers came in. A woman put an infant's board book on the counter, and Rick rang up the sale. When she'd left, I said, "As for why Todd Harrison came to my house: yesterday you left the library at the same time as he did. Did he say anything about where he was going next or what he might have been planning to do?"

"Nothing like that. We walked to our cars. He suggested I get extra copies of the first book in the Frighteners series in for the festival. I said I wanted to see what the number of attendees was likely going to be before placing the final order."

"Did anything seem to be bothering him?"

Rick glanced around. Seeing that no one was paying us any attention or in need of his help, he lowered his voice and said, "The news report said he might have been murdered. Is that true?"

"It's a possibility, yes."

"If anything was bothering him that might have led to his death, Lucy, he didn't show it. Not in front of me. No reason he should confide in me. We got on fine the few times he came in here, but we were not friends otherwise. As for the festival, he was a professional. Been writing for a long time. Had some considerable success. He would have come to the festival and likely enjoyed it, but it wasn't all that important to him. Not like other authors I could mention, who are absolutely desperate to get their time on the stage."

"You mean Ruth Vivac and Shannon McKinnah?"

"Shannon's okay, but Ruth's a pest, always needing to know how many books of hers I plan to stock and offering to help get them in. She always has been demanding, wanting window and center table space, her books facing out on the racks. I try to cut her some slack. Her books aren't bad at all—better than many—but there's a lot of luck involved in having success in the publishing world, and she hasn't had it."

The chimes rang again, and two young girls came in. They were about fourteen, long skinny legs, short shorts, good teeth, and big round eyes. One had her long dark hair festooned with colorful beads, and the other's was cut very short and dyed a startling shade of purple.

"Todd!" cried the long-haired girl. "Oh, thank goodness. You have his books." She grabbed the topmost book with both hands and held it to her chest. She closed her eyes and breathed deeply.

"He died," the other girl said to Rick and me. "Did you hear? I simply can't believe it. Todd was the best writer ever in the entire history of the world."

"Mr. Shakespeare might have something to say about that," Rick said under his breath.

"I want them all," the first girl said. "I mean, I have the whole set already, like, but these ones are . . . the last." She choked back a sob. Her friend put her arms around her and they hugged.

Rick winked at me. "Todd had a strong fan base. There's been a run on his books today."

Chapter Six

Rick wasn't exaggerating when he said Todd Harrison had a strong fan base.

A sizable number of cars were parked on the street in front of our house, but at first I thought little of it, assuming one of the neighbors was having a party.

However, that wouldn't account for the mound of flowers piled on our front steps. I left Charles in the car and walked over to study them. Carnations tied in bunches with ribbons or still wrapped in cellophane, teddy bears, other stuffies, even a couple of well-thumbed paperback copies of Todd's books. Messages were propped among the offerings to the effect of *RIP Todd* and *TH4Eva*.

I wondered what we were supposed to do with it all. People had left the offerings out of respect. Would it be disrespectful to gather them up and throw them out? The stuffies might find a home at the hospital or a women's shelter, and the books could go to the little free library, but the flowers wouldn't last long. Most of them already looked like they'd been out in the heat all day with no water. Which they had.

I decided to talk it over with Connor before acting, and went back to the car to collect Charles. Charles might live with Connor and me, but he is most of all the library cat. As the library cat, he has his job to do, and that involves coming to the library every day. A charming but extremely tiny apartment is situated on the fourth floor of the lighthouse tower. After my first day at work, Charles simply followed me up the twisting iron staircase to the apartment and settled into the window seat. When Connor and I bought our house, I moved out of my lighthouse aerie, and Louise Jane moved in. Charles, however, clearly wanted to come with me. Initially that presented a bit of a problem in that I don't live close enough to the library to walk to work (carrying a cat), and felines are not known for being fond of riding in cars or being put in their cat carriers for the journey. After some initial disagreements, and badly scratched hands, Charles finally settled down, realizing that if he wanted to go to work, which he did, he had to get into his carrier.

I won't say he's happy about it, but he has accepted the situation. Much to the relief of my shattered nerves.

I lifted the carrier out of the back seat and brought it into the house. I let us in by the kitchen door, put the carrier on the island, and opened it. Charles flew out as though propelled by a spring, but rather than jumping onto his cat tree or searching the food bowls for any leftover breakfast scraps, he lifted his ears, twitched his whiskers, and headed straight for the living room.

Curious, I followed.

The scene outside the windows froze me in my tracks. Late in the afternoon, a clerk at the police station called Connor to let him know they were finished on our deck and our stretch of beach; Connor texted the information to me, and I was thinking it would be nice to have dinner on the deck tonight.

This evening, instead of uniformed officers and forensic people crawling all over our property and environs, there were . . . teenagers.

Must have been about twenty of them, ranging in age from preteen to kids in their last summer before college. Two boys, the rest girls. They stood silently in a semicircle on the beach, facing our deck. Heads bowed, clutching flickering candles.

I picked up Charles, opened the sliding door, and stepped onto the deck. "Hello? Uh, hello? Can I help you?"

"Shh," a girl said through a waterfall of heavy black hair. "We're praying."

"Oh," I said. "Sorry." Then I wondered how long they'd been here and how much longer they'd stay. People were watching from the beach, and a few approached, obviously wondering if this was a beach wedding or something.

"Primrose," I said, "is that you?"

The girl in the center of the semicircle lifted her head. Primrose Peterson, long legs, gangly arms, slim hips, thick golden hair tied back in a tight ponytail. Her face was tear streaked, her blue eyes red, black eye makeup running down her cheeks. She wore shredded denim shorts with the pockets hanging out, flip flops, and a T-shirt featuring a drawing of a wild-haired, large-chested woman in skimpy battle armor accompanied by a snarling wolf. "Mrs. McNeil. Hi." She wiped at her face, smearing her makeup even more.

"What's going on here?" I asked.

"A vigil. For . . . for Todd." Primrose burst into tears. The girl next to her wrapped her arms around her, and they wept together. Another girl let out a moan. Rather dramatic, I thought, as though she were a wailing banshee of Irish legend. A boy stood at the edge of the circle, slightly back, not quite part of the group. "We . . . uh . . . my friends and I wanted to pay our respects." He held a candle, but he had not been crying. If anything, I thought he looked slightly embarrassed. I estimated him to be around sixteen or seventeen, of average height, slightly overweight, black hair cut very short, clear pale skin, a prominent nose, and watchful dark eyes.

"That's okay. I guess," I said. "But . . . this is my home."

They were on the public beach. I couldn't order them to leave as long as they didn't step over the row of small white stones marking the property line. But a group of candle-bearing, weeping, banshee-imitating teenagers was not conducive to me enjoying an after-work drink with my husband. "Do you plan to stay for long?"

"Not long," the boy said. "Come on, Prim. You've paid your respects. Let's go."

Some of the girls were carrying flowers, a single carnation. Others clutched books.

Primrose stepped forward first. She crossed the line of stones without noticing them, and placed a single red rose on the second step. Then, one at a time, the others laid their offerings to make a pile.

They re-formed their circle, hands clasped together, heads bowed. The boy edged toward Primrose and lightly put his arm over her shoulder.

"Todd," she said.

"Todd," the group repeated.

The boy gently turned Primrose, and together they walked away, heading toward the path through the dunes. The others followed in a long, solemn line.

Not entirely solemn, however, as one of the girls said to another, "We still on for that movie tomorrow?"

"My dad's making noises about needing more family time, but he'll get over it."

And then they were gone, leaving their offerings behind them. Onlookers on the beach shrugged and went about their business. I let out a long breath. Teenagers. No harm done. They'd been polite and respectful; they'd made their pilgrimage, left their offerings, said goodbye to their idol.

From the front of the house, I heard the sound of girlish laughter.

I walked down the steps and picked up a book. Not at all to my surprise it was by Todd Harrison, the cover illustration a realistic drawing of a sword-wielding warrior woman with her dog/wolf. Not the same picture as on Primrose's shirt, but close enough.

I'd leave the flowers here but drop the books at the little free library box in Nags Head tomorrow along with the ones left at the front. I hoped Primrose and her friends would appreciate the gesture: let someone else get enjoyment out of Todd Harrison's books.

* * *

Connor got home not long after our visitors left. The first thing he said when he came in was, "Is our house turning into a shrine?"

"I certainly hope not. I hate to tell you, but that pile on the front steps isn't the worst of it." I told him about Primrose and her group.

He groaned. "I hope that doesn't turn out to be a bother. The last thing I want is an author groupie encampment set up underneath our deck."

"The disadvantage of bordering public land. We won't see them again. They got it out of their system, and they won't be back. They'll be onto the next thing. Some of them were already making plans to see a movie tomorrow. It's my turn to make dinner tonight, and I'm doing chicken fajitas. Which means I have time to enjoy a drink on the deck first. Care to join me?"

He pulled me close and said, "No place on earth I'd rather be."

* * *

First thing the following morning, we cleared all the offerings off the steps. The flowers were little more than a limp mess, so we felt no guilt at throwing them into the composter. Connor bagged the books and toys to take them to the charity shop in town.

I wasn't scheduled to start work until ten, so after tidying up out front, I enjoyed a breakfast of granola, yogurt, and fresh berries with Connor, kissed him goodbye, and settled at the table with another cup of coffee, to send emails to a couple of college friends I keep in touch with. I was trying to lure them to OBX for a fall vacation, and to that end, I sent pictures of the beach at sunrise, taken from our deck. That task finished, I checked the online news for updates on the killing of Todd Harrison. Nothing but standard police talk about an investigation being underway, being confident of an arrest, and asking anyone who might have seen something on our stretch of the beach around that time to come forward.

Tributes to the author filled his publisher's social media pages, and his agent had put out a statement to the effect that the literary world had lost a brilliant mind cut short all too soon. As a librarian, I know a fair amount about what's going on in publishing, and I had heard of Todd Harrison before talk of him coming to our festival. But although he had some considerable success, he wasn't, in the scheme of things, all that big a name. He was certainly no Stephen King or George R.R. Martin. He'd published four books in his YA fantasy series, the third of which hit number one on the *New York Times* bestseller list about four years ago. Numbers for the fourth book, which came out two years later, hadn't been as good. Two years is a long gap between books in a YA series—hard to keep the fans engaged and excited without a book a year.

His agent's statement went on to say that Todd's newest book, which would "take his writing in an entirely new and revolutionary direction and take his millions of fans around the world on a ride such as they've never before experienced," was close to being completed, and plans remained in place to publish it early next year.

All sorts of over-the-top comments, some bordering on ecstatic, some complaining that the series hadn't been brought to a satisfactory conclusion, followed the final statement.

I was about to follow a virtual trail to Todd's online fan clubs, when a whine from Charles reminded me it was almost time to go. I closed my iPad, downed the dregs of my coffee, and struggled to my feet.

Half an hour later, showered and dressed, lunch packed, I was searching for the cat when a knock came from the front door. Charles loves going to the library, but he also loves playing find-the-cat. I always threaten to leave him behind, but I haven't done so yet. I suspect he knows my tricks.

Charles appeared out of nowhere, as though summoned by a magician, and ran ahead of me to answer the bell.

I opened the door to see a woman I didn't know standing on the step, her face set into unsmiling, serious lines. A man stood slightly behind her. He was also not smiling, and he held an enormous black camera in his hands, strap dangling. A bulging camera bag was slung over his shoulder. Slightly behind him was another woman, carrying an iPad. She was young, not much older than the teens who'd been here last night, dusky skin, dark eyes, thick black hair tied in a neat French braid falling almost to her waist. She gave me a nervous smile.

"Mrs. Lucy McNeil, I presume?" The older woman thrust out her hand. Her hands were freshly manicured, the long nails painted a deep, dark red. Her light brown hair, expertly highlighted with streaks of caramel, bounced around her thin shoulders. She wore a summer-weight skirt suit of pale green over an emerald silk blouse and strappy high-heeled sandals. She was a couple of inches taller than me, and the shoes gave her even more height. Green glass jewelry glistened from her ears and around her neck. Her teeth were so blindingly white, I almost reached for my sunglasses.

"Yes," I said.

"I'm Heather Harrison."

I sucked in a breath. "Mrs. Harrison. Oh dear. I mean, my condolences on your loss."

The man focused his camera on my face. The young woman shifted her feet.

Heather twisted a handkerchief between her fingers. "You must think this is most inappropriate, me calling on you so unexpectedly. I hope you can forgive me."

Charles stood between my feet. He hissed. Heather looked down. Her face cracked in an attempt at a smile. "A cat. How . . . nice."

The man took a picture of Charles. Charles hissed at him too. I couldn't stand here with the door open. Charles would soon get bored of the visitors, and he might take it into his mind to have a stroll around the neighborhood. I stepped back. "Would you like to come in?"

"Thank you." Heather and her followers came into my house, and I shut the door.

"What can I do for you, Mrs. Harrison?"

"Call me Heather, please. I've been told my husband died here, in your lovely home." Her accent was North Carolinian, almost the same as that of my own husband. She did not introduce me to the others.

"Not in the house itself," I said. "Who told you that?"

She didn't bother to answer, and it didn't really matter. Although the police had never officially stated the precise location of the author's death, local gossip knew. As, obviously, did Frighteners fans. "I was hoping you'd be so kind as to let me have a look around. To see where it happened. I'm having trouble accepting it. I've been to the hospital, yes, but still . . . I thought, here, I could say a final word to my darling Todd."

I hesitated. Her coming to my house was slightly creepy, but I understand people grieve in different ways. I could also understand that she'd gone to the trouble of dressing perfectly, shoes and jewelry and everything, if she'd been brought up to believe one dressed suitably for all occasions. I could even understand that her eyes showed little signs of copious weeping, and her face didn't appear to be ravaged by grief, because, again, everyone grieves in their own way. I could understand if she brought a friend or a relative with her, to offer emotional support, although the dark-haired woman seemed too young to be a friend, and I could see no family resemblance between them.

What I couldn't understand was why she'd bring a cameraman. This guy didn't look to me like a friend of the family or a pal of Todd's. He wore a golf shirt, multi-pocketed khaki pants, loafers with socks. His hair was black with a handful of silver strands, cut short, and he'd shaved this morning. He'd not said so much as "Hello."

"I suppose that would be okay," I said. "But I don't want your friend taking pictures. Can you put that down, please, sir."

He looked at Heather. She gave him a nod, and the camera was lowered.

"On the deck," I said. "Please. After you."

Heather and the cameraman walked down the hallway.

"Sorry to intrude," the young woman said to me in a low, nervous voice. "I hope it's okay. Us dropping in unannounced like this?"

"It's fine," I said.

"Thanks. I'm Layla. I'm Heather's PA."

The young woman slipped quietly down the hall after the other two. I followed. I checked to see if Charles was also going to follow. The look he gave me was entirely disapproving. I might have made a mistake inviting these people into my home. Heather's husband died here two days ago. I knew nothing about the woman. Had she killed him and returned to clean up any evidence she'd left behind? Had she not killed him, but wanted revenge on the person (in other words, me) who had done nothing to save him?

I assured myself that in either of those cases, she wouldn't have brought along a person to take photographs.

She was just a grieving widow.

Although why a grieving widow brought her personal assistant and a cameraman with her, I didn't know. Then again, I've never had a PA. Maybe that's sometimes the "personal" part of the job.

"You have a lovely home," Heather said to me.

"Thank you. It's an Outer Banks original, built in 1923, reclaimed and updated by my husband and his father."

As part of that update, Connor and Fred knocked down non-load-bearing walls dividing the kitchen from the living and dining areas, creating an open and welcoming space. At this time of the morning, sunlight streamed through the east-facing windows and the sliding door onto the deck. Dust mites danced in the air.

"We . . . he . . . was on the deck," I said.

Heather crossed the living room. She pulled at the door, but it was locked. She flicked the lock without asking permission or even looking at me for approval. She stepped outside.

The traditional Unpainted Aristocracy pattern has a covered and enclosed veranda running around three sides of the house. We'd removed the roof from the section at the back to get the full sun but kept the two enclosed sections on each side. We were looking forward to eventually having children, our own or visitors, sleeping on the screened porch on hot, humid summer nights, as OBX children have done for generations.

Connor and I had furnished the deck with new but not overly expensive outdoor furniture. A glass-topped table surrounded by eight chairs, the cushions now tucked away in plastic bins. A big black grill, Connor's pride and joy. Terracotta pots and ceramic urns overflowing with flowers and variegated ivy, my pride and joy.

Heather stood there for a long time, simply looking around. The cameraman had gone onto the deck after her. Layla hung behind.

Then Heather turned and spoke to me. "Lorraine Kittleman. I don't suppose she happened to pay a call on you the other night. The night Todd died?"

The question came out of nowhere. "I know Lorraine, but she's never been here, to my home. Why would you ask that?"

"Did you perhaps see her in the neighborhood? Watching your house maybe?"

"What's she got to do with anything?"

"She was being a pest. Wanting my husband's attention. Trying to get Todd to have a relationship with her. Poor, innocent Todd told her repeatedly to leave him alone, that he wasn't interested, but she simply wouldn't get the hint. I told him to take out a restraining order, but he was simply too nice. Nice. And naive."

I shook my head. "I don't think you're right. Lorraine was at the meeting at the library, when Todd was there on Tuesday afternoon, to discuss the festival. Her band's providing the music. I noticed nothing at all out of the ordinary between them."

"Todd didn't want to go to extremes, but at last he decided he'd have to drop out of your little festival if you didn't get rid of Lorraine and her so-called band." Heather turned back to the view. "Perhaps Todd wasn't the only naive one. Nick, get one of me with the beach in the background."

"I said no—"

"One little picture won't hurt," she said. "I want a panorama of the beach, Nick. And me, small, almost frail. Get the deck floor in to set the location."

Nick whipped up his camera and snapped away. Heather stood against the railing, staring out to sea. In the distance, people walked along the shore or relaxed in their folding chairs. Children dug in the sand, and a handful of brave souls ventured into the waves.

Heather turned and stared into the camera, her face ravaged with grief. Nothing frail about her.

Layla said nothing.

"That's enough." I was still gripping Charles. "I have to get to work."

"Yes, your work. At the library," Heather said. "I'm sure they won't mind if you're late."

"They might not mind, but I will."

Charles spat.

"What are all those flowers?" She pointed to the ragged bunch on the step. "Fans probably. Todd did have his fans."

"Why don't I take a couple shots from the beach?" Nick said. "You on the deck with the house in the background?"

"That'll work. Good idea. Get some with the flowers. Show how much Todd was loved. I'm surprised they haven't left any of his books."

"No more of this. Please," I said. "I'm sorry, but I said you could see the place where your husband died, but I also said no pictures. I'd like you to leave now."

She studied my face. Nick looked between us both. Charles spat again. I held tightly onto him, afraid he'd take a leap at her, claws extended.

"Are you ordering me off your property?" Heather asked.

"I think—" Layla said.

"When I want you to think," Heather said, "I'll tell you. And that's not now. You can go and wait in the car."

Layla almost sprinted down the hallway. I heard the door slam a second later.

"I'm not ordering you to do anything," I said. "I'm asking you to leave so I can get on with my day."

"Ah yes, an exciting day of filing books. Your husband is the mayor here, isn't that right? Perhaps I could come back this evening when he's home. Nighttime shots would be very dramatic."

"I'd rather you didn't do that."

"We'll see. Very well. You don't need to show us out—we'll go this way. Does that row of little stones mark the boundary of the public beach? Get some shots of me with the house in the background, Nick. Make sure the deck is prominent."

She stepped over the flowers and climbed down the steps. Her heels sunk into the sand, but she didn't take off her shoes. Nick followed her, not bothering to go around the flowers, but crushing the blooms beneath his feet.

I watched as Heather Harrison walked about ten feet onto the beach, and Nick positioned himself to face her so my house was behind her. She struck a pose; he lifted his camera.

I realized that Charles and I would be in the picture if I didn't move.

I made sure the door was locked firmly behind me.

Only after they'd gone did I realize I hadn't asked Heather if she knew why her husband had come here the other night. Had he gone home after the meeting, sat down to dinner, told her what was on his mind, and left? Did he spin her that story about Lorraine? For what possible reason? If he wanted to drop out of our festival, he didn't need an excuse. He could have said something else had come up. He could even have said he couldn't be bothered.

It likely didn't matter. Heather would tell me what she wanted to tell me, whether it was true or not. Heather Harrison had her own agenda, and until I knew what it was, I intended to stay well out of her way.

Chapter Seven

I was late getting to work, and I apologized profusely. Bertie was on the circulation desk in my place, and she said, "Don't worry about it, Lucy. Everyone's entitled to be late now and again."

I put the cat carrier on the floor and opened the door. Charles emerged. I'd had no trouble at all getting him into the carrier today. He clearly knew I was bothered and not up to playing games.

I'd hidden behind the living room curtains, watching as Nick took pictures of Heather and my house. That hadn't taken long, and they'd left, whereupon I crept to the front and peered out the window of the den. They'd gotten into their car and driven away without a backward glance.

What on earth had that been about?

I considered calling Connor and letting him know what happened, but I decided against it. Nothing had actually happened, aside from people behaving strangely. They did leave when I told them to. Nothing I could do if people wanted to take pictures on the beach. Our house is likely to be found in holiday photo albums and framed pictures of smiling families enjoying their vacation all over the world.

"Are you okay, Lucy?" Bertie asked. "You're a bit pale."

"I'm fine." I smiled at her. "It was upsetting. What happened the other night. I guess I was thinking about it as I drove in."

"Don't forget the seniors' class about keeping themselves safe online is at eleven."

"I'm looking forward to it," I said. And I was. I'd worked closely with the banks and the police to develop a program, specifically directed at seniors, to teach them how to recognize scams and react to malware when they were online.

The class went well, and my "students" paid keen attention to what I had to show them. "What bothers me, Lucy," one of the ladies said as they packed up the materials we'd prepared for them, "is the simple fact that there are people in the world prepared to cheat elderly people out of every cent they have. How do they sleep at night?"

"I do not know, Mrs. Jones," I said.

"Makes it easier, I suppose, if they don't have to face their victims while stealing from them."

"Always been plenty of nasty people in the world," Tim Snyder said. "Whether they came face-to-face with their victims or not."

They walked out the door, some with the assistance of adult children or caregivers, others leaning on canes. A few skipped nimbly down the steps.

Theodore Kowalski held the door and greeted almost everyone by name, which they did in return to him. Theodore's family had been in the Outer Banks as long as Louise Jane's and Connor's had, and his mother had always been active in the community.

"Good afternoon," I said. "What brings you here today?"

I always enjoyed visiting with Theodore. He scraped together a minimal living as a book collector and dealer and was a keen patron and promoter of the library.

Today he was dressed in a lightweight summer suit with a paisley cravat tied jauntily at his throat. The stem of his pipe poked out of his jacket pocket, and the scent of tobacco clung to his clothes like a noxious aura. He didn't smoke, nor did he need the assistance of the glasses perched on his nose to see, but he thought those things made him look like the scholar and gentleman he wanted to be. "Nothing. I mean, nothing in particular." His eyes darted around the room, his fake English accent slipping a bit.

A true Outer Banks original, Teddy thought appearing to be older than he was, more English than he was, smoking more than he did, with worse vision than he had, gave him a distinguished air.

In truth, it made him look a bit of a fool, but as he was a genuinely nice, kind man, everyone simply accepted his eccentricities.

He came into the room, glancing nervously around. A volunteer was at the circulation desk, patrons browsed the stacks, one of my class members was waiting in the magazine nook for her ride to arrive. Footsteps and laughter came from the children's library on the second floor. Louise Jane and Denise were working in the rare books room at the top of the back staircase. At the moment Charles was nowhere to be seen.

Theodore edged toward me. He jerked his head to one side. I lifted my shoulders and held up my hands, meaning I didn't understand. Another jerk of the head.

"Do you want to speak to me privately?" I asked.

He started, put his fingers to his lips, and bobbed his head rapidly.

"Okay. I'll be in the back if you need me," I said to the volunteer.

"What's gotten into Teddy?" a patron said as she dropped her books on the desk. "He looks even more wired today than normal."

"Theodore Kowalski," the lady in the magazine nook called, "you tell that mother of yours I expect to see her at euchre this week. It's been too long."

"Yes, ma'am. I will, ma'am." Theodore dipped his head and slunk out of the room. Confused, I followed.

He waited for me at the door of the staff break room, and when I walked in, he closed the door firmly behind me.

"Would you like a glass of tea?" I asked.

"No. I mean, no thank you, Lucy."

"Is something the matter?"

"Yes, I very much fear so. Although it is not necessarily a problem right now, but such has the potential to become critically so."

"Huh?"

He dropped heavily into a chair. I cautiously sat across from him.

"You might not be aware, Lucy, but Lorraine Kittleman and I have recently become . . . close."

Everyone in this half of North Carolina was aware Teddy and Lorraine had started seeing each other. Everyone in this half of North Carolina was wondering what had taken them so long. They'd been good friends in school, to the point that their mothers had their hopes up. But Lorraine moved away to try to make it as a classical violinist, and Theodore stayed. Her dreams of musical stardom on the great stages of the world didn't come to fruition, and she changed career direction to become a high school teacher, keeping her musical passion alive as the fiddle player and inspiration behind a popular dance band. The two reconnected at my wedding, where Teddy had been a guest and Lorraine and her band provided the music.

"I'm pleased to hear that," I said. "I like Lorraine very much. She and the band are playing at our YA authors festival."

"And thus you have arrived immediately at the crux of the problem, Lucy, as you so astutely always do."

All I was doing was trying to make polite conversation, to allow Teddy time to compose himself and get to the point. "And?" I prompted.

He tugged at his cravat. Even a lightweight summer suit must be stiflingly hot in this weather. "Lorraine called me a short while ago. She was, to put it mildly, distraught."

"Why, what happened?"

"It's related to that man who died at your house, Lucy. The police paid a call on Lorraine this morning. They had questions."

"I'm sure it was just routine. Lorriane left the meeting early, but she was still one of the last people, that we know of, to see Todd before he died."

"It was more than simple routine, Lucy. Detective Watson himself came, not just someone to take her statement. He told her he'd been informed that Lorraine had been stalking Todd."

Heather Harrison. She'd asked me about Lorraine. Told me Lorraine had been bothering Todd. Had Heather then gone to the police with her accusations? "Stalking? That's preposterous."

"I know. Lorraine has absolutely no idea who would say such a thing, or why." He leaped to his feet and began pacing the room.

"Did she tell Detective Watson so?"

"She did. She doesn't know if he believed her."

"He has to believe her. It's not true." Although, I had to admit, if only to myself, I didn't know that. Not for sure. I thought back to Tuesday's meeting. Todd and Lorraine had sat on opposite sides of the table. This table. I'd been the last to arrive, and everyone was already seated. I'd been introduced to the only person I didn't know—Todd—and the meeting immediately got underway. Everything had gone well. Extremely well, I thought. Better than these sorts of things often do. Todd was going to be the main attraction, and the other authors were fine with that. Rick from the bookstore was delighted at the bestselling author's participation. The clown was going to be a local woman who played at children's birthday parties and the like and had been at other library functions over the years. Same for the face painter. Both of them hadn't come to the library in person, but participated by Zoom. My cousin Josie's bakery would have a booth offering freshly baked goods and cold drinks for purchase. Josie hadn't made the meeting, in person or virtually, but I stood in for her, and no one had any arguments or difficult questions. Louise Jane was in charge of arranging the rental of chairs, setting up the small stage on the lawn, hiring a sound engineer. She'd done that before, and she expected no issues this time. Louise Jane would have a turn on stage in her role as local storyteller. Again, no objections and no questions.

Lorraine attended to represent her band. She had to leave early, full of apologies, and did so after hearing what time the band would be needed and how long they had to perform, and making some practical arrangements with Louise Jane.

The entire meeting was efficient, short, to the point, and soon over. I left thinking it would be nice if all meetings were as successful and agreeable.

I'd noticed nothing at all in the way of tension between Todd and Lorraine. Or between anyone else. At one point, she said something about everyone being excited about the return of the local boy who'd done good, and he smiled at her and joined the general laughter. Because she left early, I hadn't thought to ask her if she knew what Todd had been planning to do on leaving the library or if anything seemed to be bothering him.

I absolutely refused to believe Todd's death had anything to do with something that happened at that meeting.

Then again, as I've been reminded on other occasions, what I believe is totally irrelevant.

Maybe Lorraine had confronted Todd before the meeting, and for reasons of his own he kept up a brave front in front of us. Could that be what Todd wanted to talk to me about? Heather said he was going to drop out of the festival if Lorraine was part of it.

If so, he had to be a pretty good actor to keep that smile on his face as he talked to her and the rest of the group and fully engaged in preparing for his participation.

"Lucy?" Theodore said.

I gathered my thoughts and gave my friend what I hoped was a bright smile. "You and I both know Sam Watson is a good detective. He was given a lead, so naturally he followed it up. If there's nothing to find, he'll soon realize that."

"What do you mean 'if'?"

"Just a word choice, Theodore. That's all."

"Lorraine is worried."

I didn't ask if she had reason to be worried. If she had been "stalking" Todd Harrison, the last person to know would be Teddy. "Police attention is always uncomfortable, even if one is totally innocent."

"I don't like your continual use of the word 'if,' Lucy."

I threw up my hands. "Teddy, why are you even talking to me about this? I'd never met Todd before Tuesday, and prior to that I hadn't seen Lorraine in months."

He stopped pacing. He put his hands on the table and leaned toward me. He was only in his mid-thirties, much the same age as me, but the clothes, the glasses, the pipe, made him look a good deal older. He'd recently had some work done on his teeth, I noticed. They were straighter, and the brown stains were gone. "We want your help, Lucy."

"We? You mean you and Lorraine? What do you think I can do?"

"You've solved cases for the police before."

"I wouldn't say I *solved* them. I might have arrived at the correct conclusion shortly before they would have."

"Pure semantics. Will you help Lorraine?"

"I don't honestly know that I can. I have no avenue of inquiry, I don't—" I stopped midsentence, and he noticed.

"You don't what?"

I was going to say I knew nothing about Todd Harrison and his life or who might have wanted to kill him. But the words died when I realized I did know at least one thing. His wife's behavior this morning had been more than just an odd way of grieving. If I accepted that Lorriane was not stalking or pestering Todd, or begging him to have an affair with her, then I had to ask why Heather was saying so.

Was she making that story up out of whole cloth for some unknown reason?

Or did she believe it because Todd had told her so? And if he told her that, and it wasn't true, why would he have done so?

"I'll have a chat with Sam Watson," I said. "At the least I can tell him I sensed nothing untoward between Lorraine and Todd. I had a visitor this morning, which might be relevant. I'll tell him about that too."

"Visitor? Who?"

"I won't say now. Leave it with me, Theodore. I'll let you know what I find out."

And with that, I was committed. Once again.

Chapter Eight

"I was highly disappointed when you announced the book club would not meet this month or the next," Theodore said as we walked back to the main room of the library.

"Too many of the regular members are either going on vacation or have summer plans and holiday visitors. It just seemed easier to cancel. We'll start again in September."

"Perhaps a scaled-down meeting," he suggested. "You and me and anyone else who is free."

"I don't—"

"It's been a long time since I read a book about Robin Hood. The books by Howard Pyle are considerably out of date, but copies should be available for someone prepared to engage in a dedicated search."

"Robin Hood? I hardly think that would be appropriate under the circumstances, Teddy."

He blinked at me from beneath his clear spectacles. "What circumstances?"

"Todd Harrison's killing."

"Oh yes. That. I assume you are referring to the bow and arrow used. I heard about that. Seems a most unusual way of killing someone in this day and age. I can see some might speculate it has a Robin Hood connection. I suppose that's what put it in my mind. I'll start the hunt for the books now, and we can call the meeting for when you've tidied up the case. Cheerio, Lucy. I'll look forward to your report. Lorraine is of course on summer vacation from school now, so she should be free almost any time to answer your questions." He started for the door. Then he stopped and turned around. "It might be better if you speak to her directly and as soon as possible. Let's say the bar at Jake's when you get off work."

He left. I was finally able to close my mouth.

* * *

Heather Harrison spoke to the police earlier today. I wondered if she told them about the visit to my house, and if so what sort of spin she'd put on her rather odd behavior.

Only one way to find out.

I made a phone call, and then I knocked on Bertie's office door, and stuck my head in when she called, "Come in."

She looked up from her computer with an expression of such relief it was obvious she was glad of the interruption. She put her reading glasses to one side and rubbed her eyes.

"Is this a bad time?" I asked.

"Budget. Always a bad time." She smiled at me. "But a necessary evil."

"No budget, no money. No money, no salaries. No salaries, no librarians."

"No librarians, no libraries."

"I apologize for getting in late today, but I have to apologize again. I've thought of something to do with the death of Todd

Harrison, and I called Sam Watson about it. He's coming in because he wants to talk to Ronald and Louise Jane as well. I hope that's okay."

"To talk to the police? Of course it's okay. You know that. I can watch the children's library while Ronald's busy. Not only do I love every chance I get to be in the children's library, but I can hope the budget will finish itself while I'm away. Denise can manage without Louise Jane for a while."

* * *

When Sam Watson arrived at the library, I called Ronald and Louise Jane, and they both came down. We gathered once again in the staff break room.

When we all had cold drinks in front of us, I said, "Heather Harrison, widow of Todd, came to my house this morning. Did you know that, Detective?"

"I did not. What time was this?"

"Nine thirty. I was about to leave for work. That's why I was late getting here this morning."

Ronald and Louise Jane exchanged glances.

"What did she want?" Watson asked.

"She said she wanted to see the place where her husband died."

Louise Jane squealed and clapped her hands in delight. "A believer! She's planning to make the attempt to get in touch with his lingering spirit. Excellent. Did this contact happen, Lucy?"

"Not exactly. I—"

"If you give me her phone number, Detective, I can call her and suggest my assistance. Sometimes the presence of an outsider can facilitate—"

"No." Watson said. "I am not going to do that. Lucy, please continue."

Louise Jane fell back in her seat with a puff of air and a disapproving pout.

"Far from hoping to commune with his spirit," I said, "she wanted to take photographs of herself at the site of the incident." I went on to relate what happened in as much detail as I could without overdramatizing (enough of that, thank you, Louise Jane), including the presence of not only her personal assistant but a photographer as well.

"That is interesting," Watson said when I finished. "She didn't tell me about the visit, and I've no reason to believe, at this time, it's directly connected to any motives behind Harrison's death. But I do have to wonder why she didn't mention it to me. Judging by the timing, she would have come directly to the station after leaving your place. She didn't have a photographer or anyone else with her, although she might have left them outside."

"What line of work is she in that she has a PA following her around?" Ronald asked.

"You told me she was an unemployed journalist," I said to Watson. "It's possible she's mentoring an unpaid intern. The woman was young enough to be a college student or an intern. She didn't look at all comfortable in her job."

"Why did you make a point of asking Louise Jane and me to be here now?" Ronald asked. "Be quiet, Louise Jane, and let Lucy answer."

Louise Jane continued to pout, but she said nothing.

"Because Heather made an accusation to me about another person, and I believe she said the same to Detective Watson. Before this goes any further, I thought we should talk, in front of the detective, about what happened at the meeting on Tuesday. Ronald, Louise Jane, did either of you notice tension between any of the participants? Perhaps someone trying to avoid someone else? Or alternatively, someone trying to get close to someone else? Surreptitiously or otherwise?"

"Shannon and Ruth can't stand each other," Ronald said. "I've told you that. They sat about as far apart as you can get in this room. Which, come to think of it, was quite the dance as they both wanted to be as close as possible to Todd."

"Anyone else wanting to be close to Todd?"

Ronald shrugged. "Rick from the bookstore made a big deal of shaking the guy's hand and saying how pleased he was that Todd had agreed to be part of the festival."

"What are you getting at, Lucy?" Louise Jane asked.

"I suspect I know," Watson said, "and it's a good question. Louise Jane, any observations to share?"

She shrugged. "Not really. Now we're talking about it privately, I can tell you I'm not entirely pleased at being the opening act. It's hard to speak in front of a cold audience."

"It has to be that way, Louise Jane," Ronald said. "Shannon and Ruth will follow you, with some music between their presentations, and then Todd will be interviewed by me before another musical set, and finally Bertie's closing words. We tossed a coin, Detective, to decide the order of the two women authors. No one objected."

"Do you have an answer to the question, Louise Jane?" Watson asked.

"I didn't see anyone behaving either in a way that was overly friendly or overly hostile to anyone else. And as you know, I am a keen observer of the human condition. If there had been any underlying tension, I would have picked up on it immediately."

No one said anything in response to that.

"Lucy arrived late, and Lorraine Kittleman left early," Ronald said. "In neither case was there any drama around it. Lucy was delayed by a patron, and Lorraine had a doctor's appointment to get to."

I was pleased Ronald mentioned Lorraine without being prompted. And that he clearly stated there'd been no drama around her departure.

"Would it surprise you to hear Todd was threatening to pull out of the festival if certain conditions were not met?" I asked.

"It would do considerably more than surprise me," Ronald said. "I didn't have the slightest idea he was thinking anything of the sort. He seemed perfectly fine with everything as we discussed it. Why? What sort of conditions?"

I looked at Sam Watson. He nodded. "Point made, Lucy. I might have another chat with my informant. For lack of a better word."

"You can't leave us in the dark, Sam," Louise Jane said. "What exactly are we talking about here?"

"Is that why he came to your house that night, do you think, Lucy?" Ronald asked. "To discuss these *conditions*."

"I don't know why he came to my house, but I don't see how it could have been about withdrawing from the festival. You're the one who arranged for him to be part of the event, so surely he'd tell you first if he decided to drop out. Not me. Although I suppose it is possible something happened in the interval that made him change his mind, and he couldn't get in touch with you immediately. He did mention he knew where I lived only because I'm married to the mayor."

"I agree it seems a stretch," Ronald said. "He wouldn't even have to tell me himself. All the initial arrangements were made through his publisher."

"Four hours passed between Todd leaving the library and showing up at my door, Sam," I said. "Do you know what he did in that interval?"

"He most likely went home at some point, but we don't know when or how long he stayed there. His wife was out; she claims she left the house around five thirty for a dinner meeting. She says the kitchen was clean when she left, but an empty bottle of beer, a dirty glass, and a crumpled-up bag of chips were on the counter when she returned sometime after nine. She also mentioned, for what it's worth, that Todd is normally an excessively tidy individual. For him not to wash his glass and throw his trash out before leaving the house indicates he had something on his mind. Perhaps he came to a decision about this something and immediately acted on it."

"All we need to find out now," I said, "is what that something was."

"I can attempt—" Louise Jane began.

"No, thank you," I said. Earlier I'd considered telling my coworkers about the teenagers hanging around our house. Now I was glad I hadn't. I couldn't take a chance on Louise Jane deciding to join them and lead them in a séance in an attempt to contact the dearly departed author. I shuddered as I thought of Connor's reaction to that.

"You okay, Lucy?" Watson asked. "You've gone pale all of a sudden."

"Yeah, fine. Just had a thought I didn't care for. Nothing to do with any of this."

He pushed his chair back. "Thank you all for your time. I'll be in touch."

He left. Ronald and Louise Jane stared at me.

"It would appear," I said, "I've been drawn into this against my will. The widow Harrison paid a call on me this morning, and she told me Lorriane Kittleman had been bothering Todd to the point that he wasn't going to be part of the festival if she was in it."

Ronald laughed. Then he read my face. "You're not kidding."

"I am not. She went to the police and made the same accusation to them. Sam paid a call on Lorraine, who denied the whole thing. I wanted to try to clear that up. As much as possible, anyway. People don't always act out their dramas and conflicts in a public setting."

"Weirder and weirder," Louise Jane said.

Chapter Nine

As arranged, I met Teddy and Lorraine at Jake's Seafood Bar shortly after the library closed for the night. I'd texted Connor to say I was going for an afterwork drink and wouldn't be late.

He replied: *Let me know when you're on the way, and I'll turn on the grill.*

My cousin Josie is married to Jake Greenblatt, brother of Butch and owner and head chef at Jake's Seafood Bar, one of the best and most popular restaurants in Nags Head. On a pleasant evening in the summer, the place was hopping when I arrived, and a lineup had formed at the door, waiting for a free table. Fortunately, I didn't need a table, as a seat was waiting for me at the bar. Teddy and Lorraine had arrived first and left a spare stool between them at a corner of the shiny mahogany counter, where the three of us could talk easily and in some privacy.

I gave Lorraine a quick hug, hopped onto my stool, and ordered a glass of white wine. "How are you doing?" I asked Lorraine.

"Better than I was a few hours ago. Sam Watson rattled the heck out of me, and I called Teddy in a panic soon as he left.

When I calmed down, I realized I don't have anything to worry about, as what Detective Watson said is totally not true. I apologize for dragging you out here." She gave Theodore a fond smile. "Teddy can be protective."

The look he gave her in return was one of sheer adoration. He puffed up his chest, just a bit. He was still wearing the pale blue summer suit he'd had on this afternoon, but at least he'd dispensed with the cravat. You don't see many cravats at Jake's Seafood Bar these days.

"Not a problem," I said. "I'm happy to help if I can, although I truly do not know what you two think I can do. Do you know of any reason Heather would have made those accusations? I assume you know it was Heather, Todd's wife, who spoke to the police."

"You can ask the right questions, Lucy," Theodore said. "See, Lorraine? It's as I told you. Lucy knows how to immediately get to the heart of the matter."

"Questions don't always lead to answers," I said. "But sometimes they do. Back to Heather?"

"Yeah, Detective Watson didn't out and out tell me it was her, but easy enough to guess," Lorraine said. "She's got a screw loose is all I can say."

"Have you met her?" The waiter brought my drink, and I smiled my thanks. Theodore and Lorraine both had mugs of beer in front of them. The bar was inside the building, and my back was to the wide windows and the spacious open deck overlooking Roanoke Sound and Roanoke Island beyond. In the wall of glass facing me, over the heads of the diners, I caught a dancing reflection of blue water and light from the soon-to-be-setting sun.

"Never had the pleasure," Lorraine said. "I knew Todd from the old days. He was several years older than me, but he hung around with my oldest brother in high school. I had, I will readily admit, a bit of a crush on him back then. A crush, I will also readily admit, that didn't last much longer than one teenage summer. He moved away after finishing school, as I did a couple of years later, and I literally never thought of him again. Not until recently."

"Did you know him back then, Teddy?" I asked.

"I did not. I didn't move in the same circles as he and Lorraine's sports-minded brothers."

I hid a smile. Even then, I guessed Theodore had been quite the nerd.

"Todd went away to college," Lorraine said, "as so many Banker kids do. Including me. I was pleased when I heard he'd moved back and how well he was doing as a writer. About two months ago, shortly before school let out for the summer, I sent an email to his author web page, reminding him of who I was and saying I'd like to catch up over a coffee sometime. For old times' sake. I wasn't so much interested in talking about the old days, but I had the idea of getting him in to speak to my class when school starts up again. He could tell them about his writing career, maybe, or give a workshop. He replied, and we met for lunch. He said he'd be happy to come to school, and we arranged to talk again closer to the time. No more contact until he called to tell me he'd been invited to your authors festival, and he heard my band and I were providing the music. We had a laugh about how our career paths had gone in unexpected directions, and we met again about a week ago for lunch, to talk about the festival and other happenings this summer around here. That was the sum total of my contact with him until the meeting at the library on Tuesday."

She stretched her hand across the countertop, past me, to Theodore. He put his on top of it, and they looked at each other for a long time. I drank my wine and shifted on my stool.

"The very idea that I was, of all things, stalking him, is preposterous," she said. "I'm perfectly happy with what I have now." She smiled at my friend. His smile in return outshone the light of the sun reflected in the mirror.

"Did he say anything to you about his wife or his marriage?" I asked.

"Nothing specific, but I got the impression they were not in a good place. She's exploring the possibility of taking a run for state senator, and he wasn't happy about the idea."

"Really? Senator?"

"That's what Todd said. It's why they moved back to North Carolina, so she could take advantage of being a local girl. He didn't come right out and say it, but it was obvious to me he wasn't thrilled at the idea of being a political spouse. That means a lot of attention and a lot of pressure. Not to mention time he'd rather spend on other things. You must know that, Lucy."

"On occasion, yes. Although being mayor of Nags Head isn't equivalent to being a senator, and I can largely keep myself out of the limelight."

Limelight. Heather and her perfect clothes and her cameraman.

Surely she wasn't planning to use her husband's death to promote her political ambitions?

If so, how would accusing Lorraine of being a stalker help her?

"He gave me the impression he wasn't all that happy in Nags Head. It's not for everyone, is it? Particularly over the winter when it's so quiet. He missed the hustle and bustle of New York City a lot and said so."

"Did you get the feeling he was planning to go back? Leaving Heather and her political plans behind?"

"No, I didn't. He didn't say anything to that effect, whether he was thinking about it or not. I thought he might be lonely here; he'd lived in New York for a long time, and all his friends must still be there, plus his writing circles. Stuck in a marriage he's not comfortable in, his wife pursuing her own agenda. He was happy to have someone to grumble to. I thought little of it. We all grumble and complain, and then we carry on and live our lives."

"I don't grumble and complain," Theodore said.

Lorraine gave him another warm smile. "That's true. I'm sorry Teddy dragged you into this," she said to me. "He overreacted only because I overreacted."

"Better overreact than underreact," he said. I agreed.

"Ronald, Louise Jane, and I told Detective Watson we saw no undercurrents of antagonism between you and Todd. There wasn't even a hint that Todd didn't want you and your band playing at the festival. He appeared to be perfectly happy with the plans we'd made."

"Why then—" Theodore began.

"I simply don't know," I said. "Lorraine, did you and Todd talk privately before the meeting started? Did you get the sense anything was bothering him on Tuesday?"

"No and no. I would have suggested we go for a coffee or something after the meeting, but I had my doctor's appointment to get to. I told Sam Watson that. Unfortunately, the doctor's no alibi for the time of Todd's death, because I left her office about six. I have no other alibi for that evening. I went straight home from the doctor and stayed in for the rest of the night. I didn't see Todd again or speak to him."

"Lorraine and I talked on the phone," Theodore said. "Around the time in question. I'll tell the detective that."

"I don't know how good a phone conversation is as an alibi these days, Teddy. I could have been anywhere when you called."

"Something must have happened to bring him to your house that night, Lucy," he said.

"I'm beginning to think I'll never know what that was about. Maybe he wanted my Aunt Ellen's recipe for lasagna and couldn't wait until morning. She does make an awfully good lasagna."

Chapter Ten

"Forgot to mention, we're having visitors later tonight," Connor said to me as he stood over the grill, flipping the burgers. I paused in laying out the salads, buns, and condiments.

"Visitors? Who? When?"

"A clerk at the police station called me this afternoon. They're bringing some archers around later to check out the scene and see what they can determine about what might have happened the other night. They'll be here around nine, so as to get the same light as it was at the time of Todd Harrison's death."

"Do we have to do anything?"

"No. We don't even have to be here, she told me. They won't need to come inside."

"Might be interesting," I said. "I don't know if I've ever met anyone who's an archer. Not a common sport."

The burgers were delicious, but I could only eat about half of mine, and I picked at my salad. My stomach had been bothering me a bit over the last few days, and I often didn't feel like having much to eat. This was not necessarily a bad thing. Since marrying Connor and enjoying his hearty home-cooked meals several times a week, I'd put on a few unwelcome pounds.

Connor looked at my plate. "Not good?"

"Very good, but I've had enough. This stuff with Todd and Heather might be getting to me more than I realize. There's something personal about it—personal to me, anyway. He came here, to our house, and here he died. And now his wife's poking around and making personal insinuations about me."

"Let's hope these people from the archery club can tell us something."

* * *

They couldn't, but it was interesting watching them. Two people came, a man and a woman, both in their mid-fifties, both tall and lean, with short gray hair. He had a neat silver goatee, and she had a line of gold rings running up her right ear.

Butch Greenblatt came with them, and he introduced us to Robert and Eileen Cook.

The bows they carried looked nothing like I'd expected from watching Robin Hood movies. Made of metal rather than wood, with a network of complicated gears and pullies, they were huge and intricate.

"This type is a compound bow," Eileen explained. "Good for hunting."

"The same type of bow we found in the dunes," Butch said.

She held up an arrow. I had an image of the one in Todd's chest and looked away. Connor put his arm around my shoulders. This arrow had blue and yellow fletching. It was about two feet long, with a point much like that of a bullet.

Butch had brought what looked like a sandbag with concentric circles drawn on it. He carried it onto the deck and stuffed it into a chair at the exact spot where Todd had been sitting. We'd switched the living room lights off and turned on the one over the deck, making everything as close as possible to the way it had been on Tuesday night. The weather was the same—clear with a light breeze off the ocean.

We gathered on the beach in front of our house, about twenty yards from the deck, at the spot where the police had found scuffed sneaker marks.

"An arrow was embedded in the wall," Connor said as Robert and Eileen studied the ground and assembled their equipment. "Can we assume the first shot was a miss?"

"You said only one person was on the deck at the time?" Eileen asked Butch.

"That's right."

"Then it was most likely a miss, and so they fired again. The light's good enough to see the person clearly and for the shooter to know if they'd made the hit, so no need to fire another."

"Wouldn't Todd have heard something?" I asked. "And run for cover?"

Eileen's laugh was an amused tinkle. "If he heard anything at all, it would have been nothing more than a whoosh of air. He would have taken it for a bug flying past. If he paid any attention."

"That," Robert said, "is the great advantage of bows and arrows versus firearms. They don't make a sound. People walking past on the beach, like those ones"—he waved his hand to indicate the nightly strollers—"wouldn't have paid the slightest bit of attention, never mind it alerting the victim."

"How much skill would it take?" Butch asked. "To hit him from here on the first or even the second shot?"

"Not a great deal," Eileen said. "A compound bow isn't difficult to learn or to handle, and if we're standing where you think the archer stood, the target's close and clear."

"Not a great deal," Robert repeated, "but the archer would have needed some experience. You don't pick one of these up off the street and know how to use it. Mishandling can be dangerous. Accidents can and do happen, even to experienced archers if their attention wanders."

"I can't even tell which is the front of that thing," I said. "I assume you pull back the string, like in the movies, and let fly."

"The technology has changed a lot since the twelfth century," Eileen said, "but the principal is exactly the same."

When I thought of a bow, I imagined a length of soft wood formed into a curve and fitted with a taut length of string. These ones were made of aluminum, jammed with intricate interweaving parts, cables, and two little things at each end that looked like wheels. The arrows fitted into the frame of the bow, presumably for easy carrying.

"Ready when you are," Butch said.

"Ladies first," Robert said.

I took care to keep myself well out of the way as Eileen took position. She selected an arrow, fitted it into the bowstring, and then she slipped her hand into a sling attached to the contraption and stood perpendicular to the deck and the target, her legs and back straight and tight. She gripped the center of the bow with her left hand, wiggled her fingers, adjusted her hand slightly, and extended the bow in front of her. She shifted her feet and pulled her right arm holding the bowstring all the way back so her hand was directly beside her face. She peered through what I assumed was a sighter. Her focus was intense.

"Eileen and I have top-of-the-line bows," Robert said while she was getting into position, "but for today we borrowed a couple of lighter and less expensive ones to match what you think the killer used. Now remember, we've got a lot of experience in doing this. We'll have no trouble hitting anything that close."

"Famous last words," Connor said, and we all laughed, Eileen most of all.

"So true," Robert said. "Officer Greenblatt wanted a demonstration at the place and approximate time the incident occurred, and we're here to provide that."

A handful of people wandered up the beach to see what was going on. They all kept a respectful distance.

"We're assuming," Butch said, "our shooter didn't stand around talking about what he was doing or demonstrating it to a bunch of curious onlookers. How long would it have taken him to get set up?"

"Seconds," Robert said. "If he knew what he was doing. And he'd have been a fool to try it if he didn't."

"Any reason you're saying 'he'?" I asked. "Could an average woman have done it?"

"Average," Eileen said, "like me?" She released the bow. It flew silently through the night air, striking directly the center of the innermost circle on the sandbag.

One of the onlookers applauded. Another grabbed her child by the scruff of the neck to keep her from venturing closer.

"I guess that answers your question, Lucy," Butch said.

Robert picked up his own bow, followed the steps Eileen had taken, and fired the shot. Another hit, so close to Eileen's arrow they almost touched.

More applause from the beach this time.

"Thanks for coming out," Butch said as the couple began packing up their equipment.

"Can I get the arrows for you?" Connor asked.

"That'd be good, thanks," Robert replied.

Connor ran up the steps and plucked the two arrows out of the sandbag.

"Did you learn anything, Officer Greenblatt?" Robert asked.

"I'll tell the detective what happened here, but I can't say if it'll help much. Not if these things are easy to use and readily available."

"Robert and I could have done that blindfolded and standing on one leg," Eileen said. "If you want to see some fancy shooting, you're welcome to come out to our club one day. We're not hunters, just target shooters."

Connor handed them the arrows; we shook hands, and the Cooks took their leave.

Butch shook his head. "I don't know if that helped the case any, but it sure was interesting. I might give it a try myself someday."

"They mentioned their club," I said. "Are you having any luck tracing the person who was here the other night?"

"The detective's got people making calls all over this part of the state, but nothing's come up yet. Problem is, we don't have anything to go on. Not if the person of interest didn't specifically ask about how to shoot a person in the dark at a beach house. Nothing on tracing the bow itself either."

Chapter Eleven

Friday was my day off work. I planned to spend the morning grocery shopping and running normal household errands. In the afternoon, I intended to take my book out onto the deck for a few hours of reading and relaxing in the shade of the big umbrella. I'd put on my bathing suit and run down to splash in the surf if and when the spirit moved me. I've never been much of a cook—that's not a skill my housekeeper-employing, social-climbing mother thought I needed to know. Connor does most of the cooking in our house, but I'm trying to expand my admittedly limited repertoire. Today, I planned to pop a pork shoulder into the slow cooker, with plenty of onions and herbs, and let it gently cook while I enjoyed my afternoon, and then we could have a delicious pork roast for dinner.

As so often happens, my carefully considered plans came to naught.

Around eleven, Charles was snoozing on the cat tree while I unpacked the groceries, when Bertie called. "Lucy, I'm sorry to bother you at home on your day off, but something has happened I think you should know about."

Imagining misplaced books or ill employees, I said, "Not a problem. I've just gotten in from doing the grocery shopping."

"A woman was in here earlier. She was asking about you."

"About me? What do you mean 'asking about'?"

"Todd Harrison's widow. Heather. She said she met you yesterday."

"She did, but it wasn't a comfortable meeting. What did she want to know?"

"I didn't care for the direction of her questions, Lucy. Fortunately, Ellen was on the desk this morning, and she had the sense to immediately tell Mrs. Harrison she didn't know anything about anything, and she called me to come out." Ellen meant Ellen O'Malley, my mother's sister. "Basically Mrs. Harrison said she heard you were often invited to become involved in police cases."

I was starting to get a bad feeling about this, but I simply said, "And?"

"It's no secret that here at the library we've had more than our share of unfortunate events. It's also not a secret you've been able to help the police on occasion. I told Mrs. Harrison that. When she started asking what sort of unfortunate events, I referred her to sources such as the local newspapers. Then she changed direction to ask about you personally, Lucy—your work history and if you'd been involved in similar situations in your previous jobs." Bertie cleared her throat. "I was already getting uncomfortable, but then she asked why you'd left Boston and a good job at the Harvard libraries. I said that was a personal matter, none of hers or my business. She then had the nerve to ask me if there had been any—and I quote—'notable crimes,' at Harvard in the time you were working there."

"She's been checking up on me," I said. "Otherwise, how would she know I worked at Harvard? It didn't exactly come up the only time we met. But my bio on the library staff page mentions it."

"As you say, checking up, yes. Even your involvement with the earlier police cases didn't get as much mention in the news as it might have."

"For which I'm eternally grateful. I don't have to account to her, and neither do you, but for the record, there were not any so-called 'incidents' when I was at Harvard. Not in the library, anyway."

"By this time Ellen was prepared to get fully engaged in the discussion. As you can imagine, she would have been less than polite."

"I can." I thought fondly of my aunt. She of the fabulous lasagna. I was closer to Aunt Ellen than I was to my own mother. Always have been.

"I cut Ellen off," Bertie said, "thinking it might not be wise to let Mrs. Harrison know of your relationship. I asked her to leave, telling her I did not engage in gossip about my staff. She informed me she was entitled to stay as long as she wanted, as we are a public library. Before I could remind her, I have authority to limit access to anyone I choose, she said she'd leave. And she did so."

"Good. Hopefully she won't be back."

"We can hope. There is, unfortunately, something else. A nervous young woman, who didn't say anything the entire time, came with her. Also a man with a camera. It looked like a professional camera. More than a phone or a point-and-shoot, anyway."

Not good. "Oh dear," I said.

"He took pictures of the inside of the library as soon as they arrived, before Ellen knew what was going on. I told him no more photographs, but after they left, he took quite a few of Mrs. Harrison standing in front of the lighthouse."

I had no idea what Heather Harrison might be after, but I didn't care for thoughts of where this might be going.

"When she first introduced herself to me," Bertie continued, "I naturally offered my condolences on the death of her husband. She accepted them, but then she launched directly into the questions about you, Lucy. She asked me if I knew of any reason why you would have invited Todd to your house that evening."

"That's not what happened! I didn't invite him! I didn't even know he was coming!"

"I know that, and I told her so. She brushed my objection aside. I thought you should be aware she's asking about you."

"Thanks for handling that. And thank Aunt Ellen for staying out of it. I'm sure it's nothing and Heather won't be back."

"If she does, I have grounds to order her off the premises and call the police if she won't leave. She is clearly interested in one of the staff on a personal level, not coming here because she wants to select a book for her holiday reading."

Was Heather now going to start stalking me? The way she accused Lorraine of bothering her husband? Might that have been some sort of projection on her part?

"Thanks, Bertie. I've no doubt she got the message loud and clear. I suspect she's floundering around, trying to find meaning in her husband's death, and as I was the one near him when he died, she's morbidly curious about me."

"I don't know, Lucy. The cameraman is a concern."

When we'd hung up, I looked at Charles. "All's well that ends well, right, little buddy? Bertie gave her the boot, and she got the message."

But it would appear that Heather Harrison didn't entirely get the message.

At one o'clock, I was reading over the recipe for my pork roast and assembling the ingredients when Josie called.

"Hey, what's up?" I asked. It was unlike Josie to call at this time, peak busy hour at the bakery and café, but she might have taken a brief break to check in.

"Nothing much, but something happened, sweetie, that has me worried. I thought you should know."

My heart fell into my stomach. "Let me guess. A woman has been poking around and asking questions about me?"

"How did you know that?"

"It's becoming a regular occurrence. Did she give you her name? What did she say?"

"She told Alison at the counter she wanted to speak to me. She referred to me by name, so I came out. She told me her name's Heather. She knows you and I are cousins, and she knows you spend a lot of time in here. And that I spend time with you."

"Heather Harrison. What was she wearing?"

"Does that matter?"

"I'm beginning to think it might."

"She wore a suit. A skirt suit in a pale blue with a dark shirt. Very nice. Heels, makeup, hair done. Totally out of place here. Even the businesspeople we get coming in before work or wanting a quick lunch dress business casual. Some even dress as though they're heading straight to the beach after work, which they probably are. She looked like a cable TV host ready to go on camera, not like anyone on vacation. To add to the TV image, she had a guy with her with a fancy camera. He took some pictures."

I groaned. "Can I take a guess that she had questions to do with my criminal history?"

"I wouldn't put it exactly like that, but it seemed to be the direction she was going. She asked how often you and Sam Watson met here at the bakery. I didn't give her the chance to ask any more questions. I told her I had to get back to work, and none of my employees would be able to take the time to speak to her. She tried to argue, but I just walked away. I immediately sent a text to all my staff, reminding them that gossiping about customers is grounds for being dismissed."

"I don't know what to say. Except thanks."

"If I see her or her cameraman again, I'll let you know. Alison told me he took some pictures when they first came in, before the woman asked to speak to me."

"I'm sure it's nothing to worry about," I said.

"I'm not so sure, sweetie. Don't hesitate to call the cops if she comes near you. She's creepy."

"Was anyone else with them?"

"I noticed a young woman, late teens or early twenties, hanging back. She didn't say anything. I wasn't entirely sure if she'd come with them or if she was trying to get close to hear what was going on."

"Thanks for this, Josie."

"You take care, sweetie."

I dropped onto a stool at the island. I didn't know what to think. Why on earth would Heather Harrison have any interest in what I got up to? Lorraine had said Heather had political ambitions, but I couldn't see it helping her if she "brought me down." I literally was a nobody. I was married to the mayor of our town, yes, but even he was pretty small fish in a big state and even bigger country. That Connor had no plans to run for mayor again, or to seek higher office, was generally known in political circles around here. Plenty of people still thought he wasn't serious or he'd change his mind. Did Heather also think that? If so, if she thought Connor might be an eventual rival of hers, she was certainly jumping the gun. The campaign for the party nomination to replace the sitting state senator was coming up. Connor wasn't even associated with that party, so he couldn't be secretly planning to run. Shouldn't she deal with any potential rivals for the role first?

No point in speculating. I had no idea what was on the woman's mind. And I hoped never to find out.

I got to my feet, reached for a carving knife, and set about quartering the pork roast. Very satisfying. I chopped onions and garlic and ground and pounded and mixed spices, also very satisfying.

Chapter Twelve

When the meat was in the cooker, doing what it had to do, I sat down again. I no longer felt like reading on the deck and splashing in the waves. I wanted to dismiss Heather Harrison's attentions as those of a grieving woman who'd soon find another outlet for her grief, but I couldn't. The question about me meeting Sam Watson at the bakery bothered me more than anything else. Josie's was a hugely popular spot. It wasn't far from the police station, so plenty of cops and civilian clerks got their morning coffee and muffins there or stopped in to grab a quick lunch.

What was Heather Harrison trying to get at?

I reached for my iPad.

Heather Harrison (née McAllister) had been born in Raleigh, North Carolina. She'd gone to Chapel Hill, where she met fellow student Todd Harrison of Nags Head. She'd majored in journalism in college. Following graduation, the couple married and moved to New York City. Heather initially got a job at a radio station and eventually at one of the city's lesser-known daily newspapers. She was laid off, along with most of the staff at that paper, three years ago. She then started a podcast specializing in the politics of New York State and North Carolina. According to what I could find, the podcast was small in listenership, although she occasionally got some high-powered politicians or influential pundits onto the show. She hadn't broadcast anything new for nine months, which, from what I knew, would be around the time she and Todd moved to Nags Head.

The couple had no children. Todd's writing career took off several years ago, enough that he'd been able to quit his own job. In New York, as well as working on her podcast, Heather was involved in several charities, mostly to do with the arts, serving on the board of some of those charities. I found pictures of the couple in their younger days at various fundraising events. In quite a few of those pictures, they were posing with well-known political figures of both parties. Todd always looked slightly uncomfortable, standing stiffy next to his wife, glass in hand, frozen smile on his face, whereas a beaming Heather was clearly in her element.

Two years ago, one of the charities Heather was involved in became embroiled in scandal. Some of the funds they'd raised, supposedly in support of a struggling youth art project in a poverty-stricken neighborhood, had instead been directed to the daughter of the main sponsor of the project. The whistleblower was none other than Heather Harrison herself, and she'd gotten a lot of favorable press out of it. She was widely quoted as saying that corruption was the root of all evil and had to be stamped out wherever it was found, and those issues became much of the focus of her podcast.

Then, nine months ago, Heather informed her listening audience that she and her husband would be moving back to their "beloved" North Carolina, where she would continue to fight "tooth and nail" against corruption and influence.

Todd was quoted in a literary blog saying that as "true Southerners," he and his wife needed to return to the authentic life of their roots, free from corrupting big-city influences. I wondered if those were Todd's words or Heather's. He was the one with the "name"; her moment in the spotlight of publicity had faded with the change in the news cycle.

I looked up from my iPad at the sound of a key in the door and Connor calling, "Honey, I'm home." I'd spent the entire afternoon doing research. Good thing the dinner didn't need my attention. If it had been in the oven, it would have burnt to a crisp.

"Something smells good." Connor dropped his laptop case on the island and planted a kiss on the top of my head. Then he stood back, narrowed his eyes, and said, "You okay, Lucy?"

"You're perceptive this evening."

"I hope that when it comes to you, I can always tell if something's wrong."

"Not *wrong* exactly, but worrying." As I'd been looking into the affairs of Heather and Todd Harrison, the back of my mind had been wrestling with whether or not to tell Connor what was going on. The matter was decided for me. I'd promised never to lie to him, and I was not going to start now.

"Get yourself a beer, and have a seat," I said. "It's a long story."

When I finished, he said, "How much of this does Sam know?"

"None of it, far as I know."

"He needs to, honey."

I winced. "Someone asking questions about me is annoying, and I'll admit slightly worrying, but hardly a police matter."

"Except that his name was specifically mentioned to Josie, right?"

"Yes."

"Then he needs to know." Connor pulled out his phone.

"Before you call," I said, "Heather Harrison hasn't been around to your office or asking questions about you?"

"Not that I'm aware of," he said.

"I'm surprised you've been left out of it. Whatever it is. If Heather has political ambitions, and she's planning to campaign as a fighter against political corruption, you'd be a good target."

He raised one eyebrow. "Because I'm so corrupt?"

"Sorry, no. Not what I meant. Good thing I'm not the politician in this family. If Heather's after me, the best way to get to me might be through you."

"Maybe she isn't after you, but after something or someone else. It's well known I don't intend to run for office again. I'm not worth her worrying about." He put his phone on speaker and dialed.

"Connor," said the voice on the other end.

"Sorry to bother you if you've gone home for the day, Sam, but Lucy has something we think you should know."

"Hi," I said. "I'm on speaker."

"As it happens I was about to give you a call. Better I come over. I suspect I have an idea as to what you have to say."

"Okay. We're at home."

Watson hung up.

"I guess he knows," Connor said.

Might as well finish preparing dinner while we waited. I went to the pantry and gathered a few potatoes. I'd mash the potatoes and sauté a nice bunch of asparagus to accompany our roast. I was popping the peeled potatoes into a pot of boiling water when we heard a car drive up and footsteps climbing the kitchen steps. Connor opened the door to admit our visitor.

"Beer, Sam?"

"Better not. This isn't exactly a social call." The detective was not smiling, and his eyes were guarded.

Connor glanced at me as he said, "Take a seat, then."

Watson did so. "First, tell me why you called me, although I'm pretty sure I know."

"Heather Harrison?" I asked.

"Yup."

I related the story—stories—as told to me by Bertie and then Josie.

"Yeah. Okay. Here it is. I've been told to stay away from you."

"What?" Connor said.

"I'm obviously breaking that order by coming here, but I decided you need to hear it directly from me. The chief called me into his office a short while ago. This Heather Harrison, wife of the late Todd, has been making accusations against the police department."

"Accusations about what?" Connor asked.

"Incompetence. Favoritism. About being too friendly with some residents, turning a blind eye, playing favorites. She's hinting, so far, that the police are not fully investigating the death of her husband because it might involve people close to certain people in the department."

"Meaning you and me," I said.

"No names mentioned, but yes. I didn't know she'd been to the library and Josie's today, but it fits the pattern. She's looking for the dirt, and the chief doesn't want her to find any. Not that there's any dirt to be found."

"It's been three days since Todd was killed," Connor said. "Does she expect an arrest already?"

"I don't know what she expects," Watson said. "If anything. The current state senator has announced that he's not going to run again, because of ill health. The seat's wide open, and Heather Harrison has her eye on it. The chief is worried she's laying the ground to run on the basis of cleaning up corruption and influence in local law enforcement."

"I did some research online today," I said, "and that's similar to what I found."

"I've heard nothing about this," Connor said.

"Early days yet, but the chief says it's an open secret. She's been shaking all the right hands, going to all the right functions, starting to raise money, looking for campaign staff and volunteers. He was at a social gathering not more than a week ago, and she made a point of introducing herself and saying, without coming right out and stating it, that she hopes for his endorsement. He politely replied that he has no political affiliation. He now thinks that might have been a mistake."

"Was Todd at this social gathering?" I asked.

"The chief didn't meet him, if he was."

"I think I know the event," Connor said. "I was invited but I couldn't make it. Looks as though that was a wise move on my part. I have no wish to become embroiled in state politics."

"Lorraine told me she got the feeling Todd wasn't happy about Heather's political ambitions," I said. "He didn't want to be a political spouse. Is it possible she—"

Watson raised his hand. "I'm sorry, Lucy. I truly am. But I can't hear what you have to say on this matter."

"Why not?"

"I've been told to stay away from you. To pay no attention to your—and I quote—'attempts to interfere.'"

I sputtered in indignation.

Connor did more than sputter. “You must be kidding. Lucy has been of enormous help to you, and thus to your chief and the entire department, these past few years.”

“I know, I know. Again, what can I say, but I’m sorry. It’s only because I’m getting close to retirement, and I don’t much care anymore about the political aspect of things, that I’m here in your kitchen right now, and I didn’t hang up on you earlier.”

“Your chief always has been a—” Connor began. Again Watson lifted his hand. “I might agree with you, Your Honor, but I can’t let you say it. It’s irrelevant anyway.”

“What about Connor?” I asked. “Never mind the death of Todd Harrison or any problems Heather has, or is making up, with the police department, but do you think she’s likely to go after Connor? In his role of mayor, I mean.”

“I don’t care, Lucy,” Connor said. “Let her.”

“I can’t say,” Watson said. “She might not. Connor’s made it clear he doesn’t plan to run again, so he’s not a worthwhile target. She’s a political neophyte. She lived in New York City for a good number of years, and that’s got to count against her despite any talk of North Carolina being her home. She’s working hard to get known here, yes, but she needs something concrete to run on, and I fear incompetence and lassitude in local policing might be it.”

“That ties into something I read. She reported a member of the board of a charity she was with in New York for embezzling. That got her some highly favorable press. I wonder if it put the idea of a campaign slogan into her head.”

“Entirely possible,” Connor said.

"Having been widely praised for uncovering a genuine case of corruption, she's desperately trying to find another. And if she can't find it, she'll make one up."

"Let's not jump ahead of ourselves," Connor said. "She may decide not to take this line any further. There are plenty of real problems for a wanna-be candidate to get herself in front of."

"One more thing before I go." Watson looked genuinely uncomfortable. He shifted on his stool and then looked directly into my eyes. "I truly hate to ask you this, but I will in the interest of full honesty. Did you kill Todd Harrison, Lucy?"

I said nothing. What could I say? Even Connor was struck speechless. He found words before I did. "We're saying 'sorry' a lot here tonight, Sam. I'm sorry, but you need to get out of my house."

"It's okay, Connor," I said. "Detective Watson, I did not kill Todd Harrison. And no, I do not know who did or why."

"Thank you. I wanted to hear it from you, Lucy. Whispers are swirling to the effect that you sometimes . . . make trouble so you can be the hero."

Chapter Thirteen

Connor and I stared at each other. Charles had kept to his cat tree, watching and listening. The moment the door closed behind Sam Watson, he leaped onto the island and from there into my lap. He rubbed his little face into my chest, and I gave him a ferocious hug.

Connor stood up. "The potatoes are going to be overdone."

"I don't care about the potatoes."

He turned the stove off. "That has got to be the most ridiculous thing I've heard in a long, long time. Whatever you do, Lucy, do not confront this Heather person. If she tries to approach you, walk away. Call the police if you have to. If you see her anywhere near the property, call me immediately, and then the police."

"I will," I said. "Sam might have ordered me not to share my thoughts, but I can't help thinking them. If Heather's prepared to use her husband's death as a way of climbing onto her preferred political hobbyhorse, what's to say she didn't decide to put things in motion herself?"

"I see what you're saying, Lucy. If she did kill him, Sam will find it. We don't know if she has an alibi. Even if she does, it might have been a contract killing, or she got a friend to do it. Everything of that sort leaves a trail, and Sam's good at following trails. However . . ."

"However?"

"Can she possibly be that dumb? Or that desperate? She has to realize the police will be thinking exactly the same as you are. She's put herself directly under the spotlight."

"Maybe she doesn't think it matters," I said. "Not if the local police are as lazy and incompetent as she seems to think."

My husband shook his head. "I doubt she believes a word of what she's saying. She's hoping the voters will believe it, and then they'll want her to clean it up."

"I'm going to give Teddy a call. I don't know what Lorriane has to do with this, but I should warn them."

"Go ahead. Do you feel like dinner?"

"Not really, but we should eat something. What's that noise?" Charles was still on my lap, but he'd come to attention. His ears were up, his blue eyes round, his whiskers twitching. I heard the sound again. Voices, coming from the back of our house. And not just one or two voices, as though people were taking a shortcut to the road.

I stood up and put Charles down. He ran ahead of us as Connor and I went into the living room. For a moment I thought our deck was on fire. I blinked and refocused.

Candles. Dozens of candles, flames flickering in the dying light of the day. About thirty people were gathered at the foot of the steps, clutching lit candles, heads bowed.

Connor groaned. "I really, really do not want to deal with this."

"Let's just close the drapes and ignore them," I said.

Before we could do so, a girl stepped forward. She put her foot on the bottom step. And then, ever so slowly, she began to climb. Others followed her in a solemn line while more spread out at the foot of the steps.

"Nope," Connor said. "Not happening."

He opened the door. I swept Charles up and ran to the bedroom. I dropped the cat, shut the door before he could realize he was about to be locked in, and dashed back to the living room.

It resembled a scene from a horror movie. Connor, flames flickering around him, standing tall and resolute, protecting his home. The hordes of the undead (or possessed teenagers) with their fires and their focus.

"Hi, Mr. McNeil," a girl said. Candlelight shone on her face, casting deep shadows into the crevasses. Yup, real horror movie stuff. "Never mind us." Her voice was very young.

"I do mind you," he said. "You can't bring those candles onto the deck."

"We won't be long," another girl said.

"You got that one right."

Some of the kids had pulled the hoods of their sweatshirts up, no doubt liking the image this created, but most of them were in regular summer clothes of shorts and T-shirts, flip-flops or untied sneakers, unbound hair or bouncy ponytails. As earlier, almost all were girls, with a couple of boys hanging back.

"Primrose," I said to a girl at the front, "what is going on?"

"Hi, Mrs. McNeil. Hi, Mr. McNeil. The police report said Todd died here around nine. It's been three days. Three days is an important period of time in the world of the Frighteners."

"What on earth is a Frightener?" Connor said.

"Todd's sorcerers. In his books, like."

"The Frighteners must gather three days, to the hour, after the death of their leader," a girl at the back helpfully added. "Or the world will fall into chaos."

"Suppose they don't know when the death happened?" I asked.

"But . . . well, they just do. They always do."

"You can gather in your own homes," Connor said. "Not here. You are trespassing."

"But this is the spot. We have to be at the spot."

"It's okay, Mr. McNeil. We won't hurt anything."

One of the girls stepped forward. Connor edged backward, unsure of what to do. Clearly, he didn't want to find himself in a brawl with a pack of Nags Head teenagers. She leaned over and put her candle on the floor of the deck, muttering something indecipherable. She had nothing with which to secure the candle, and it immediately toppled over. Fortunately, a gust of wind caught it, and the flame was extinguished. "Oops," she said. "Sorry."

"I am not asking; I am telling you to leave. Now," Connor said. "I'll call the police if I have to."

"Even worse, Primrose Peterson, I will call your mother," I said. The police had been told not to have anything to do with me. I hoped that didn't include responding to a 911 call.

Primrose hesitated. The girls behind her shifted their feet and avoided looking directly at us. The one who'd dropped her candle slunk away, leaving it rolling uselessly across the deck.

The boy who'd been here with the group the other day ran up the steps. He touched Primrose's arm. "We're good here, right, Prim? You don't know the exact spot where Todd died. Maybe it was down here, on the beach. Next to these rocks?"

"I suppose it could have been," she said.

"Close enough," a girl at the back called. "Even the Frighteners don't always know for sure."

First Primrose, then another girl, stuck the bottom of her candle into the sand. The others followed before forming a circle and holding hands. They murmured something indistinct. A couple of them wept.

The boy who'd led Primrose away stood behind her, not joining the circle. He looked at Connor and gave him a nod.

I glanced at Connor and saw him mouth, "Thanks."

A girl wrapped Primrose in her arms. "It's okay. Why don't we go to my place and listen to music and read some sections of the book to each other?"

The boy pulled Primrose's friend's arm away. "Leave her alone, Simone. Can't you see she's upset?"

"We're all upset here, Noah," Simone snapped back. "Pardon me for caring."

Noah put his hand on Primrose's shoulder and whispered something into her ear.

"Not tonight, thanks, Simone," Primrose said. "Maybe tomorrow." She wiped tears from her eyes. and then she turned and walked slowly away with her friend, heading toward the water. He took her hand, and she left it in his. The others followed, leaving their circle of burning candles behind. Simone fell in behind them.

Connor headed for the steps, but I called him back. "Leave it. The candles will extinguish themselves soon enough." Many of them had already flickered and gone out. "If they see you interfering, they might come back to object."

"I do not want to have to deal with this. Of all the ridiculous things."

"They're teenagers, Connor. They'll soon move on to the next thing." I'd said that on Wednesday. Obviously it hadn't worked out as I had so confidently expected.

"Let's hope our house is still standing when they move on," he said. "Not much I can do about a bunch of kids standing on the beach, but those candles worry me. If we hadn't been here to stop it, they could have set the deck on fire."

"What do you suggest we do?"

"I'm going to call the police. Not Sam, but someone needs to know what's going on."

* * *

Connor called the police station and told the dispatcher he needed someone to come around and check out what was happening here.

The dispatcher sent our good friend Butch Greenblatt. Obviously she wasn't aware we were trying to avoid any suggestion of favoritism or influence peddling.

"Did you know there's a whole lot of dead flowers stacked on your front step?" Butch asked when he arrived.

"We are, it would appear," I said, "a site of pilgrimage. Which is what we want to talk to you about."

Our roast pork dinner sat on the counter, cold and forgotten, and I offered Butch a glass of tea while Connor explained exactly what happened earlier tonight.

"I can have a patrol checking this stretch of beach more than usual," Butch said. "You're right about those candles being a fire hazard—for sure if the wind is strong and blowing toward the houses. I don't suppose you know if these . . . what? Frightening People? Whether the bunch from the books are on a three-day cycle?"

I groaned. "The Frighteners. I certainly hope not. That's an idea, though. I can find out. Ronald might have read the books or know someone who has. Maybe there's a counterspell to chase them away."

"I am not going to try to beat a bunch of obsessed teenagers at their own game," Connor said sharply.

"They'll find something else to worry about," Butch said. "Soon enough."

"Perhaps not soon enough for us," Connor said.

"Tell me about it. Since word went out that Todd was killed by an arrow fired from a bow, we've had every one of our frequent callers phoning in with so-called 'hot tips.' Plus, folks keen to tell us they saw a neighbor, who they've always had suspicions about, creeping around in the shrubbery, firing arrows at cats or dogs. Not a single thing has panned out, but we have to check every tip. Total waste of time."

"Back to the teens," I said. "Primrose Peterson seems to be the ringleader. I threatened to have a word with her mother, but I'm not sure if that's a good idea. Mrs. Peterson has been known to overreact to what her daughters get up to. And when she overreacts, she usually achieves the opposite of what she intended." As proof of that, despite Mrs. Peterson's determination to make her daughters into literary scholars, the eldest Peterson girl was now at college on a soccer scholarship. I smiled to myself at the thought of how proud Mrs. Peterson suddenly became. She who'd tried so hard to turn the girl from sports.

"What are you smiling at all of a sudden?" Butch asked me.

"Just thinking about teenagers. Teenagers and their parents. That boy, the one who talked Primrose into leaving—Noah, someone called him—I don't know him. Did you recognize him, Connor?"

"No."

"That might be an avenue to take. I can say something to Mrs. Peterson about what a nice young man he is.""

Butch put his glass on the counter next to the sink. "I'll file a report of what you told me. Don't worry. We'll keep an eye out."

"Thanks for coming," Connor said.

Butch grinned. "All part of the service, Your Honor."

"Maybe not mention that," I said.

"Mention what?"

"That you came out tonight because Connor's the mayor."

"I didn't come because Connor's the mayor. I came because it's my job to address the safety concerns of the citizenry. Is something wrong?"

"No," I said. "Nothing wrong. I won't ask you to let me know if you hear any gossip, or otherwise, around the station about me."

"Lucy!" Connor said.

"In my defense," I said, "nothing wrong with Butch talking to Steph."

"I have no idea what's going on, and I don't think I want to know," our friend said. "But I'm sure I'll find out soon enough."

"I'll walk you out," Connor said. "Something I want to get from the garage."

The men left and the door swung behind them, but it didn't swing all the way closed. It just happened that the abandoned roast was on the counter next to the door, and it needed my immediate attention. I edged closer to the door.

"Didn't want to say in front of Lucy," Connor said, "but that Harrison guy was not just on the deck. He was in our house."

"I'll beef up patrols on the road too," Butch said.

Chapter Fourteen

Connor and I finally got around to eating our cold, greasy pork, dry, lumpy mashed potatoes, and burnt asparagus.

"I'd like to find out more about Todd Harrison's fans," I said. "Someone has to be organizing these outings to our house. They had a big crowd out tonight, and they didn't all just happen to spontaneously arrive at the same time bearing identical candles."

"Forewarned is forearmed," he said. "We can probably assume it was arranged online. Think you can find that?"

"I should be able to. Teenagers these days have no problem airing everything in public, least of all their taste in popular culture."

"See what you can find." He pushed his half-finished plate aside. "I'll do up the dishes, and then I have some reading to do for a meeting in the morning. Before that, I'll get rid of those flowers. If they're left where they are, they'll only attract more."

I looked at my own plate. I also hadn't finished my meal. Despite that, my stomach wasn't feeling too good again tonight. Stress, most likely. It's never easy being accused of being either a criminal mastermind or a corrupting influence on the local authorities. "Another cooking failure."

He pulled me close. "You had more than enough things on your mind tonight, honey. Try making that again. I'm sure it's delicious."

He carried the used dishes into the kitchen, and I got my iPad and settled back at the table in the dining room.

It was late, and all was dark outside, the only noise waves rushing to shore as the tide rolled in. I love little more in life than that sound. I hope I never get so used to it I stop noticing it.

I also love this old house; I love what we've done with it to make it our home; I love the life Connor and I are building here.

The thought of Todd Harrison bringing his problems, whatever those problems might have been, here, to us, and of Primrose and her crowd disturbing our peace with their fantasy world made me very angry indeed.

I opened the iPad. I had no trouble finding Todd Harrison's online fan clubs. Clubs plural. Branches were scattered all over the country; all around the world. From what I could tell there was only one "official" club to which Todd himself had contributed occasionally. I was asked to verify my love of Todd by typing in the title of my favorite book by him, and to agree to the rules about not promoting other books or authors. I knew the title of Todd's most recent published book, and I had no intention of promoting anyone at all. So I was in.

A solid black banner filled the top of the page. Then, a recent picture of the author and his dates. Two women's names, which I didn't recognize, administered the fan club. They wrote a post expressing their adjective-riddled shock at his sudden and tragic (more adjectives) death, and asked fans to leave comments in memory of Todd and his work. Hundreds of people had done so.

I scanned the comments quickly but saw nothing other than expressions of surprise and grief. Nothing that might indicate someone knew more about his death than was in the news, or that they might be celebrating it. I had no quick and easy way of telling where the comments originated, unless the commenter provided that information. It would take me days to check the individual identity of every one of them. And this was only the official fan page. Countless others filled the social media world.

I scrolled down the page, moving back in time as I read earlier postings. Todd had dropped in about a week ago, mentioning he would be a guest of honor at an upcoming fantasy and science fiction conference in Texas, and hoping to meet many of his fans there. Plenty of comments expressed either dismay at not being able to attend, or joy at the prospect of having a drink in the bar with the celebrity or attending a panel Todd would be on.

Scrolling further down, I found some pictures of the pier not far from here, used to illustrate Todd saying how happy he was that he and his wife had come home to Nags Head. A lot of fans then posted pictures of their own favorite beaches, and Todd commented on a handful.

Prior to that, nothing other than postings from the author and the site administrators with news about rereleases, translations, Todd's public appearance, and the like.

Nothing was said about our festival. I wondered if Todd planned to post those details the night he died. Might he have come to my house wanting promo material or further information he could share? It was possible but highly unlikely. I have a library email address, and surely something like that could have waited until morning.

I left the "official" page to see what else I could find in the way of fan pages. I found a lot. Not much distinguished one from another, except many were in languages other than English.

Finally, I landed on the Outer Banks chapter. Once again I had to answer the question about what I loved most about Todd and agree to the rules, and I was in. The page was administered by Primrose Peterson and a girl whose name I didn't recognize.

Like all the other pages, the social media site led with news of the author's death and the shock and grief of his devoted fans. As he'd died in their area, they were able to show a picture of where Todd had breathed his last. Fortunately, the photo had been taken at night, from the beach, and showed not much more than a generic beach-house deck. More photos taken in the daytime of the beach that "Todd so loved." A picture of Todd and Heather in happier times. A request to respect Heather's privacy in "this difficult time."

Someone commented on that request, with a few bad words about Heather. Some fans had gone to the Harrison home to express their condolences to the widow. Apparently, according to the comment, Heather didn't have the courtesy to speak to the mourners herself. Instead, she sent her PA to answer the door and tell the callers to "get lost." I thought of the silent young woman who'd accompanied Heather when she came here. I doubted she'd actually said, "Get lost," but that was the gist of the message.

I couldn't fault Heather for not speaking to them. If the fans arrived en masse, bearing their candles and proclaiming the extent of their sorrow, anyone would send them away. The grief of the fans was a fraction of an inch deep, and for many it was a way of showing off, a dramatic display of mourning, not truly mourning someone they didn't actually know. Soon enough, most of them would go on to other things, and Heather would know that.

I skipped down, searching for mention of the gathering on Wednesday, the day following Todd's death. And yes, they gave our address. I swore under my breath. The post provided not only the location but also the time, and requests for people to bring "objects of remembrance and tribute."

Scrolling back up to Thursday morning, I read plenty of comments about how meaningful it had been to visit the spot where Todd had breathed his final breath.

But then, to my considerable dismay, someone reminded everyone that the only way to truly honor Todd as he deserved would be to follow the required mourning schedule by gathering every seventy-two hours following the death for a year. *A year!* She then asked who would be attending on Friday.

A couple of commentators said they had plans for that night. Sorry. A couple more said they'd done their bit. Sorry. A few were all in, including Primrose, who started a new post with meeting time and instructions.

I sat back with a sigh. This couldn't go on for a year! I didn't want to call the cops on a bunch of well-meaning, not to mention *literary*, kids. Primrose seemed to be a ringleader. I'd been reluctant to have a word with Maureen Peterson, but I might have to. She could, as has been stated, overreact at times.

I scrolled back up to the top of the page to see if anything new had been posted.

Primrose asked if anyone had thought to invite Mrs. Harrison to the mourning gatherings. The replies came quickly:

I saw her at my mom's hairdresser and asked her.

Not interested. Rude about it too.

Forget her. Todd deserved a better life companion than her.

I was about to leave the page, when a comment caught my eye. Under a picture of Todd at a bookstore, signing books, someone said:

Talentless jerk. The world is better off without him, and you bunch of losers need to get over yourselves and get a life.

The comment had gone up less than five minutes ago. I assumed as soon as the moderators saw it, they'd take it down. It was signed by Jane Smith.

Almost certainly a pseudonym.

I briefly wondered if this "Jane Smith" might be Todd's killer, but I soon dismissed the idea.

Easy to make unkind comments from the anonymity and safety of your own computer, but not so brave if she (or he) didn't use their real name. But that's the nature of social media these days. As the saying goes, "On the Internet, no one knows you're a dog."

I did a quick search for Jane Smith on the fan club page, but I found nothing. When I went back to the top, the comment was gone.

The site moderators were quick. Considering the amount of attention their page was getting and that school was out for vacation, they likely had the time to spare and the determination to devote all that spare time to the task at hand.

I searched further on social media pages for Jane Smith.

Turns out there are a heck of a lot of them. And far more than I had the time, or the patience, to check up on. I have computer skills adequate for a person of my age and my profession, but I am in no way capable of digging any deeper than what's available to everyone in the general public. From what I could find, on the site that hosted the fan club, this Jane Smith had zero followers and was following zero people. The profile was set to "private," meaning that without the aforementioned hacking skills, I couldn't find out any more.

No matter, I thought, as I closed my iPad. Some people are mean simply for the sake of it, and the internet gives them the privacy to be so.

Chapter Fifteen

"Good news," Ronald announced the following morning. "Jacob Rose has agreed to be attend the festival."

"You must be kidding," Shannon said. "He's nothing but a hack."

"Nowhere near good enough," Ruth said.

Ronald's face fell. He'd been quite pleased at getting the up-and-coming YA author to agree to be part of our festival. As he said to me while we waited for the others to arrive, the prospect of a summer weekend in Nags Head had done the trick.

The two local authors, the bookseller, Ronald, and I were gathered once again, in the meeting room of the library, to hear of the new development.

"He's better than nothing," Rick said.

"You think I'm nothing?" Ruth snapped.

"I think you're a popular, small-press local author, Ruth. Even you admitted we need a draw."

"I've changed my mind. Look, if we don't have the likes of Todd Harrison, then why not support these local authors you're so dismissive of?"

"I'm hardly—"

"I'll do it."

"You?" Shannon snorted. "You'll do what? Step into Todd Harrison's shoes? You'll fall flat on your face. And not for the first time either."

"My work in progress is almost finished. It will make an excellent main stage reading at the festival. I can—"

"If anyone should be taking Todd's place, it's me," Shannon said. "After all, his new book was originally mine."

Ruth laughed. Ronald and Rick studied the papers in front of them. "What do you mean?" I asked. "Do you have a copy of it? His newest book's not published yet."

"The entire concept of that book was my idea," Shannon said. "Mine."

"Yours?" Ruth snorted. "You've never had a decent idea in your life. All you've ever been is a copycat. And not a very good one at that."

"Todd Harrison took my idea. He stole it." Shannon's voice began to rise. "He did an interview recently on a podcast, and he talked about it. I knew right away it was mine. My idea. My book. I'm getting a lawyer, and I'm going to fight for what's mine. So there!"

"Funny, you never mentioned anything about that when Todd was alive to refute your allegations," Ruth snorted.

"I intended to. I was hoping we could settle this amicably, but I didn't get the chance. He died."

"My point exactly," Ruth said. "He died, so you saw a chance to grab the credit when he couldn't defend himself."

Shannon stood up. She leaned across the table. "That's not—"

Ronald closed his briefing folder. "This meeting is over. You do what you think you have to do, Shannon, but please don't involve any of us here at the library. In the meantime, Jacob

Rose is the headliner of our festival. Lucy's going to make changes to the posters and the online notices. I'll send you photos and a bio of Rose, Lucy. This will be the last chance for changes. If either of you have decided you have better promotional opportunities elsewhere, please let us know by the end of today. Rick has to order the books, and time is running out, right, Rick?"

"Yeah. I do. For what it's worth, Rose is a good pick. I've heard he's an excellent public speaker and puts on a good reading."

"I'm an excellent public speaker," Shannon said.

"Too bad your reading is trash because you're reading from your own work," Ruth said. "Maybe you can get Shannon here to forget about flogging her little books, and she can read from Todd's new book. The one *she* wrote. *Not!*" Ruth laughed.

"Adjourned," Ronald said. Normally Ronald was the most easygoing of men. As suited a children's librarian who put up every day with rebellious or disturbed children, and even more rebellious or disturbed parents. In all the years I've worked here, I'd never before seen him genuinely angry. He was getting there now. The color of his face was close to the red of Spiderman's costume as featured on today's tie. Before he exploded, I hurried to stand up. "That's settled then. Good. I'm looking forward to meeting Mr. Rose."

The door flew open and Louise Jane fell in. "Sorry I'm late. Alarm didn't go off." She looked around the room. "Has someone died?"

"Bad choice of words, Louise Jane." Ronald got to his feet and stormed out.

"I'll fill you in later," I said.

"Ruth," Rick said, "I'm having trouble getting the needed number of copies of your first book. Why don't you come to the store now, and we can talk about it?"

Ruth and Rick left. "That's understandable," she said in a voice designed to be heard behind her. "*The Might of the Stone* has been so popular, my publisher is having trouble keeping up with the demand, particularly with the number of people wanting to read it in preparation for my reading at the festival."

"They printed one copy," Shannon said to no one in particular. "There's been such a rush, they've had to double the order."

"Thanks for coming," I said in my cheeriest voice. "Have a nice day."

She didn't move. "It was my book, you know. Todd's. I was about to find myself a lawyer when he died. Now I'm afraid they'll think I had something to do with his death, and his fans will turn on me."

I said nothing. Legally, ideas cannot be copyrighted. Not many, if any, ideas are truly original. Classic stories are reformatted and changed and reproduced and retold all the time. How many interpretations of *Pride and Prejudice* or the tales of King Arthur are out there?

"You believe me, don't you Lucy?" Shannon asked.

"I can't say," I said. "I've never read any of Todd Harrison's work." I didn't say I'd never read any of hers either.

"Louise Jane?"

"I might agree. If I knew what you were talking about."

"I suggest you send Ronald a quick email," I said. "Remind him you're excited about being part of our festival and you know he's doing his best to make it a success. We do need all hands on deck here."

Shannon sighed. "Okay. I can do that. I am looking forward to it. Although I don't know why he had to invite *her*."

When she'd left, Louise Jane eyed me. "Tough meeting?"

"That's an understatement. I thought Ronald was going to explode."

"That would have been messy."

"Remind me again why we do these sorts of things."

"For the love of literature, Lucy. There's an idea. If Ronald's having problems with the authors, I'd be happy to step in and tell two stories. Maybe three."

We found a barely recovered Ronald chatting to Mrs. Peterson at the bottom of the spiral staircase. Her two youngest daughters, Phoebe and Roseanne, played with Charles on the stairs.

"I'll be up in a minute," Ronald said. "Why don't you go ahead."

"Come along, girls," Mrs. Peterson said.

"Come along, Charles," Phoebe said, her pitch and tone so much like her mother's, I had to choke back a laugh.

Then I had an idea. "Ronald, did you tell Mrs. Peterson Jacob Rose is going to be our festival star? Why don't you give her some of his books to take home for Primrose? I'm sure she'll adore his writing."

Mrs. Peterson's eyes lit up. "A new author. How exciting. I have to admit, I'm getting tired of hearing about that Todd Harrison. Not to make light of the poor man's death, but enough is enough. She's draped her bedroom door in black crepe, and Al had to order her to blow out all the candles she littered the floor with before she sets the house on fire."

"They can get carried away at that age," Ronald said.

"I'm only glad she has her friends to keep her grounded," Mrs. Peterson said as she and her daughters climbed the stairs. Charles leaped onto the railing and preceded them. "I wasn't at all keen to have that Noah Carpenter hanging around earlier in the summer, but now that he seems to be back in Primrose's circle again, I've realized the boy does have a sensible head on his shoulders."

"I still don't know what happened before I arrived," Louise Jane said to me.

"Earlier, Ronald told us Shannon and Ruth can't stand each other, but they'd made a truce for the sake of the festival when they heard Todd was coming. That truce seems to have ended."

"And how," Ronald said.

* * *

On Saturdays in the summer, we close at five o'clock. A few minutes before five, I was on the circulation desk, checking out books for the last of the day's patrons.

Mrs. Peterson and her daughters had left earlier, almost staggering under the weight of the books in their book bags. Ronald sent me publicity information about our new featured author, and I planned to prepare the advertising materials on Monday.

Bertie doesn't usually come in on Saturdays, nor does Denise. Louise Jane had finished work for the day and skipped merrily up the stairs to the Lighthouse Aerie, winking broadly and ensuring I knew she was searching online for a quiet, secluded, yet luxurious seaside cabin to rent for her upcoming vacation.

Ronald came down the stairs, briefcase in hand, as the final patron of the week departed. I stood up and gave my back a good stretch. "Any plans for the weekend?"

"Nothing in particular. It's supposed to be nice, so we're hoping to get some serious beach time in. You?"

"Probably standing guard over my property with a shotgun broken over my arm, watching out for villagers bearing torches and pitchforks." I'd told Ronald about Primrose and her gang although I hadn't dared tell Louise Jane for fear of where she might take the fans' enthusiasm. I'd also decided not to tell Primrose's mother—not yet. Not until the situation got genuinely critical and it was a matter of calling the Petersons or the police. Ronald, who'd read the books in Todd's Frighteners series after extending the invitation to the festival, reluctantly told me that elaborate death rituals and extensive mourning periods were part of the world Todd had created between the pages.

"Rumor had it he was giving up the Frighteners series and working on a new book that would take him in a totally different direction," he said now. "Risky thing to do considering the single-minded fan base he had. Remember how angry everyone was with George R.R. Martin because he was taking so long to finish the *Game of Thrones* books?" He chuckled. "I'll say one thing for Todd. He was mighty brave to agree to come to our festival. The Frighteners fans, like Primrose and her bunch, would have given him a stern talking to if they thought he was abandoning the series."

"Do you think it will ever get published? The new book."

"If it was almost finished, it likely will. The publisher will be keen to get it out there while news of Todd's death is still fresh. Enjoy your Sunday, Lucy, and try not to frighten any villagers."

We walked to the door together, me intending to lock it after Ronald. Before we reached it, it swung open and a man came in. He was of average height, average weight, average age. Thinning brown hair cut short, dressed in khaki pants and an ironed blue-and-white-checked shirt. He carried a small leather over-the shoulder case. "I made it. Whew! I wasn't sure if I'd get here before five."

"Hello," I said. "I'm sorry, but we're closing now. We reopen Monday."

Ronald hesitated, not wanting to leave me alone until we knew what this man wanted.

"I realize that. I just got in from New York City. Long trip. Bad traffic. I'm here about the YA literary festival. Is the person in charge still around?"

"That would be me. Ronald Burkowski. You are?"

The man thrust out his hand. Ronald took it and they shook, and then he introduced me. "Lucy McNeil, assistant library director." The man shook my hand also. His was hot and clammy.

"Great, great. I'm Bill Pratchett. William Pratchett and Associates. I'm the literary agent of the late Todd Harrison."

"Pleased to meet you," Ronald said. "What can we do for you, Mr. Pratchett?"

"I heard from Heather—Mrs. Harrison—that you've removed Todd from your festival lineup. Is that correct?"

"Well, yes." Ronald said. "He is . . . unable to participate."

"Physically unable, perhaps, but not in spirt. I'm hoping you can continue with the original format. Heather would be delighted to represent her late husband and to read from his work."

"I don't think that would be a good idea," I said. "Ronald did you tell Mrs. Harrison our plans?"

"I called her to express my condolences when I got word he'd died. I believe I said I was sorry he wouldn't be able to appear and he would be sorely missed."

"Did she say anything about possibly taking his place at our event?" When Heather confronted me at home, and later spoke to Bertie and to Josie, nothing had been mentioned about the festival, and certainly nothing about her assuming her late husband's place.

"Nothing to the effect of what Mr. Pratchett's suggesting."

"She was in shock, of course. Shock and now deep mourning," Bill said. "Understandable. I must admit the shock was considerable for me as well." He paused briefly. "Such a tragedy. Continuing with his participation, in spirit, would be a tribute to Todd. A mark of respect for how much he's done for your community, specifically, and the world of literature in general."

"Not to put too fine a point on it," I said, "but Todd Harrison moved away for college and didn't come back until a couple of months ago. He hasn't done anything for our community. As for the world of literature, he had his niche, but he wasn't Margaret Atwood or Toni Morrison."

Ronald was looking at me with something approaching shock. After making snide insinuations to my boss about me, and open accusations to the police, I wasn't going to turn around and invite Heather Harrison to speak in front of a lawn full of our patrons. I had little doubt she'd manage to turn her grief-soaked reading into a political speech about her own merits.

"Besides," I said, "another author has agreed to take Todd's place. We don't have time for them both."

"We might be able to—"

"Nope. Not gonna happen. Let's talk later, Ronald. I have to get off home now. My husband expects his dinner to be on the table on time."

Bill turned from me and spoke to Ronald. "I'm sure we can come up with a mutually beneficial arrangement. Todd's newest book was being kept under wraps to allow the buzz to build. His publishers know it's going to be an international sensation. Think of the publicity your little library here would get if Heather can be convinced to read a section from it in public for the first time."

"Meaning you haven't spoken to Heather about this yet?" I said. "Don't bother. It's not a good idea. Good night." I edged forward a couple of inches. Bill edged away from me. Another couple of inches and he was standing on the step.

I shut the door in his face.

Ronald stared at me. "Lucy? What on earth was that about? The idea's worth considering."

"No, it isn't. Let me get my bag, and on the way out I'll tell you what else has been happening."

Chapter Sixteen

When Connor got home, he shoved a bunch of carnations, wrapped in cellophane and loosely tied with a thin black ribbon, at me. "Here you go."

I studied them. Edges browning, color fading, stems limp. "Thanks. I think."

"I found them on the front step. No card, so judging by the color of the ribbon, I assume they're meant for Todd. Thank heavens he didn't write a series about a florist."

I tossed the flowers in the trash.

"That's not the worst of it," Connor said. "Mike from across the street waylaid me when I was picking up the flowers."

"Waylaid you about what?" I asked.

"He wants me to do something about the number of people knocking on his door and asking for directions to the place where Todd Harrison died."

"Oops."

"Oops, indeed. Apparently some of the so-called mourners have been told it's the last house on South Old Oregon Inlet Road before hitting the town limits, but they weren't told which side of the street. He put a sign on the door saying, 'If you're here about Todd Harrison, go away.' I gather his sign didn't have the desired effect."

"What did you say?"

"What could I say but apologize and tell him there isn't much I can do. I was able to tell him the police have increased patrols on this street, but that didn't mollify him. I suggested posting a no trespassing notice, and he said he didn't want his kids' friends thinking they weren't welcome. Besides, his wife runs her bookkeeping business out of their home. She has clients popping by all the time. I won't say he was angry, Lucy, but he was annoyed. This can't continue."

"Let's hope the furor dies down before too much longer. Mention was made of having Todd's wife read in his place at the festival, but I shot that idea down flat. That wasn't my reason, but it's a good by-product. The less we talk about Todd, the sooner his fans will lose attention."

"We can only hope," Connor said.

By profession my husband is a dentist. He intends to return to his practice when his time as mayor is up, and to keep his practice open and his hand in, he sees favored patients on a part-time basis and does some pro bono work. He'd been at the dental office all day, and we agreed to order a pizza for dinner tonight.

He helped himself to a beer and poured me a glass of wine. "Dare we sit out on our own deck this evening?"

"I have good news and bad news. First, Mrs. Peterson took books by a new author home for Primrose. Maybe that will get her interested in something else. I get the feeling Primrose is the ringleader, or at least *a* ringleader, of that group. If Jacob Rose's books meet their approval, Primrose might be able to convert the entire fan club to the new author."

"I assume that's the good news. The bad news is?"

"According to Ronald, in Todd's books the people on the good side have to gather to mourn their fallen leader for a year. Every third night for a year."

Connor groaned. "I dread having to tell Mike that."

"If such is the case, and the fans are following the pattern, we should be okay on our own deck tonight. It's not a third night since Todd died."

We took our drinks outside and sat together, enjoying the warm soft night, watching the activity on the shore and farther out at sea. Charles was allowed to join us wearing his halter and a short leash fastened to the leg of the table. Lights came on in the house immediately to our left. A plane flew overhead. People walked through the incoming surf. "My mom wants us to come for Thanksgiving," I said.

"Do you want to go?"

"No."

"Are we going to go?"

"Yes. We had last Thanksgiving with your parents, so I guess it's mine's turn. I wonder if I can talk Ellen and Amos into coming. I'd love to have Josie and Jake and the baby, but Thanksgiving is such a busy time for them both, with the restaurant and the bakery."

"Feel like a walk before ordering the pizza?"

"I'd like that," I said.

I took our glasses inside and put Charles into the house. I kicked off my shoes, locked the deck door, and joined my husband on the still-warm sand. We walked slowly down to the shoreline, holding hands in the long, slow twilight of a summer's evening. Families picnicked on the beach; a few determined people were still trying to catch some fish. Kids shouted and splashed in the waves. The town limits end not far past our house, and the long empty length of Cape Hatteras National Seashore begins. It was quieter there, away from the hotels and vacation rentals of town. I let the gentle surf wash over my feet, and I felt most of my cares wash away with it. The police would find Todd Harrison's murderer. Primrose and her gang would soon forget Todd. Heather Harrison would take her political ambitions elsewhere.

"Ready to turn back?" Connor asked me.

"I am."

* * *

After dinner, Connor went to the den to watch some sports thing on TV. I sent an email to my mom saying we'd be delighted to come to Boston for Thanksgiving. Ronald's message with the new author's details sat in my inbox, and that got me thinking.

Shannon McKinnah claimed Todd Harrison had stolen her idea. Todd's agent wanted to begin promoting the forthcoming book. I wondered if Heather Harrison would find a way to use Todd's death to advance her political career. I'm still close to a college friend who works in publishing in New York, It wouldn't hurt, I thought, to ask her if she had any inside gossip. It was past nine o'clock on a Saturday night, but she had a six-month-old baby, so she was unlikely to be out clubbing in Manhattan.

Hey, Michelle. Lucy here. Do you have a few minutes for a chat? If not now, anytime.

The reply was instantaneous: *Perfect timing. Just got Tammy down. Finally.*

I gave her a call. After a few minutes of general gossip about mutual friends and filling each other in on our own lives, me telling her she should come and visit next summer when Tammy could play on the beach, and her reminding me that New York City was the best city in the world for a weekend escape, I got to the point.

"Your company publishes a YA author named Todd Harrison, right?"

"Yes, we do. Did you hear he died? Hey, I've just made the connection. He lived in Nags Head. Did you know him?"

"I'd met him, yes. He was due to appear at our YA authors' festival in a couple of weeks."

"I hope it doesn't derail your event."

"He'll be missed, but we're going ahead. We have other authors scheduled to appear. Did you ever work with him?"

"No, I didn't. I'm not in either YA or fantasy, but we talk about our projects over drinks or lunch all the time. What do you want to know?"

"I'm not sure I know what I want to know. Ever hear any rumors that he wasn't the author of his own books?"

"No. Is that true?"

"I don't know or not know. A woman here is saying she provided the inspiration behind the new book."

"Forget that, Lucy. People are constantly crawling out of the woodwork claiming big-name-author stole their idea. They insist all they want is to be mentioned in the acknowledgments, that plus a million bucks to drop the lawsuit. They're usually shown the door mighty fast and told to feel free to do what they want to do."

"Usually? But not always?"

"Always, in every case I'm aware of, Lucy. As for Todd Harrison himself, he was a solid mid-list author. He had a bestseller a couple of books ago, but later books didn't do as well. Between you and me, his editor was considering discontinuing his series."

"I've been told he left that series and was working on something else. It was, apparently, getting some buzz."

"And it was. All this is secondhand to me, Lucy, but that's what I heard. I don't know if a contract's been finalized yet—I can check on that—but from what I hear, his editor's interested in taking a chance on a new book from Todd. It's not the start of a series, but a stand-alone."

"What's the status of the book right now?"

"I can't say for sure. Last I heard it hasn't been delivered yet."

"If the publisher's showing solid interest, that must make his agent happy."

"Seems to me I heard something about that. Can't quite put my finger on it. What's his agent's name, do you know?"

"Bill Pratchett."

"That's it. I know him. One or two of my authors had been with him at some time."

"Not any longer?"

"Not if they stay with us for any length of time. He's strictly small potatoes, and from what I've heard, not very good. Come to think of it, Todd was likely his biggest client. Pratchett has trouble keeping junior agents at his agency, and that means continuity and follow-up often falls through the cracks. Unless something's changed that I don't know about. Which is entirely possible. Since having Tammy, I'm not nearly as clued into the gossip network around the office as I once was. No going out for drinks after work and all that. I don't usually even join the gang for lunch, as I'd rather work through my lunch hour and get home on time." She sighed. "I miss it sometimes." Then she laughed. "But only sometimes. Nothing's better than having Tammy. What about you, Lucy? Motherhood in the cards yet?"

"Early days for us still."

"Time passes."

"That it does. Thanks for this, Michelle."

"Keep me posted. I've heard the police think Todd was murdered. That's tough."

"Seems so. Before you go, what's likely to happen with the new book now that the author's not around to promote it? Will it get published?"

"If I took a guess, I'd say yes. Presuming they like it enough to make an offer, they'll want to rush it into print to take advantage of Todd's death being in the news. I know that sounds callous, but it's business. I can ask around, if you'd like me to. Everyone's talking about it because of Harrison's death."

We sent greetings to each other's husbands and hung up. I didn't think I'd learned anything new, and I didn't know what any of it meant anyway. But every piece of the puzzle can lead somewhere. I almost started dialing another number before I realized I couldn't do that. Once, I would have told Sam Watson what I'd learned. But now . . . Now I was on my own.

I stood up and went to the windows overlooking the deck, the beach, and the ocean beyond. To my infinite relief I saw no sign of teenage mourners. Dare I hope they'd given up and would leave us in peace?

I could hope. But it was a Saturday night in the summer. Kids of that age had beach gatherings to go to, movies to see, dance parties to join. For some of them, even family dinners to reluctantly attend.

Not yet time to put down our guard. I closed the drapes against the night.

Chapter Seventeen

Sunday morning, I was in the kitchen, rattling pots and pans and gathering breakfast ingredients. The library was closed, but Connor planned to put in a half day at his dental practice. I'd do my wifely duty and make a big breakfast we could enjoy out on the deck before he left.

First thing, I put the coffee on, and then I popped a tray of bacon in the oven and placed a pan of sausages on the stove. I got out tomatoes, onions, and herbs and chopped them up to mix in with the scrambled eggs. I melted butter in a frying pan and dropped slices of wheat bread made at Josie's bakery into the toaster.

I poured myself a cup of coffee and took that first welcome sip. I then decided I didn't feel like coffee after all. I poured the contents of my mug into the sink and put the kettle on. A nice light green tea would be just the thing this morning.

I assembled a tray with dishes, cutlery, butter, jam, and hot sauce. The sausages spat fat, and my stomach rolled over. I swallowed heavily. I took the bacon, brown and crispy, and also spitting fat, out of the oven.

I really didn't feel too good. A piece of toast with a dab of Aunt Ellen's homemade raspberry jam would be about all I felt like for breakfast.

I served up a huge plate for Connor and carried the tray outside.

He accepted a fresh cup of coffee with a smile. I put the plate in front of him. His eyes widened. "Gosh, Lucy. Do you seriously think I can eat all that?"

I sat down. "Gotta fuel up for a long day at the salt mines."

Charles snoozed in the chair next to mine, and I gave his head a rub.

"As do you. Is that all you're having?"

"I'm not too hungry. Besides, I have to save room for all the tasting I plan to do."

I was due to spend the day at Aunt Ellen's, helping her prepare her contributions for the upcoming hospital fundraising bake sale. Ellen's daughter, Josie, is a professional pastry chef. I am not. I'm not even much of a baker. But Josie had her own place to run and her own customers to bake for, and I can follow instructions as well as the next person. Almost as well as the next person.

"I hope," Connor said, "you'll learn to make pecan squares the way Josie does." He patted his flat belly in anticipation.

"I suspect that's a closely guarded secret. The recipe is probably in a bank vault somewhere, kept under lock and key."

I started feeling quite a bit better once I had a few sips of green tea and nibbled on my toast and jam. Connor and I lingered over our breakfast and coffee for a long time, enjoying each other's company while watching the ocean and the beach come slowly to life, and made plans for a night out later.

Eventually Connor stood up, kissed me, wished me a good day, and left.

I was hunting for my car keys, prior to saying my goodbyes to Charles, when the phone rang. Aunt Ellen. "Hi, honey. I've only just discovered I'm almost out of butter. I can't imagine how I could have forgotten. I can't have a baking marathon without butter. I can slip out to the store, but if you're on your way . . ."

"Sure, I can get it. How much do you need?"

"Get four pounds. We're going to need a lot. If you go to the store opposite the café, you can drop in and get us a couple of drinks. Extra-large frozen mocha latte for me, please. And tell them not to skimp on the whipped cream."

"Happy to. See you soon."

"She probably forgot the butter on purpose," I said to Charles. Aunt Ellen did love her icy latte.

Butter purchased, I dashed across the road to Josie's Cozy Bakery. At ten o'clock on a hot sunny Sunday it wasn't too busy. Meaning the line didn't stretch out the door and down the sidewalk. I slipped inside.

About half the tables were taken. Three or four people waited at the end of the counter for their order, and two customers were ahead of me in the line. Alison gave me a wave when she saw me come in, and called, "Are you here to see Josie, Lucy?"

"No. Just getting a drink order."

She smiled at the next customer and asked, "What can I get you?"

I glanced idly around the room, checking to see if anyone I knew was here.

Someone was.

Shannon McKinnon sat at a high-topped table made out of a reclaimed ship's barrel. A large black and white framed photograph of the Bodie Island Lighthouse at night, the powerful beacon warning ships at sea to stay clear, hung on the wall above her. Four stools covered in blue and white cloth were pulled up to the table, but she was alone. She didn't have a drink or food in front of her, so I guessed she was waiting for someone.

She saw me watching and gave me a small wave.

"Lucy?" Alison said.

"A medium low-fat latte please and an extra-large frozen mocha latte with plenty of whipped cream."

"On your way to Ellen's are you?" she said, and I laughed.

I headed to the end of the counter to wait for my order, hesitated, and then kept walking. "Shannon, hi. I hope you've decided to still participate in our festival."

"It wasn't me who threatened to quit if I didn't get my own way," she said.

"Okay." I edged backward. "Have a nice day."

"I'm sorry, Lucy. Let me rephrase that, I'm greatly looking forward to it."

"I'm glad."

"Never mind me," she said. "I'm feeling pretty nervous. I have a meeting with a big-time agent in a couple minutes."

"Good luck."

She dug in her tote bag and brought out a book to show me. The cover wasn't particularly appealing, mostly murky shadows against a dark background, but her name was prominently displayed. "I've managed fine so far without an agent." She laughed so nervously I knew she was lying. "Why should I give some smooth-talking New Yorker fifteen percent of my hard-earned income, right? But now . . . Now I'm at the point where it's time for me to move into the big leagues. If someone like Todd Harrison can get a six-figure advance, why can't I, right?"

"Totally," I said.

"Lucy, your order's up!"

"Be right there." I half turned and then I stopped. "You're meeting a New York agent today? Is his name Bill Pratchett?"

"Yeah! He's Todd's agent. He's going to be looking for new talent, right? He got here yesterday to meet with Heather and make plans for the release of Todd's new book. Which, as I might have mentioned, is partially my book. I sent him an email last night, told him all about myself, and asked if we could meet." She picked up her book and balanced it in her hands.

I put my bag of butter on the floor under a spare stool and sat down. "Do you intend to make a claim for authorship of Todd's book?"

"I do. I'm sure once this Bill Pratchett reads my book"—she held it up—"he'll realize I can write as well as Todd ever did, and understand how I provided the idea for Todd's book."

"You don't need my advice, Shannon, and I'm not in publishing, but wouldn't you be better to start fresh with this agent? It's unlikely he's going to want to hear what you have to say otherwise."

"Why wouldn't he want to hear it? It's the truth."

Because he won't want to get into a legal battle with all the complications that entails, I thought, but didn't say.

"I'm early—nervous I guess—so I have time to tell you what happened. Todd and his wife moved to Nags Head about eight or nine months ago, right? Not long after he arrived, he gave a talk at the library in Manteo. I went to it. He's a big name right? I always believe in hearing what successful authors have to say. Not that I'm not successful, in my own small way"—embarrassed giggle—"but you know what I mean."

She leaned across the table, inviting me into her confidence. I leaned toward her, willing to be invited. "To be honest," she continued, "I thought his talk was deadly dull. A lot of people came, and I could tell they were getting restless, the kids in particular. It's difficult to keep the attention of teenagers. That's one of my strengths. The kids love me. And my books, of course. Anyway, after Todd's talk and signing, as he was getting ready to leave, I approached him. I told him I was a writer too, and I suggested we go out for a drink. Don't take it the wrong way, Lucy. I knew he was married. I'm married too." I hadn't thought anything of the sort, but I wondered why Shannon rushed to mention it.

"We went to a bar on the beach. I was hoping to get some tips on promotion from Todd; maybe he'd offer to introduce me to his agent or his editor. Instead, all he talked about was himself. The more he drank, the more maudlin he got. His last book was flop; he was afraid his publisher was going to drop him. Sales of the most recent of the Frighteners series were far lower than they needed to be to justify the size of the advance. I have to say, Lucy, I was shocked to hear that. I thought he was such a big success, and everyone says that series is a giant hit. Goes to show, right? Anyway, he told me he wanted to write something completely different. Have a fresh start. Break from expectations, and all that. But absolutely nothing was coming to him. So I foolishly told him what I was working on."

"And?"

"And that was that. We finished our drinks and left. Then, what do you know, I was listening to this podcast all about fantasy fiction, and they were interviewing Todd. They mostly wanted to know about the Frighteners series, but when they asked him what was next, he started talking about the new book."

"When was this podcast? Before Todd died?"

"Yeah. A little over a week ago maybe. Todd would be appearing at the library festival, same as me, so I tuned into the podcast, wanting to get some idea of what he might talk about. He didn't sound at all like he did the night he talked to me. This time he was excited, upbeat."

"Don't read anything into that, Shannon. Todd would have been interviewed many times about his books. I'm sure he knew how to play that game."

"No, he was super enthusiastic when he talked about his forthcoming book, about how excited he was, and how original and groundbreaking the new book would be. He said he was going to go deeper and darker than he'd ever gone before."

"You thought it was the same as your idea?"

"Totally! At first, I thought he'd been inspired that night in the bar, and how exciting would that be for me, but then as he went on, I was shocked, Lucy, absolutely shocked. It's exactly the idea as I told it to Todd. I might as well have written it myself. I did write it myself!"

"A couple of sentences about the concept is not a book, Shannon," I said. "An author takes an idea and makes it their own."

"He stole that idea from me!"

"How far along are you in your own book? The one with this . . . idea?"

She glanced away. "Not as far as I'd like. Unlike some writers, I can't produce the first draft of a book in eight months. I can't make a living from this—not yet—so I still have to go to work.

My husband doesn't always understand that I need to devote time to my writing. I backed out of going to his mother's birthday party in the spring so I could have some writing time, and he was mad about that. Not that his mother cares if I come or not."

I didn't ask Shannon to tell me about this idea she supposedly gave to Todd. I didn't want to know, and I didn't want to one day be accused of using her idea. Not that I have any intention of ever writing a book. Or any talent, if I even wanted to. I took some creating writing courses in college, and got solid Cs for effort.

"Did you speak to Todd about it?" I asked.

"No. I didn't get the chance. I thought it would be best not to rush into things. I wanted to think it all over and find the right time to have a chat with him. I got busy with work and stuff, and then we met at the meeting at the library. We went around the table and introduced ourselves. I don't know if he even remembered me. He didn't act like it. It wasn't the place for me to talk to Todd—not about something so important, and not with that Ruth Vivac sitting there gloating."

"What about after the meeting broke up? Did you talk to Todd about it then?"

"I wanted to suggest we have coffee, or maybe even go to that beach bar again as a way of jogging his memory. But he was talking with Rick from the bookstore, and then he got into his car and drove away. I didn't have the opportunity to talk to him, but I had his private email address from the messages Ronald's been using to organize the festival. When I got home, I sent him an email right away." She dipped her head. "I never heard from him."

"That's . . . too bad."

"Yeah, I sat up for a long time that night, waiting for his reply. Then, in the morning, I heard he'd died."

"Did you explain to your husband why you were waiting for a phone call or email that night?" I asked. That might seem like something that was none of my business, but I was really asking if Shannon had an alibi. Someone who could say she was home at nine o'clock, sitting up, waiting for a reply that never came.

"He was away. He and his brothers go to Vegas together every July for a week."

So, Shannon didn't have an alibi.

"Hello there," a man said. "You're the lady from the library." Bill Pratchett stood by our table. "Nice to see you again."

"I'm Lucy, yes."

"And this must be Shannon. Bill Pratchett."

Shannon jumped to her feet. "Mr. Pratchett, I'm absolutely thrilled to meet you at last. I just know we're going to have a very fruitful relationship."

"That," he said as he unwrapped his case from his shoulder, put it on the table, and dropped onto a stool, "remains to be seen. I'll have a coffee. Black, no sugar. And a cookie or muffin or something."

"Right, right." Shannon bustled off.

"Discussing the festival were you?" he said to me. "Have you considered my proposal?"

"No and no. I don't want to go into any details, and I won't, but Heather Harrison was asked to leave the lighthouse library on one occasion. Meaning, she's not welcome back. Not in any capacity."

"Might that have something to do with the fact that you were the last person to see her husband alive?"

"The last person other than his killer. How do you know that?"

"Heather told me. He died at your home. Under suspicious circumstances."

"Coffee and a sugar cookie." Shannon put the drinks on the table. She'd bought coffee for Bill and herself, and nothing for me. That was okay, as I wasn't planning on staying any longer.

"I'll leave you to your meeting," I said.

"Nice talking to you," Shannon said. "I brought one of my books for you to read, Bill. Can I call you Bill? I know you'll love it. It's exactly the type of high-fantasy, intricately crafted world-building Todd Harrison was so successful at." She shoved her book toward him. Bill lifted one eyebrow and barely gave the book a glance. He drank his coffee as Shannon blundered on. "Before we get into that, I want to be completely honest with you. I intend to tell Todd's publishers that his newest book, the one not out yet, was my idea, and I want co-credit. It will make things so much easier, don't you think, if you represent me too?"

Bill stared at her. I stayed where I was, curious as to how this scene was going to play out.

He put his cup down. "Is this some sort of a joke?"

Oblivious to his tone, she prattled on. "Not at all. Why would I be joking? You see, one night Todd and I went to a bar. He told me he wanted to do something new and different, but he was having a bad case of writer's block, and so to cheer him up, I told him all about my new book."

Bill grabbed the cookie and stood up. "Not interested."

"But, but . . . you have to be interested. I'm telling you your biggest writer plagiarized my idea."

Bill turned to me. "Did you put this person up to this?"

"Don't look at me," I said.

"Todd Harrison passed away less than a week ago." Bill spit out the words. "His new book is close to completion, but not yet finished. Nevertheless, it is already predicted to be next year's biggest book in fantasy. And not just YA fantasy—they're bringing it out to a larger audience. Negotiations are already underway for foreign language rights and movies and TV."

"That's good, right?" Shannon said.

"I do not need to be tied up in a frivolous lawsuit brought by a failed woman writer who thinks a drunken night with a popular author is her ticket to fame."

I didn't know what being a female author had to do with it, but I said nothing. Shannon's mouth opened and closed. Tears gathered in her eyes.

"I'm here, in your charming little seaside village, to work with Mrs. Harrison on getting Todd's magnus opus completed. A considerable amount of work remains to be done, but we're confident it will get done. With no participation from the likes of you." He held back the index finger of his right hand with his thumb and flicked the digit at Shannon's book. He then picked up his coffee and walked away.

Shannon stared after him, tears dripping down her cheeks. I felt dreadfully sorry for her. Bill Pratchett didn't have to be anywhere near that rude. A simple explanation of how hard, to the point of impossible, it would be for her to sue Todd's estate over a vague idea expressed in a bar late one night with no witnesses, not even the writer who went on to write the book. He could have made an insincere offer to consider her work, and then left.

"I'm sorry," I said. "If you're ready to go, why don't I walk you to your car?"

She slid off the stool and gathered up her book. She held it briefly to her chest and took a deep breath. "It was a good idea. But now, when—if—I finish my book, everyone will think I stole the idea from Todd Harrison."

"It will be your own," I said. "There are no original ideas."

"Lucy!" Alison called. "You forgot your order."

"I'll be back for it."

I left the bakery with Shannon. Bill Pratchett stood on the sidewalk a few doors down, sipping the coffee Shannon bought for him. I steered Shannon in the opposite direction.

Directly toward Ruth Vivac, waving to someone beyond us as she hurried down the sidewalk.

Shannon gasped. Ruth looked at Shannon. Shannon looked at Ruth. Ruth lifted her pointed chin and sailed on past. They said nothing to each other.

"Bill!" Ruth cried a moment later. "Thank you so much for agreeing to meet me at such short notice."

Shannon sucked in a sob.

"What's your book about?" I asked, because I could think of nothing else to say.

"It's post-apocalyptic. Almost all human life on earth is gone, and a band of courageous young people, the last of their families and community, work together to create their own brave and hopeful new world. They mostly hire themselves out as hunters, food providers for older people or women with small children who can't hunt for themselves. But, of course, all is not well. It wouldn't be much of a book would it, if everything was perfect?" She let out a nervous laugh. "When one of their own falls afoul of a gang of roaming pillagers, they're forced to join forces with one of the villagers and fight back."

"Sounds interesting," I said. "Where's your car?"

Shannon pointed to a small white compact neatly parked in front of a hair salon.

So far, I'd heard nothing the slightest bit original about this story. The success of the book, or not, would all be in the creation of the world and the portrayal of the characters and the skill of the writing.

"The main character is this girl, one of the villagers who's being exploited by the bad gang. She's something of an outcast and everyone thinks she's slow. But when the group is threatened, they rely on her and her skill with a bow and arrow to save them."

Chapter Eighteen

I stopped in my tracks and grabbed Shannon's arm. "Bow and arrow. This book is about archery?"

"Oh yes. That's an important part. Hunting for food with bows and arrows requires a great deal of skill and patience. That's why my character is so—"

"Are you an archer yourself?"

"Not yet. Once I get down to writing the actual details of the book, I want to take some lessons, so I can describe it all properly. I haven't had the time, so far."

"Is that one of the things you told Todd about?"

"Yeah. That's why I know for sure he copied my idea. Why are you so interested in that part of it? The characters are—"

"Gotta run. See you at the festival."

* * *

When I got home, I dove for my iPad. From the top of the cat tree, Charles opened one eye and stared at me. Seeing as how nothing exciting was happening and treats were not being offered, he closed the eye again.

I'd read Todd Harrison's official biography and his list of books in preparation for the festival. I went back to his website for a closer look. It had been updated with news of his death and thanks from his wife, Heather, to fans for their condolences.

I searched online for information about Todd. So much popped up about his death, I changed the search parameters for several months prior to now, but not including this week.

Eventually I found what I was looking for. At a bookstore signing in Buxton last month, Todd briefly talked about his exciting new project. The book was a "post-apocalyptic novel about hope and despair in a brave new world." That was it, nothing more.

Shannon said her book was about a "brave and hopeful new world." The similarity in phrasing did more to prove my point than establish Shannon's claim. *Brave New World* is the title of the classic novel by Aldous Huxley, published in 1932. The phrase is a commonly used one, often employed by people not aware of its literary origins.

The bookstore printed the gist of Todd's remarks in a blog post, along with photos of the author surrounded by books and readers. In answer to a question about the amount of research he does for each book, he told the audience he'd learned archery for the new work.

My phone rang. I glanced at the name on the display. Aunt Ellen. The butter. The baking day.

"I am so sorry," I said. "I forgot."

"You forgot between an hour ago and now? Did something happen?"

"No. Yes. I got thinking about the Todd Harrison situation, and off I went, down the rabbit hole."

"If you're busy, Lucy, I can manage on my own. But I do need the butter."

I'd last seen four pounds of butter sitting beneath a table for four in Josie's Cozy Bakery. Ellen's and my drinks remained unclaimed. I hoped the bakery staff had given them to someone worthy while they were still hot. Or cold in Aunt Ellen's case.

"Give me half an hour," I said.

I wasn't supposed to contact Sam Watson, but I needed to tell him about these archery lessons Todd had taken. He might already know about that, but he might not. Robert and Eilleen Cook, the couple who'd been here the other night, checking out the scene, were from the nearest club. I didn't know if the police asked them if they'd met Todd there, but even if they hadn't, he could have gone somewhere else. Was it possible his death had nothing to do with his books, but he'd made an enemy at an archery club?

Unlikely, I thought. Surely anyone he'd fought with to the point of that person wanting to kill him, would have the common sense not to use the weapon—and an unusual weapon at that—they were both practiced in.

Then again, no accounting for how intelligent, or not, some people might be.

It was Sunday. If I wanted to talk to Detective Watson, I should call his private number. He'd never objected before. I made the call.

"Lucy?" he said.

"This is Mrs. Lucille McNeil, concerned private citizen. I have information that might be pertinent to a crime. If you are off duty, sir, I can leave a message with the dispatcher."

He sighed. "Go ahead, Lucy."

"Did you know Todd Harrison had experience in archery?"

"I did not. His wife never mentioned it. How do you know this?"

"I've been doing a little research. On my own time, again as a concerned citizen, not because I'm investigating or anything, but because I'm curious."

"I get the point, Lucy. What have you learned?"

"His new book, the one not out yet, is about archery. The characters hunt and fight with bows and arrows. He told the audience at a book signing not long ago he joined an archery club to get his facts straight for the book. What I read didn't say where the archery club was. I thought you might want to know about it, that's all."

"I do want to know. Thank you for calling. In return, I'll tell you that our attempts to find the person who bought the bow likely used in the attack on Harrison have come to nothing. Nothing unusual or special about it. Generally available, commonly used. Not expensive. No license or background check of any sort is required to buy one or the arrows it uses."

"The people from the archery club who came here the other night told us the shot on Todd didn't require a great deal of skill. Did Butch tell you that?"

"He did. I was hoping we were looking for an Olympic-class athlete, but that doesn't appear to be the case. Anyone who has even a minor amount of experience, enough to know how to handle the equipment safely, could have made it. With enough luck, it might have even been someone with no experience."

"Speaking as someone with no experience whatsoever, I couldn't have picked that thing up and fired it. To start with, I wouldn't have been able to figure out which end was which, never mind fit the arrow, hold it straight, take aim, and fire. All without making a lot of fuss and noise that would have attracted attention, not the least from the individual sitting in firing range."

"Good to know."

"Thanks, Sam."

"Thank you, Lucy. You take care, and . . . if you have anything more to share, please feel free to call me. Any time."

I hung up, smiling.

Ruth Vivac and Bill Pratchett were nowhere to be seen when I got back to Josie's. I found my butter and ordered another round of drinks, and went to Aunt Ellen's house for a baking marathon.

Chapter Nineteen

Connor and I enjoyed a pleasant night out at Jake's Seafood Bar. We sat at a table for two at the edge of the veranda as fishing boats returned to harbor and the big, round orange sun set over Roanoke Island. In the distance, the fourth-order Fresnel lens of the reproduction Roanoke Marshes Lighthouse flashed its rhythm. I had a flashback to one of my first dates with Connor, in this very restaurant, where, over hush puppies and the seafood tray, he talked about the history and importance of lighthouses and how much he loved them. About the writing on the wall at Currituck Beach Light, farther up the coast, which says "to illuminate the dark space." I believe I began to fall in love with him that night.

"Treat from the kitchen," the waiter said as he placed a platter of those hush puppies on the table between us, along with our drinks. Jake knows how much I love the tasty little lumps of dough. "Ready to order?"

Connor asked for the ribs, and after much dithering and consulting with the waiter, I decided to have the crab risotto. My stomach had settled down, and I'd been able to sample the freshly baked goods we'd made at Aunt Ellen's. I was looking forward to my meal.

When the waiter left, as I dipped a hush puppy into the spicy sauce provided and took a bite, I told Connor what I'd learned from Shannon earlier and that I'd called Sam Watson with the information. "He seemed almost pleased to hear from me. I hope that means some of the pressure is off him regarding his association with me, the criminal mastermind."

"Don't take this lightly, and don't jump the gun, Lucy. As we were cleaning up the office before leaving, Irene told me the buzz in the political world is that Heather Harrison is about to announce her run for the state senate seat coming empty."

Irene is Connor's dental assistant.

"For what it's worth," he continued, "Irene's husband is active in their party association, and he's not happy about Heather. He calls her an outsider, an opportunist, and an upstart."

"No one thinks it's in bad taste, her throwing her hat into the ring so soon after her husband's death?" I asked.

"*I* think it's in bad taste, but what I think doesn't much matter. It's not entirely a new idea on her part; she has been taking some of the preliminary steps. I'm not surprised she's going to try to use the situation to her advantage."

"Making me wonder, once again, if she took it upon herself to arrange this advantageous situation."

"Don't say that to anyone else, Lucy. You don't want a libel suit. As for Sam, let him take the lead. Leave him alone, and don't press him. Now, on to more important things. What did you make at Ellen's, and did you bring any samples home?"

* * *

Mondays in the summer are slow days at the library. Ronald is off, and we have no scheduled children's programming. Denise and

Louise Jane both work part-time, and Denise doesn't come in on Mondays. Bertie was in her office, door closed, still wrestling with getting the budget finished prior to a board meeting this afternoon, and Maureen Peterson was the volunteer in the children's library. Charles was taking advantage of the empty chair by the magazine rack to have a snooze.

Louise Jane skipped happily down the stairs around eleven, carrying a mug of coffee and her laptop. "I have found the most perfect place for my private" big wink "getaway."

"That's nice," I said. "Where?"

"Let me show you. It's gorgeous." She dropped the computer onto my desk, but before she could open it, Theodore and Lorraine came in.

I blinked. For a moment I scarcely recognized my friend. Teddy wore baggy pink-and-green-checked shorts displaying a pair of excessively knobby knees, and a short-sleeved T-shirt revealing an almost complete lack of muscle structure. Flip-flops were on his feet, and he wasn't wearing his glasses today. Lorraine wore an attractive, flowing, multicolored beach dress over her bathing suit, a straw hat on her head, and enormous sunglasses on her face.

"We're on our way to the beach," Theodore announced.

"Coulda surprised me," Louise Jane said. "I hope you brought lots of sunscreen, Teddy."

"I did, yes. Why do you say that?"

"No reason," she said.

His skin was so white, it was almost fluorescent. Lorriane smiled at him. "I made sure he has lots."

He pulled a book out of his beach bag and handed it to me. "I managed to locate two copies of this." *The Merry Adventures of*

Robin Hood by Howard Pyle. The cover showed the titular character, wearing a green tunic and leggings, about to fire an arrow from a bow considerably less mechanical and sophisticated than the ones Robert and Eileen demonstrated the other night.

"Why did you do that?" Louise Jane said.

"For book club."

"We're reading that in book club?"

"No, we're not," I said. "I told you, Teddy, I think it's in bad taste, considering what happened to Todd Harrison."

"I told him that too," Lorraine said.

"A classic novel is a classic novel for a reason," Theodore said. "The tales are timeless. The value of great literature is because it is so closely reflective of real life, of the human condition, unchanging down through the ages."

"I still don't think—"

"Todd Harrison wasn't killed by a bunch of merry men skipping merrily through the glen in green tights and tiny green hats with feathers stuck into them," Louise Jane said. "I'm with Lucy. That's an inappropriate choice."

"Will you at least read the book, Lucy? Then you and I can discuss it in our private book club."

"You have a private book club?" Louise Jane said.

"No," I said.

"Only for the summer months while the regular club isn't meeting," Theodore said. "As an indication of what I mean by 'timeless' in modern terms, the Sheriff of Nottingham might be considered a politician either corrupt or attempting to twist events for his own purposes. We can discuss that, and the populace rising against corruption under the leadership of what we loosely call the hero. And then—"

"Let's not start the meeting at this very moment," Louise Jane said.

"Count me out," Lorraine said. "Now and later. Come on, Teddy. There's a wave out there with my name on it."

"Actually," I said slowly, "I've just had an idea. Have you read *Brave New World*?"

"By Aldous Huxley? Of course. A true classic of dystopian fantasy that illustrates perfectly my point about continuing relevance."

"I read it many years ago in college," I said. "I can try to refresh my memory. Louise Jane, do you know it?"

"I can't say I've read it, but I know the basic story. Everyone does."

"Exactly," I said. "Everyone does, in some shape or format. Dystopian fiction is hugely popular right now. In YA as well as adult literature. Think of *The Hunger Games*, or *The 100*. Everyone is searching for the brave new world, but not understanding that if we take all our problems with us, the new world won't be all that brave."

"Your point?" Louise Jane asked.

"My point is, that would be an excellent topic for our festival: Searching for Brave New Worlds in YA Literature." Ideas began tripping all over themselves in my head. "Maybe a panel discussion with all the authors, including Louise Jane. Theodore, you could moderate."

His eyes lit up. "That . . . that would be marvelous, Lucy." *Robin Hood* was forgotten in an instant.

"You need to run this past Ronald and Bertie," Louise Jane said. "We don't have a panel discussion on the schedule, and from what Ronald says, he might not want Ruth and Shannon on stage at the same time. Plus, Ruth writes mystery novels, not fantasy, so she'll feel left out."

"True. We'll drop the authors and just go with Theodore and Louise Jane. I'll moderate. We'll keep it short, maybe half an hour. If we talk about the appeal of dystopian fiction in YA, then we fit the mandate of our festival. As a bonus, we can throw in a nod to Todd Harrison's forthcoming book and thus remember he was supposed to be attending."

Louise Jane and Theodore looked at each other.

I had not the slightest doubt that Louise Jane would agree, but Theodore hesitated. "I'm not much of a public speaker," he said at last.

"Nonsense," Lorraine said. "You love nothing more than to talk about books. And this will be a talk about books, with your closest friends, that just happens to be in front of an audience. Pretend they're not there."

He broke into a huge grin. "Excellent plan. I'm in."

"I'll run the idea by Bertie and Ronald, and if they agree, we have some reading to do," I said. "I think we have one copy of the book lying around somewhere."

Theodore already had his phone out. "Checking now." His fingers flew.

"Then again," Lorraine said to me with a sigh, "maybe that isn't such a good idea. I am hoping to have a beach day today, remember."

"The wonders of modern technology, my dear. I have it now, and will begin my concentrated reading this very afternoon."

"Dibs on the library copy," Louise Jane said. "Lucy, you'll have to hunt one down."

"I'm thinking," Theodore said, "that I might be able to incorporate some of my ideas about Robin Hood into my talk. When you think about it, what Robin and his men accomplished in Sherwood Forest, defeating the Sheriff of Nottingham and returning to the rule of law under the true king, did create a brave new world that worked for them and the residents."

"We only have half an hour, remember," I said. "That might be off topic."

"Also remember," Louise Jane said, "it's going to be a panel discussion. You are not giving a lecture. I am not going to talk about Robin Hood."

Lorraine gave him a fond smile. "I'll help him prepare. Which means keeping you to the subject at hand, Teddy."

"Great," I said.

As they gathered up their beach things in preparation for leaving, I remembered something more important than even our festival. "Before you go, have you heard anything more from the police about Todd's death?"

"Nothing," Lorraine said. "The idea that he and I were romantically involved, willingly on his part or otherwise, was preposterous to begin with, and they won't find anything to the contrary. In fairness, if I must be fair, in her grief his wife is searching for meaning behind his death and grasping at the first idea that comes into her head."

"It's good of you to think that way," I said. "But don't let your guard down yet. She has her own agenda, rather like the Sheriff of Nottingham."

"My point exactly!" Theodore said.

Once they'd left, Louise Jane said, "Do the cops honestly think Lorraine had something to do with the death of Todd?"

"Accusations have been made. No matter how groundless those accusations might be, they have to be followed up."

"Like the time they were after me because the tires on my van were worn."

"As I recall there was more to it than that."

She sniffed. "Whatever. Have a look at what I found." She opened her computer to show me information about the beach house she'd rented for her little getaway, and I was suitably impressed. Gorgeous house, on the beach, fabulous views, beautifully decorated, remote and private. A weekend-long stay cost far more than Louise Jane should be able to afford on her part-time librarian assistant's salary, but no doubt Tom Reilly would be paying. Let's just say I suspect his dealings in fine art do not always fall on the respectable side of the law.

Louise Jane went back upstairs, and a few patrons wandered in, returned their books, selected new ones, and wandered out again. Charles rolled over, yawned mightily, and went back to sleep. No one needed my help, so I had time to work on preparing and distributing the updated promotional materials for the YA authors festival. As part of the description of events, I added "Panel Discussion," hoping Ronald wouldn't shoot down my idea. I was printing out a copy for Bertie to show at the board meeting later, when she came into the main room.

"My head is about to explode. Am I getting old, or is the budget harder to deal with every time?" Bertie always starts the day with her long gray hair pinned neatly into a bun at the back of her head. Now, tufts stuck up in all directions, showing where she'd run her fingers through her hair in frustration.

I indicated the poster slowly emerging from the printer. "I've done up new material reflecting the change in lineup at the YA festival. Here's a sample of the poster you can show to the board. Once they've approved it, I'll distribute copies to each of them and ask them to spread the word, and do the same for all our media contacts."

Bertie picked the paper up and studied it. "It looks good. I had a couple of calls over the weekend, asking if the festival would go ahead. I was pleased to tell everyone it would." She tapped at the line I'd added. "Panel Discussion. Is that something new?"

I explained my idea briefly, and she gave me a smile.

"It's up to Ronald, but I think it's a great idea. The topic is relevant, and I always think it's important to make sure young people know the things they think they invented have been around for a long, long time. Thanks, Lucy. I'm putting a fresh pot of coffee on. Can I bring you one when it's ready?"

"Yes, please."

The main door to the library opened. I turned with a welcoming smile, and the smile died.

Heather Harrison, dressed in one of her power suits, this time in a shade of lime green that would have looked awful on anyone else but seemed to suit her. She held her phone in her perfectly manicured hand. To my infinite relief her cameraman was not with her. To my surprise, Bill Pratchett, Todd's agent, was. Layla, Heather's ever-present young PA, slunk in after them.

Bertie put the poster onto the desk. "Good afternoon, Mrs. Harrison," she said politely. "What brings you here?"

Heather smiled at us both. "Your festival is going ahead, I understand."

"It is," Bertie said. "Lucy and I were just discussing it."

"Wonderful. So brave of you to attempt to continue. I don't know if you've met Bill. This is Bill Pratchett, Todd's marvelous agent."

Bertie nodded politely. Bill did the same in return. Charles awoke from his nap and came to join us. He hissed at Heather and arched his back.

"Such a lovely cat." Her smile was strained to the breaking point.

I have always maintained Charles is an excellent judge of character. He's let me down once or twice, but this time he was spot on. An image flashed through my mind of Heather Harrison as the Sheriff of Nottingham. That particular shade of green might have been very fashionable in Robin Hood's day. I hid my smile.

Bill Pratchett leaned over and held out his hand. "Hey there, little buddy." Charles gave it a dismissive sniff, and then he turned his back and jumped onto the desk. Bill straightened up. The shadow of a smile crossed Heather's assistant's face as she watched the cat.

"I was hoping to get a chance to discuss the matter of the festival lineup directly with you, Ms. James," Heather said. "Bill spoke to . . . this lady and your children's librarian—such a charming gentleman—the other evening, but they were less than receptive to our idea."

"Your idea?"

"I suggest we pay a small, tasteful tribute to my darling Todd at the festival. As a special way of honoring him, I'd like to read from his yet unpublished book. I know how much festivalgoers will love that. Todd was, after all, the main reason many, if not most, of them planned to come. Isn't that right?"

Bertie threw a look at me. I took it to mean she was suggesting I take the lead, so I did.

I stood up. Charles hissed. I smiled. "Mrs. Harrison, as kind as it is of you to make the offer, we have to decline. We'll have a word in recognition of Todd at the beginning of the afternoon and ask for a moment of silence to remember him. Unfortunately, as I've already explained, we won't have time for you to read. I heard you're running for political office. Is that correct?"

"I'm mulling the idea over, yes. I have not yet fully made up my mind."

"We're a public library. Owned by the town and thus the citizens of Nags Head. The library can't appear to be in the position of favoring one candidate, or one party, over another. I trust you understand."

"I do not understand. I will not be campaigning at the festival. I'm honoring my late husband by offering to read from his work."

I had not the slightest doubt Mrs. Harrison would manage to turn all of that "honoring" into a speech on her own virtues. Behind her back, the PA rolled her eyes. She obviously agreed with me.

"Todd's book is going to be the biggest thing in publishing next year," Bill said. His eyes landed on the festival poster on the desk. He swept it up and gave it a good shake. "You're going to replace Todd Harrison with Jacob Rose? The man's not even in the same league, never mind those two small-town women writers you have."

"Do you have a problem with women writers?" Bertie asked calmly.

"What? No. I'm saying they're small fry, that's all."

"We're a small library putting on a small festival for the benefit of residents and visitors. We always feature local writers whenever we have the opportunity, and we are proud to do so."

Bill waved the poster in the air. "Along with some unheard-of, so-called 'storyteller.' What a pathetic lineup."

As if she'd heard she was being insulted, Louise Jane appeared on the stairs, a heavy map book clutched in her hands.

"I've allowed Lucy and Ronald complete control over the authors festival," Bertie said. "Their decision is final. Thank you for coming in and expressing your opinion. You are, of course, welcome to attend, as is everyone who loves books."

Bill sputtered.

Layla edged toward the desk and held out her hand. Charles sniffed at it.

Heather pushed a button on her phone. A moment later the door opened, and Nick, her cameraman, came in, bag slung over his shoulder, the large black Nikon in his hands. The camera strap dangled loosely in front of his chest.

I threw a panicked look at Bertie.

Nick held up his camera.

"Put that thing down," Bertie ordered. "No filming."

"We won't be long," Heather lifted her chin and straightened her spine for the benefit of the camera. "I have a question for Mrs. McNeil here. Mrs. McNeil, did you kill my husband?"

I stared at her. "What sort of a question is that?"

"A very practical one. You have a reputation around this town of being of enormous help to the police over the years. Do you enjoy being the object of so much admiration and respect?"

"I don't—"

"Makes me wonder, Mrs. McNeil, what lengths you would go to in order to maintain that reputation. Have you found that the Nags Head police, particularly Detective Sam Watson, sometimes rely on you more than they should? Detective Watson is an older gentleman, I couldn't help but notice. No doubt he's appreciative of the chance to cruise into his well-deserved retirement."

"Heather, I don't see that this—" the young woman began.

"When I want your opinion, Layla, I'll ask for it. At the moment, I do not want it, nor do I need it."

Layla's cheeks flushed, and she dipped her head.

Charles hissed.

Bertie took a step toward Heather. "Stop this nonsense right now." She pointed a finger at Nick. "You—turn that camera off and get out of here."

Heather turned to face Bertie. Nick swung the camera toward my boss. "Ms. Albertina James, director of the Bodie Island Lighthouse Library, has it never occurred to you that the staff here at this public library are spending more time investigating police cases than actually doing the work the town is paying them for?"

"That's not true." Bertie said. "They—"

"I apologize," Heather said. "I didn't mean your staff in general. I meant Mrs. McNeil in particular."

"I–I . . ." Bertie sputtered.

Charles had come to attention. His ears were low, every hair on his back standing up, his claws out, his eyes narrow with fury. If he weighed more than eight pounds, Mrs. Harrison would have had something to worry about.

"Nick, focus on me," Heather said. When he had done so, she looked into the camera, her face composed and serious. "Small police departments are often underfunded, understaffed, and under pressure from the public and local authorities to get the case solved. It must be tempting, wouldn't you agree, Mrs. McNeil, for them to pass some of that case load off to a willing yet totally unqualified amateur?"

"I–I . . . I've only ever wanted to help."

"So thoughtful and civic-minded of you, Mrs. McNeil. Your husband, Doctor Connor McNeil, is the mayor of this town, is that correct?"

"Yes, but—"

"Therefore, ultimately he is your employer. I wonder if there's a conflict of interest there. Small towns are all too often underfunded and always scrambling for money. I'm sure it helps with his budget worries if the police don't need to put in a lot of overtime because of the help of such a keen member of the public. Even better, you don't always have to stick to the guidelines of the law, do you? Not as a concerned townsperson simply wanting to do her civic duty and help out."

"That's not—"

"Which brings me back to my question, Mrs. McNeil. If a case, as you might call it, doesn't present itself, what will you do to keep yourself in the limelight? To maintain that shining reputation of being so clever and so civic-minded."

Bill Pratchett had slunk off to stand against the wall. The poster fell out of his hands and fluttered to the floor. Following her failed attempt to control her boss, Layla stepped away, keeping her head down and her eyes averted. Louise Jane came down the steps. Nick kept filming. I feared that in the lens of his camera I would look like a fish caught on the line.

In fact, that pretty much was what I felt like.

"Or," Heather went on, "do you use that reputation to come to the aid of your friends? You are friends with a local musician and high school teacher by the name of Lorraine Kittleman, are you not?"

"I—"

"Why, I have to wonder, did you invite my husband to come to your house the night he was so brutally murdered?"

"I didn't invite him. I didn't know—"

"Did he want to talk to you about your friend Lorraine Kittleman? Did he perhaps intend to ask you to intervene on his behalf and tell Lorraine to leave him alone? She was becoming rather a pest. I hate to use the word 'stalker,' but it does seem appropriate in this case. Did you plan on killing him in advance, or was it a last-minute thing when he showed up alone and you realized you had the perfect opportunity to, once again, be of help to the police?"

Unnoticed, Louise Jane crept quietly across the floor and came up behind Nick. Before he realized she was there, she lifted the large and heavy map book and whacked it against Nick's camera. He yelped; the unsecured camera flew out of his hands and hit the floor. Louise Jane calmly put her right foot on it. "I thought I heard Bertie ask you to leave. If she didn't, I am."

"Who are you?" Heather asked.

"A storyteller. One who now has a story to tell about intimidation and bullying."

"Can I have my camera back? Please?" Nick asked.

"You can have it when you're ready to leave," Louise Jane said. "Looks like a delicate instrument to me." She leaned forward, putting her weight on her right foot. "Wouldn't want it to break."

"That's enough," Heather said.

"It certainly is," Bertie said. "I'd like you to leave now. If you refuse to do so, I will call the police and have you charged with trespassing. I don't think that will help your political career any."

"You won't have footage of you being dragged away in handcuffs," Louise Jane said. "Too bad."

"All this has nothing to do with me," Bill Pratchett said. "Keep your festival. Heather, I'll meet you back at the house. We have things to talk over. I want that manuscript in my hands, and I want it today." He ran out of the library.

Layla said, "About that, Bill," and went after him at an equally rapid pace.

Heather kept her eyes on my face. "Very well. We're done here. For now. I think we understand each other, don't we, Lucy?"

"I understand nothing. Particularly why you're doing this."

"You are rather naive, aren't you?"

"How can I be both naive and a criminal mastermind at the same time?" I said, thinking I was making a clever point.

She grinned and leaned toward me, her heavily applied perfume washing over me like a wave off the ocean. "The truth, my darling," she whispered in my ear, "is that you can be whatever I say you are."

Chapter Twenty

"Such a lovely library you have here. I'm a proud supporter of public libraries," Heather said to the room. "I'm sure I can count on your endorsement in the forthcoming election." She looked at Charles, sitting on the desk. He'd dropped his attack position at Louise Jane's intervention. "Such a nice cat too."

She left. Once she was gone, Louise Jane took her foot off the camera and stepped away. Nick bent over, keeping one wary eye on her, and picked it up. "This is an expensive piece of equipment. If it's damaged, I'll be calling on you."

"You know where I can be found. Upstairs in our legal section, making note of the laws to do with recording people against their specific instructions in a private setting."

He scurried after Heather, clutching his camera to his chest. The door swung shut behind him.

I dropped into a chair. Fortunately, it was behind me. Incident over and settled to his satisfaction, Charles jumped off the desk and headed toward the comfy chair to resume his nap.

Bertie said, "I have no words."

Louise Jane let out a bark of laughter and punched the air. "McKaughnan to the rescue once again. This is becoming a habit, Lucy."

"You should have confiscated the data stick," I said "He still has the video of me looking totally and completely outmatched. Not to mention entirely witless."

"I didn't know the legalities of my taking it," she admitted. "Bertie asked them to leave, and they did not, so I was pretty sure I was within my rights to take steps to encourage their departure."

"I don't normally approve of our staff attacking visitors," Bertie said, "but in this case it was necessary. I should apologize to you both. Her wave of accusations was so unrelenting, I found myself almost frozen. Witless, as Lucy said."

Two school-age children ran down the stairs, followed by their father and Maureen Peterson. The kids dumped a stack of books on the desk. I stared at them. Then I blinked, forced out a smile, pushed myself out of my chair, and reached for the topmost book. I checked the books out, gave them back, and the family left.

"What on earth was going on down here?" Mrs. Peterson said. "It sounded tense, so I encouraged Mr. Jameson to linger."

"Wise move," Bertie said. "It wasn't a scene to be witnessed by small children."

"Or by ladies of delicate sensibility," Louise Jane said. "Fortunately, that doesn't include me. Are you okay, Lucy?"

"No. But I will be."

"Go to my office," Bertie said. "Sit down, take a breath, close your eyes for a few minutes. Then you need to call Connor and tell him what happened, as his name and position were mentioned. While you're doing that, I'll give Sam Watson a heads-up. He's not going to be happy."

"Not happy at all," Louise Jane said cheerfully. "I'll try and get Teddy and Lorraine. If that woman releases any of that footage, or even just the audio, they need to know in advance."

"What can I do?" Mrs. Peterson asked.

"Hold the fort," Bertie said.

She looked pleased at being given such a weighty responsibility.

"Did Primrose start to read any of the books you brought her?" I asked. "The ones by Jacob Rose?"

"She not only refused, she accused me of being heartless and failing to understand the depths of her grief. If her father died, she asked me, would I accept a replacement before a week had passed?"

Louise Jane laughed. "Would you?"

"If George Clooney came courting, I wouldn't turn him away."

We all laughed, glad of the chance to break the tension left in Heather's wake.

"Teenagers," Mrs. Peterson said. "I thought Charity's obsession with soccer was bad. I had no idea. Primrose finally emerged from her room this morning to go the beach with the Carpenter boy, Noah. I have to say, he's been surprisingly understanding of her. They broke up a month or so ago, after he mocked Todd Harrison and Primrose ordered him never to speak to her again. All so over the top and dramatic."

"I'm sure he has an ulterior motive," Louise Jane said.

Mrs. Peterson looked so shocked at the very idea, Louise Jane hastened to add. "That's what friends are for, isn't it? To support us when we're having a tough time."

Mrs. Peterson appeared to be only slightly mollified.

* * *

Initially Connor was beyond furious when I told him about Heather Harrison's visit to the library, but when he calmed down, he advised me to do nothing. If I saw her approaching, he said, I should run away. "If she comes to the house, do not, under any circumstances, let her in."

"I'm not likely to do that," I said into the phone.

"I don't know. This sort of person can be mighty persuasive, and they talk a good game. Her background is a muck-raking journalist, remember. She's clearly transferring those skills into her political life. Regarding that piece of advice, I'll do the same. Any accusations she makes about me will be rebutted formally and in writing, in appropriate legalese. Not in a shouting match. Are you okay, honey?"

"Yes, I am." I was comfortably ensconced in Bertie's office chair, leaning back, eyes closed, Charles nestled in my lap. My heartbeat was gradually returning to normal. "Never thought the day would come when once again I'm grateful to Louise Jane."

"Louise Jane has her uses, but she needs to think things through before acting. No one was in physical danger, from what you tell me, and if she'd broken that camera, she could have found herself in trouble. I'll see you at home later. If Heather Harrison approaches you again, let me know."

We hung up. Charles purred loudly, and I stroked his soft fur.

The library was quiet. I took a deep breath, gathered my composure, and opened my eyes. The screensaver on Bertie's computer showed a series of pictures of her in various yoga poses, often leading a group. She was part owner of a yoga studio in town, and she gave classes two mornings a week. I didn't usually see Bertie ruffled, outside of budget time, or not in full control. I hadn't been the only one intimidated into silence by Heather Harrison.

A light knock sounded on the door, and Louise Jane's head popped in. "Bertie sent me with a glass of water for you." She held it up in evidence.

"Thanks," I said. "I'm okay now. How's things out there?"

"Fine. A couple of kids came in, so Maureen has gone back upstairs, and Bertie's on the circulation desk."

She put the glass of water in front of me and took a seat in the visitor's chair. "So that's the grieving widow Harrison."

"'Grieving' isn't the word I'd use. More taking advantage of the situation."

"I got who the guy with the camera was, and the older guy, Todd's agent. But who was that young woman who came in with them? She looked to be really embarrassed. When she tried to speak, Heather was awful rude to her."

"She's Heather's personal assistant. I get the impression the poor girl's terrified of Heather."

"Why does she need a PA?"

I explained to Louise Jane about Heather's possible senate run.

"That's an idea. Do you think she killed her husband to take advantage of publicity surrounding his death? So she can present herself as the tragic widow on a determined quest for justice?"

"I don't know, Louise Jane. I suppose it's possible. Anything's possible. Lorraine told me Todd didn't want Heather to go into politics. He didn't want to be a political spouse. His objections don't seem like a reason to kill him, though. Divorce isn't an impediment to political office these days."

"Maybe she needed him to fund her ambitions, he refused, and she took steps to get her hands on his estate, or whatever."

"Possible. He might have had life insurance."

Louise Jane grabbed a piece of paper out of the printer and a pen from a chipped mug, a souvenir of a long-ago librarian's conference Bertie used as a pencil holder. Charles left my lap and climbed onto the desk. He sniffed at the pen.

"What are you doing?" I asked.

She quickly drew rows and columns on the paper. "I'm making a list of suspects and notations. You need to get your thoughts straight, and then you can take your ideas to Sam."

"I can't take anything to Sam. Because of Heather's implications, he's been told to stay away from me."

"Pooh. I'm including a third column for action items." She drew a long, thick line down the paper. "Ask Sam what sort of life insurance Todd had and if he had a will. Tell him you think Heather might be trying to take suspicion off her by focusing on, of all people, Lorraine." Louise Jane scribbled on the paper. "Next?"

"Next what?"

"Next suspect. Or is Heather all you have?"

"I'm not too sure about Todd's agent, Bill Pratchett. I spoke to a friend who works at Todd's publisher, and she said it's rumored Todd was looking for a new agent." When Bill left the library, he told Heather he wanted her to give him the manuscript. If I was correct in assuming he meant the manuscript for the new book, the supposedly next big thing, clearly Bill didn't have it. Not the most recent version, at any rate. If he was to send it to the publisher, obviously he had to have it in his possession.

Was it possible the contract between the publisher and the author via his agent hadn't been finalized yet? It might be. Experienced authors usually get a contract based on a proposal or a partially completed work. But if Todd's next novel took his writing in a new direction, as he'd been telling everyone, the publishers might have wanted to see the final product first. Todd himself might have wanted to hold off signing if he thought the book was deserving of more than the publisher initially offered.

If Bill had not yet negotiated a contract, had he feared he was going to be dropped, replaced by a new agent? Would he have killed Todd to stop that from happening?

Perhaps. Todd was the goose laying the golden eggs, but if Bill feared he wasn't going to get any more eggs . . . ?

"Bill Pratchett, then." Louise Jane wrote his name down. "Next steps?"

"I don't have any. I suppose I could ask Sam if Bill has an alibi. But as I mentioned, he's not talking to me."

"We'll work something out. Next?"

"Shannon McKinnon."

Louise Jane lifted her head. "Why?"

"She claims Todd's new book was her idea. One night at a bar, over several drinks, she told him all about it and he turned her ideas into his book. She's angry about that. Anger makes people do strange things."

"How would she benefit by killing him? If she intended to take him to court, it would be a lot easier if he were alive, I'd think."

"I don't know. Action item: Shannon told me the characters in her book use bows and arrows. She said she hasn't learned how to use a bow yet herself, but that might not be true. Has Shannon ever visited an archery club? We can ask the same about Heather."

"Excellent. See? We're getting somewhere. Charles, please get off the paper. Charles, I said *move*." Louise Jane poked him with her pen. He twitched the end of his tail and remained exactly where he was. Louise Jane sighed and wrote around him. "Next?"

I thought for a long time. "As long as we're throwing ideas out there: Ruth Vivac. Once Todd was no longer going to be the main attraction at our festival, she suggested herself. Was that always her intention?"

"Possible. Anything is possible, as you so recently noted." Down went Ruth's name. We had no next steps.

"I heard what Heather said about Lorraine," Louise Jane said. "Anything to it?"

"Not according to Lorraine."

"Who is not an unbiased observer. I'll put her down with a question mark."

"That's all I can think of," I said. "Other than person or persons unknown. Todd's death might not have had anything to do with us or our festival, or even his writing career. He moved to Nags Head less than a year ago. Maybe his enemies followed him. Maybe he made new ones."

"Why was he killed at your house, do you think?"

"Might have been nothing but my bad luck. The person who killed him could have been following him for days, waiting for their chance. A deck overlooking an expanse of open beach, a dark, quiet night. No one else around, an easy escape route. They saw their opportunity and took it. Although I am inclined to think the archery business must have something to do with the book. He might have made an enemy when he was learning archery, but surely that person would know better than to draw an arrow directly at themself."

"You made a pun, Lucy."

I sighed. "Not intentionally."

"Does that strengthen the case against Shannon? If she was angry at Todd for using her idea, did she, in turn, use her idea against him?"

"Good point."

"Weird."

"So everyone keeps saying. Weird. Person or persons unknown." An image of Primrose and her friends, circle on the sand, bowed and hooded heads, flickering candles. "Do you know the origin of the word 'fan,' as in fan club or fans of an author or his or her books?"

"No."

"Fanatic. Did one of Todd's fanatic fans do away with him?"

Chapter Twenty-One

Monday night was the sixth day following Todd Harrison's death. Connor suggested we have dinner on the deck. After we finished and the dishes were done, he put on a pot of coffee. When it was ready, he poured himself a mug and took it and a book onto the deck and settled down.

"I thought that big game was tonight," I said. "The one so critical for your team to get into the playoffs."

"There will be other games," he said.

"You never drink coffee after dinner," I said.

"Sure I do. Sometimes."

I sat down. "You're worried Todd's fans will be back."

"It is the sixth night, and from what we've been told they mourn in threes."

"Other than Primrose and one or two others I recognize from the library, none of them seem to stand out in any way. Have you noticed anyone acting, shall we say, over the top?"

"The whole thing is over the top, Lucy."

"You know what I mean. Exceptionally over the top."

"As befits someone who killed their idol for some demented reason."

"You're thinking along the same lines as I am."

"It has crossed my mind that one of these kids might have done it. Did Todd rebuff their attempts to get friendly? Did he slight a fan at a book signing? Are you aware that John Lennon, of the Beatles, was murdered by a fan?"

"A fan? Really?"

"The killer was a Beatles fan who came to believe that Lennon, in particular, was a hypocrite. That his lifestyle didn't match his rhetoric. I've also heard some degree of jealously was involved. He, the killer, wanted to *be* Lennon. As obviously there isn't room in the world for two John Lennons, one of them had to go."

"You think something like that happened here?" I asked. "I don't know enough about Todd's life and his work to know if he was a hypocrite or not."

"Just pointing out the dangers of fame, that's all. I'm not coming to any conclusions."

I thought for a while and eventually said, "No, I can't see that being it. More likely, if that's what happened, the killer would be so shocked at what they'd done, they'd be keeping far away from the rest of the fan group."

"Don't try to guess how people that disturbed would think, honey. Far from being shocked by his own impulsive actions, the man who killed Lennon planned it for a long time, and he actually sat down at the scene and read a book while waiting for the police to arrive and arrest him."

"How do you know so much about this? I knew John Lennon had been murdered in front of his apartment building, but that's all."

"My parents were—and still are—huge Beatle fans. To this day, they talk about the tragedy of Lennon's death."

"Something to think about," I said, "but I don't want to look for parallels with that case. Makes me wonder, however, if the killing was planned in advance. I mean, did the killer just happen to have a bow and arrow ready at hand?"

"That might or might not be significant. If this person was an archer, and we're assuming they have some expertise, they might not always put their equipment away after practice. So yes, the bow and arrow might have been at hand when needed."

"If we go back to my original thought," I said, "that the killer might not be hanging around with the fan club, because they're keeping a low profile, it's not easy to ask who hasn't been part of that creepy bunch after the death."

"Not if you use the word 'creepy.'" Connor chuckled.

"I'm not necessarily buying the idea of the killer being a fan, but whoever it was, fan or not, might they be returning to the scene of the crime? Still trying to fit in with the group? Would a true keen fan stand out if they *didn't* attend the mourning rituals? As for asking about the group, I can do that. Talk to Primrose, I mean. Ask her if anyone in the fan club has been noticeably absent since Todd died, or noticeably present or otherwise acting out of character."

"You can ask," he said. "But my guess would be she won't know what's out of character for some of them."

"Teenagers can be more perceptive than people give them credit for." I stood up. "Although it's likely some, if not most, of them are friends mainly through their social media groups, not in person, and that's a narrow window onto someone's character."

"What are you going to do now?"

"Get my book," I said. "The sun will be setting soon, and there are worse ways to stand guard."

* * *

Connor and I read our books in a tense silence. I was pleased I'd been able to distract Theodore from wanting to discuss *The Merry Adventures of Robin Hood* by Howard Pyle. Despite his insistence that we regard the book as being pertinent today, I refused to agree. Plenty of books, historical fiction and fantasy in particular, contain scenes of archery and battles using bows and arrows. I wasn't going to avoid them all from now on. But somehow Robin Hood, above all semi-historical characters, is closely associated with archery.

Instead, I was skimming through *Brave New World*, trying to refresh my memory in preparation for the festival panel. Connor was reading a political biography. He had his coffee; I sipped a glass of iced tea. Charles, attached to his halter and leash, snoozed on a spare chair.

The sun had gone down in the west, and the sky over the ocean was heavy with clouds. Not many people were on the beach tonight. A few cars drove past on the street in front of the house.

I was finding it hard to concentrate on my book, and whenever I glanced at Connor, I could see he was as edgy as I was. Instead of focusing on what he'd earlier told me was a "thoroughly engrossing read," his head was up and his eyes constantly moving. I didn't think he'd turned a single page this evening.

Shortly before nine o'clock, a car stopped. The engine died. A door slammed. Connor sat upright. Charles's whiskers twitched.

Then all was quiet again and we relaxed. "How long do you think we need to sit out?" I asked.

"Probably not much longer. The time of the death seems to be important to this so-called ritual."

Charles jumped up. Connor said, "Shh."

"I didn't say anything."

He held up his hand. Charles remained at alert.

And then I heard it too. The squeak of hinges, the slow creak of a floorboard. A quick, whispered, "Be quiet."

Connor shot to his feet and threw open the sliding door. I grabbed Charles and unhooked his leash, and we followed.

We'd been reading in the light cast by the lantern above the door. The living room and dining room lights were off; the only light in the house, a faint glow coming from the kitchen.

Connor slapped the wall switch, and the hallway flooded with light. "What is going on here?" he bellowed.

He was facing a pack of teenage girls. They clustered in the hallway, clinging to one another, wide-eyed with shock.

My own shock began to dissipate. Not an armed intruder—nothing but a bunch of frightened girls.

"Primrose Peterson," Connor yelled, "what on earth do you think you're doing?"

Primrose dipped her head. Her fair hair fell over her face. "We're . . . we're only wanting to have a look around, Mr. McNeil."

"Have you never heard of a doorbell or the concept of knocking?"

"We didn't think you'd let us in." The speaker was the girl with beads woven into her long dark hair I'd seen at the bookstore earlier, grieving Todd.

"You're right about that. What's your name?"

"Uh . . . Jolene?"

I put Charles down and stepped forward. Charles sniffed Primrose's shoes.

"Answer Mr. McNeil's question," I said. "What do you think you're doing creeping around in our house? In the dark, no less."

"We . . . we . . . I . . ."

"Simone checked around the front," a short-haired girl said. "She said you and Mr. McNeil were on the deck, so if we were super quiet, like, we could pay our respects to Todd and then leave without you knowing we were here."

"Where is this Simone now?" Connor asked.

"Here," a nervous voice said.

There were ten of them. Teenage girls, from about ages fourteen to seventeen, with a variety of skin tones and haircuts, a few with tattoos and piercings, dressed in good but casual summer clothes. Teeth were brushed, hair was washed, shoes were clean.

"You can't keep doing this, girls," I said. "Coming to our home. Disturbing our peace."

"We only want to honor Todd as he deserved to be honored." Primrose's voice was very low. Her friends nodded. Jolene's beads clattered.

"That may be, but entering a house without being invited is a crime, and I'm calling the police." Connor pressed two buttons on his phone.

"Gosh, no!" one of the girls cried. "My dad will have a fit."

"You should have thought of that before breaking into our home. Lucy, you know Primrose Peterson. Anyone else here?"

The girls shifted uncomfortably. Simone, the one at the back, edged away. I let her go.

"Madison Thompson, you come to the library regularly. I don't recognize any of the others."

"All of you, give your names to Mrs. McNeil." Connor held up his phone. "Or I will finish this call. Lucy, audio only. For now."

I took out my own phone and opened the recorder. One at a time, the girls mumbled their names. They might not have given me their real names, but I thought they did. They were all thoroughly scared at the idea of the police contacting their parents.

"How did you get in?" I asked, keeping the recording on.

No one said anything. Much shuffling of feet and studying of the floorboards.

"Primrose, how did you get in?" Connor said.

"The side door." She pointed to her right. "The one on the screened porch that looks as though it's never used. I noticed it was slightly ajar the first time we were here, and I . . . uh . . . slipped a stone into the gap to keep it open."

I winced. She was right that we never used that door. I didn't even know when I'd last checked to see if it was locked.

Realizing Connor hadn't finished dialing 911, the girls relaxed fractionally. A couple gave me bashful smiles. One dropped to a squat and clicked her fingers. Charles approached. "This is a nice cat. Can I pat him?"

"No," I said.

Despite my tone, Charles rubbed himself against the girl's arm, and she rewarded him with a scratch between the ears.

"Now we've established you're illegally trespassing," Connor said, "I have to ask what you think you're doing coming into the house. Mr. Harrison died outside, and you know that because that's where you brought your candles and flowers on other occasions."

"Todd walked through here on his way to the deck, didn't he?" Primrose said. "We wanted to follow the path of his last steps. That's all."

"I am going to call the police, but you can leave first. I'll tell them what's been going on, but I won't mention any names. I will if I see any of you on our property again. Inside or outside. Do you understand?"

"Yes, sir.

"Yes, Mr. McNeil."

"Sorry, Mr. McNeil. Sorry, Mrs. McNeil."

They hesitated for a fraction of a second, and then a jumble of arms and legs and hair rushed for the front door.

I gave Connor a glance before following them. I was pretty sure they'd leave and not come back, but I needed to be sure.

Girls streamed down the steps and ran into the night. Most of them were on foot. Two jumped into a car; I made a note of the license plate.

A boy stood next to a car parked in front of the neighbor's house. Primrose ran toward him. "Let's go, Noah. I'm finished here."

He looked at me, standing on the step watching.

"You didn't actually break into that house, did you?" he asked Primrose. "You said you were just going around the back."

"I don't want to talk about it." She tugged at the passenger side door, but it didn't open.

"I didn't think you'd be that stupid," he said.

"Don't you dare call me stupid! Unlock this door and let's go!"

"Primrose," Jolene called, "want to come around to my place? I've scheduled a Zoom call with the Todd Harrison club in Vancouver for ten. They want to know what the funeral arrangements are and if it's going to be online."

"Will you get lost, Jolene!" Noah shouted. "Primrose came with me, and she'll leave with me. She doesn't need any more of you and your nonsense."

"It's not nonsense!" Primrose said. "You don't get to tell me who my friends are."

Noah lifted his hands. "Sorry, Prim. Sorry. I didn't mean the fan club and all. I just meant . . . well, I meant the funeral arrangements aren't up to you to make, are they?"

She relaxed fractionally. "No, they're not. I just hope his wife doesn't go and make it something private and secret, like. We all want to go. Sorry, Jolene—you'll have to tell them we don't know what's happening yet."

"Okay. Call me later. If you want to talk or something." She gave Noah a hard stare before joining her friend. They slipped away, disappearing into the night.

Noah flicked his key fob. Lights flashed, door locks clicked, and Primrose clambered into the car. He got into the driver's seat without giving me another glance, and they drove off.

Back inside, I found Connor on the phone.

"They've left, and I told them I won't do anything further about it, not unless I see them here again. Lucy taped them saying their names. No video, though."

I heard the mumbled sound of Sam Watson's voice coming down the line.

"I detect no malice in them," Connor continued, "and I don't think they're up to anything other than the sort of misplaced hero worship of kids totally bored on the summer holidays. But this threatens to get out of control, and if that happens, it's easy for someone to get hurt."

More mumbling.

"This can't go on, Sam. You've asked Lucy not to get involved, but I'd say she's completely involved through absolutely no fault of her own. An incident relating to the Todd Harrison situation occurred at the library earlier. . . . Thanks. We're here."

Connor hung up. "He's coming over."

"For once, I've tried so hard not to be involved," I said. "Despite that determination, involvement simply won't leave me alone."

* * *

It wasn't long before first one vehicle and then another pulled into our driveway. Sam Watson was driving his own car, and a police cruiser came after him.

Connor opened the kitchen door. Watson and Officer Holly Rankin came in. "Coffee's on," Connor said.

"Thanks," Holly said.

"Not for me," Watson said.

Connor poured a mug for Holly and one for himself, and we took seats around the kitchen island. Charles leaped onto his cat tree to follow the conversation.

Connor filled our visitors in on what had been happening with the fan group over the past week, leading up to this evening. He gave no names, but said, "They're mostly local kids. Lucy recognized some of them from the library. I think—I hope I made my point tonight and finally got through to them. If I see them on our property again, I will report them formally and lay charges."

"You'll have to," Watson said, "These things can get out of hand."

"In fairness—" I said.

"I don't want to be fair," Connor said. "I want them to go away."

I touched his hand. Some of the tension disappeared from around his mouth, and he smiled back at me. "Their numbers were substantially down tonight. It was a lark for most of them the first couple of times. Something dramatic and exciting to do, but then they soon went on to other things. I know the parents of the girl who appears to be the ringleader, and I told her if I see her here again, I'll tell them."

"In the meantime," Watson said, "we'll keep up an extra patrol on your street and the stretch of beach outside. Bertie James called me earlier to report the incident that happened at the library."

I nodded. "Heather Harrison, Todd's widow, is making accusations against the police department of, if not out-and-out corruption, taking the easy route."

"What sort of easy route?" Holly asked.

"Using unpaid, unqualified civilians to do work that should be done by the police. By unpaid, unqualified civilians she specifically means me. And by police, I'm sorry to say, she specifically mentioned Detective Watson."

"Why would she do that?"

"She has political ambitions," Connor said. "She's grabbed at the opportunity for a platform."

"Wouldn't the murder of her husband be enough?" Holly said. "If she has the bad taste to campaign on that."

"She needs more," Watson said. "That's to say, she thinks she needs more. On that note, she's called a press conference for ten AM tomorrow. It will be held in the town parking lot."

"In front of the police station and the town hall," I said.

"Nice background when announcing a campaign against corruption. Or incompetence. Take your pick," Connor said.

Watson sighed. "Maybe I will have that coffee after all, Connor. Okay, I'll admit I shouldn't have listened to the chief when he told me not to talk to you, Lucy. You've been of help to us in the past, and the idea that you're killing people to make yourself look clever by solving the mystery is beyond ridiculous."

Connor put a full mug on the island.

"I shouldn't have paid any attention in the first place, but even more now that it looks as though Mrs. Harrison isn't going to limit herself to one person or one accusation. She'll spread that talk as far and as wide as she can, to get traction on the news. However, that's not why I came around tonight. Back to these kids: you haven't seen anything to indicate someone's putting them up to this, have you?"

"No," I said. "I'm pretty sure they're acting on their own. Just a bunch of kids. I popped into a couple of social media accounts run by Todd Harrison fan clubs. Lots of shock and dismay at news of his death, which you'd expect. Some vague mentions of mourning in the style of the Frighteners."

"What's a Frightener?" Holly Rankin asked.

I explained the origin of the term. "No one, as far as I can see anyway, has suggested gathering with bows and arrows. So there is that. As long as we're talking, can I ask what you've learned from various archery clubs?"

"Not a lot," Watson said. "Heather Harrison gave me the name of the club where her husband took lessons. Not far from here. I paid them a call. He went a few times, spoke to members, took lots of notes, learned the absolute basics, and didn't come back."

"When was this?" Connor asked.

"Six, seven months ago, not long after he and his wife moved to Nags Head."

And not long after Shannon McKinnon shared her great idea with Todd.

"The absolute basics would likely be all he'd need to know," I said. "For writing about it, I mean."

"People I spoke to at the club said he was friendly enough, didn't show any special aptitude for the sport, and didn't appear to care. He mainly wanted to ask questions about it, try handling the bow, judge the amount of concentration and control needed to aim and keep it steady, experience what it feels like when the arrow releases. He came alone every time. Never suggested getting together for a beer after or anything like that. Since then, he emailed the woman he'd taken lessons from a couple of times, with specific questions, but otherwise, they haven't seen him in months."

"Heather didn't go with him?" I asked.

"Heather says not, and no one there mentioned seeing her. I've asked for lists of members at that club, as well as others around here, but nothing leaps out at me. No reason someone didn't learn at a club elsewhere or pick it up on their own in their own backyard. Might have even been years ago. Kids' archery sets are readily available."

"He wasn't killed with a kids' arrow, was he?" Holly asked.

"No. Compound bow, sharp-tipped arrow. Nothing special about it, and not at all rare."

"I would have thought," Holly Rankin said, "finding someone who shot someone with a bow and arrow would be a no-brainer. Turns out, I was wrong."

"Can I suggest a couple of names for you to check against these membership lists?" I asked.

"Go ahead," Watson said.

"Shannon McKinnah. Ruth Vivac."

"I know who they are, and I've spoken to them about their whereabouts following the meeting at the library the day Harrison died. Nothing stood out to me as important. Any specific reason you're asking about them?"

"Professional jealousy, most of all. They both said publicly they were absolutely thrilled that Todd Harrison would be fronting the festival, but were they? Maybe one or the other of them thought she should have been the star. I have one more question."

Watson grinned at me. "Only one?"

"For now."

"Is Heather Harrison in a financial position to mount a run for state senate?"

"Good question," Connor said.

"She is not," Watson replied, "from what I can tell, independently wealthy. At the moment she's not employed by any news sources or anyone else. The state and federal political organizations say she's gearing up her fundraising. If you're asking me if she killed her husband to fund her campaign, I have to say that would have been unwise of her. He had no income other than from his writing, and although he was doing well by publishing standards, he wasn't bringing in much more than an average middle-class income."

"Life insurance?" Connor asked.

"They both had substantial policies, yes. Those polices were taken out shortly after their marriage, which was twelve years ago. Enough to kickstart a political campaign? Perhaps, but I'm not basing an investigation on that. Many couples have life insurance. CeeCee and I have life insurance on each other."

"As do we," Connor said.

"Heather Harrison does have an alibi, by the way. A solid one. She was having a dinner meeting in Duck with representatives of her political party. They all confirm it. She was sounding them out about running, and the dinner broke up around nine. They all left at the same time. Heather drove to the restaurant by herself, but she would not have had time to drive from Duck to this house to kill her husband. The waiter confirms Heather was at the meeting as well as the time she and her group left. Here's a word of advice for you, Connor: if you're out in public representing your political party, tip well. Heather's group did not. The word the waiter used was 'insulting.' She will not be getting his vote."

"Worth remembering," Connor said.

"I don't suppose you've considered someone did the killing for her?" I asked.

"I'm considering everything, Lucy. But at this time I have no reason to believe so."

"What about Todd's agent, Bill Pratchett?"

"What about him? Is he in the frame?"

"He's here, in Nags Head. Now, I mean. I don't know if he was here last week. You might want to ask the NYPD to check into him. It's possible Todd was about to dump him. As his agent, I mean. He would not have liked that. Todd was his biggest client, by far."

"You think this agent worked with Heather Harrison to get rid of her husband?"

"No, that's not what I'm suggesting at all." I thought back to when they'd been together at the library. They'd not been overly friendly toward each other, and I could see no benefit to either of them of working together. Bill wanted the manuscript. Presumably

Heather had it, if she had access to the files on Todd's computer. If Todd had been ready to dump Bill Pratchett for a bigger and better agent, he might have told this to his wife. If so, she would know she could try to get a better deal elsewhere for the manuscript. Might that be why she was balking at handing it over to Bill?

Would Bill take drastic steps to get it? Possible. "He stood to lose a lot if Todd did take what is supposedly going to be the biggest book of the year to another agent. He might have thought that Todd's estate, which I suppose now means Heather, would find it easier after Todd's death to simply continue with the agent Todd had been using before."

"I'll see what I can find out about him." Watson smiled at me. "Anyone else you want me to check up on?"

"Not at this time," I said.

"Lorraine Kittleman?" he asked.

"Why do you mention her?"

"Because you notably have not. Heather Harrison came to the police station and made an accusation against Lorraine. No one else we spoke to has mentioned anything that would suggest Lorraine was bothering Todd, stalking him, or anything else. I hear she's currently dating Teddy Kowalski. Of all people."

"Of all people, indeed. I'm happy for them both. I haven't mentioned her because the idea of her chasing after Todd is simply preposterous."

"I'm inclined to agree. About the stalking at any rate. I spoke to Mrs. Harrison again after meeting with you at the library. I pressed her harder on her accusations against Lorraine. She didn't quite dig her heels in, but she maintained that what she told me is what her husband told her. I suspect Mrs. Harrison doesn't often back down."

"Have you considered," Holly said, "that the only thing that might be preposterous, as you call it, about it is the stalking bit? They might have been having an affair, him being a willing participant, and they managed to keep it hidden. Not only from his wife, but from everyone else. Which, I'll admit is a heck of a lot harder to do than the participants might think."

"If Heather found out what was going on, and confronted Todd," Connor said, "he could have started babbling about poor innocent him trying to discourage Lorraine's unwanted attentions and all that."

"Didn't happen," I said firmly.

Although I wasn't entirely sure why I was so firm.

Chapter Twenty-Two

Tuesday morning at the library we gathered around the computer at the circulation desk to watch Heather Harrison's press conference. That wouldn't normally be something Bertie would consider worth the attention of the entire staff as well as any patrons who happened to be interested, but as we were terrified Heather was going to show footage of us at our absolute worst, she suggested it. Forewarned is forearmed, and all that.

The entire event was surprisingly dull.

The day was overcast, the sky thick with clouds, but no wind. Heather stood at a small lectern hastily erected in the parking lot serving the town's official buildings. The police station formed an unimpressive backdrop behind her, its flags hanging limply on their poles. Heather wore a well-cut, somber gray suit with a pink blouse, and gray pumps with one-inch heels. Her hair was tied loosely back and her make up and jewelry were minimal. She thanked everyone for coming and declared that she was throwing her hat into the ring for her party's nominee for state senator. After the de rigueur brief tribute to the retiring senator, she informed the audience that her aim in seeking office was to focus on eliminating what she called "lackadaisical and uninterested" state and local officials. "These people are paid excellent salaries to do the jobs that we, the people of this great state, ask them to do for us. There's no place for skirting responsibilities and allowing informal and unauthorized people to act willy-nilly on their own initiative," she declared.

By pure, unfortunate coincidence (or maybe not), at that moment a patrol car pulled into the lot and drove slowly past in the background.

"I assume 'unauthorized' means me," I said.

"I shudder to think what's coming," Bertie said.

Heather paused, dipped her head, and then told us she'd considered holding off on her campaign in light of the sudden, tragic, unexpected death of her beloved husband. However, once she realized the police were not only failing to make an arrest, but seemed to be blundering about in the dark and once again relying on unofficial, unaccountable, unpaid resources to do their job for them, the time had come for someone to put a stop to it.

I braced myself. I knew Connor would be watching on the TV in his office. Likely Sam Watson and the chief of police too. Last night, after the police left, Connor suggested we alert my uncle Amos and our friend Stephanie Stanton that we might be in need of their services. They were partners in a law office, and the best defense lawyers in town.

And then, to the surprise of everyone watching, it was over. Heather accepted questions, but there weren't many. I wondered if she'd made a mistake in declaring her candidacy in our small town in the middle of tourist season. Everyone had more important things on their minds: either going to the beach or selling stuff to tourists to take to the beach.

A representative of a local paper asked Heather whom exactly she was talking about when referring to the police, and she answered vaguely that her first step would be to identify problems and try to work with the people involved for the mutual satisfaction of all. Another reporter asked her to name these unaccountable people. I held my breath, but Heather demurred, saying something about early days yet and not wanting to name anyone genuinely attempting to do their civic duty. Then she launched into some mumbo jumbo about her enormous respect for the majority of the members of police forces throughout our state. She concluded by thanking everyone for coming.

Layla, her hair in its neat French braid, her smile stiff and formal, stepped forward and began handing material to the assembled journalists and the few members of the public who'd bothered to stop and watch.

The screen switched to a commercial for laundry detergent.

"That was anticlimactic," Bertie said.

"It was." I closed the news stream. "I expected her to show some of the footage she took here yesterday, or a still shot of me looking like an idiot—but nothing. She started throwing out accusations and then never followed up. All terribly wishy-washy and vague. Deliberately vague, do you think?"

"She's keeping her powder dry," Ronald said. "For now. She'll mention names when the campaign fully gets going."

"I'm not so sure," Denise said. "I think she's way out of her depth. At a guess, she's not being properly advised. It's possible her party doesn't want her securing the nomination, so they're not being any help."

"It's also possible they are helping her by telling her not to throw unsubstantiated dirt around," Tim Snyder said. He'd come in, as he did twice a week, to settle in the magazine nook, flip through magazines, and snuggle with Charles. "This library's hugely popular with the townspeople. Connor's approval ratings remain sky high, and although everyone always has helpful suggestions for how the police could do their jobs better, no one has any specific complaints."

"'*Sufficient undo the day,*'" Bertie said. "Back to work everyone."

The desk phone rang, and Louise Jane answered it. "Connor for you, Lucy."

"I'll call him back." Cell phone signals within the solid stone walls of the lighthouse were erratic at best, nonexistent at worst, so Connor knew to call on the landline. I slipped outside, while the library staff returned to their jobs and patrons went back to browsing the stacks or working on the computers.

"Did you watch?" Connor said.

"'Anticlimactic' is how Bertie put it."

"Very. I wonder what Heather Harrison is playing at, but for now I'll take what I can get. I have a meeting with the chief in half an hour. I'll call Amos and tell him he and Steph can stand down. For now."

"Is it possible Heather expected something far more dramatic to happen, either the times she's been to the library or elsewhere? And when it didn't, she went ahead with her press conference without being able to drop whatever bombshell she was hoping for?"

"I don't know, Lucy. I simply don't know." We hung up and I went back to work.

* * *

Much of the talk for the remainder of the day was about Heather Harrison and her press conference. The general consensus, among library users anyway, was that she was nothing but "a bag of hot air," in the words of our loyal patron Mrs. Cunningham. "Why she thinks she can get our votes by insulting us, I have no idea. As for that other matter, Lucy"—she dropped her voice and leaned toward me—"do you know, or suspect, who killed her husband?"

"I don't know anything," I said.

"Wouldn't be surprised if she did it herself," Mrs. Cunningham said, hefting her book bag. "She seems the type to me."

* * *

In the early afternoon, I was in the break room, eating a sandwich and going through publishers' catalogues, making notes of forthcoming books we might want to get in.

In one of those coincidences that make life interesting, I read about a new book coming out by an Olympic gold medalist in archery.

I sat back and thought. It had been a week since Todd's killing. The clock was running down on the investigation. Most murders needed to be solved quickly. Police have new cases to attend to, memories fade, people move on, evidence can be inadvertently destroyed or lost.

I wondered if I'd not been taking the method of Todd's death seriously enough. I mean, really, to shoot an arrow at him? To use the method of killing he employed in his own books?

That could not be a coincidence.

I picked up the phone and called the extension for the children's library. Ronald answered. "What's up?"

"I have a quick question about Todd Harrison's books. You read some of them, right?"

"I did. I can't say I thought much of them, to be honest, but they were popular with his intended audience, and that's all that matters."

"In the published books, do his characters use bows and arrows?"

"Not that I recall. Some swordplay, lots of magic duels, hurling of thunderbolts, and the like. Some characters have knives concealed in every possible place. At least one instance I can think of where someone fires rocks from a slingshot. To great effect, I might add. I haven't read all the books, though, Lucy. Why are you asking?"

"Just wondering. Thanks, Ronald."

I continued with my train of thought. It was not a secret that Todd's new book prominently featured archery. He talked openly about it on podcasts and at least one book signing I knew about. He'd joined an archery club to get tips.

Todd's killing had to be directly related to his writing. If he had enemies in New York City or anywhere else because of something else in his life, they would not have gone to the trouble of hunting him at night on a beach in Nags Head.

If Heather wanted to kill him, surely as his wife she had plenty of better opportunities to do it. She might say she believes the police cut corners and are lazy, but she has to know that's not true. According to Sam Watson, her alibi was secure. She possibly could have hired someone to do the killing for her, but I couldn't see a contract killer using such an unusual, not to mention dramatic, method.

No, this way of killing had to be highly personal, and it had to do with Todd's writing.

I considered Bill Pratchett, the agent, but I dismissed him. If Bill killed Todd because Todd was going to take his new book to another agent, that wouldn't be *personal*. It'd be business.

Ruth Vivac? Again unlikely. If Ruth wanted to be the headliner at our festival, and she eliminated Todd to take his place, again, nothing *personal*. Just business.

Shannon McKinnon? Possible. Shannon, according to her, had a personal reason to hate Todd, and that reason had a lot to do with archery.

Which brought me, reluctantly, to Lorraine. Nothing more personal than an unrequited or failed love affair. Although, I admitted, I didn't have one scrap of evidence that Lorraine and Todd had been having any sort of relationship other than old friends casually catching up over lunch or coffee in a public place. Nothing except for Heather's nasty insinuations.

I trusted Heather no further than I could fire an arrow out of a bow.

I'd met Todd Harrison exactly twice. Once at the meeting in the library and then a few hours later when I invited him to take a seat on my deck. Not exactly a close relationship, but the man seemed to be well-spoken, presentable, competent, confident in himself. He'd been nicely dressed, well-groomed. He had some degree of fame in his own world and made an adequate income from his writing.

Pretty much the opposite of Theodore Kowalski. Occasionally hapless, often awkward; a genuinely kind, well-meaning man. Teddy with his tweed jackets and paisley cravats, clear-glass spectacles, never-used pipe, fake English accent. Teddy, with his barely hanging on book dealing business that financially wasn't much more than a hobby.

The two men couldn't be more different. If Lorraine loved Teddy, as I believed she did, could she possibly have found something attractive in Todd Harrison too?

I didn't see it. People can be complicated and contradictory and totally confusing. I've been wrong more than once. I could be wrong about Lorraine, but until something happened to change my thinking, I'd eliminate her as a suspect. For the reason Heather was claiming, at any rate.

Bertie came in and went to the fridge. She took out an apple and the jug of tea. She nodded to the stack of catalogues in front of me as she poured herself a drink. "Anything looking particularly promising?"

"A few. More than a few. No mention here about Todd Harrison's big book. Makes me think the contract isn't finalized yet."

"Do you think that's relevant to his murder?"

"It might be. His agent is pretty shifty."

"He left fast enough when Heather started interrogating us. I'd say that's a point in his favor. Speaking of being in favor, are you back in Sam's good books?"

"More or less," I said.

"If you need any time to look into this matter, you know you can take it as long as your work is covered. Heather Harrison involved a member of the library staff in her problems, and we are entitled to do what we have to do to protect our reputation."

"Thanks," I said.

"Tea?" She held up the jug.

"No thanks."

When Bertie left, I thought for a while, and then I sent a text:

Got a moment to talk?

Happy to. Long, boring day.

I phoned Michelle, my friend who worked at Todd's publishers.

"Great minds think alike," she said after we'd exchanged greetings. "I was about to call you."

"You have news of Todd Harrison's book?"

"I do. As I told you, fantasy isn't my area, but after you and I talked, I've been keeping my ears open. The manuscript came in yesterday afternoon. The fantasy editor took it home to read last night."

"Isn't that fast? He must have other things waiting to be read?"

"Fast, yes. The approximate speed of light by publishing standards. But like I told you, they've been waiting for this manuscript, and he wanted to dive in. The recent death of the author gives decisions to be made about the book some urgency."

"And?"

"And he told his assistant this morning it's the best thing he's read in years. The concept is, according to him, high-octane but also deeply emotional. Todd's gone dark and deep and created the perfect story for our uncertain times. Guaranteed bestseller written all over it. Movie and TV rights a given. Once the book is finished, which apparently it isn't."

"Did Bill Pratchett's agency send it in?"

"I think so. I guess Todd's widow or whoever's in charge of the estate wanted to get it over with. Bird in the hand and all that."

"You might want to put a word in the editor's ear that potential legal problems are swirling around that manuscript."

"Because the author died?"

"Another writer claims he stole it from her."

She snorted. "Oh, that. Pay no attention to that, Lucy. We've heard it all before."

"Just sayin'. How much work is required to get it publishable, do you know?"

"Fair amount. More than just a polish."

"Thanks for this."

"You're welcome. I'll let you know if I hear anything more. And I expect I will."

Chapter Twenty-Three

After I left work for the day, before getting into my car, I made a phone call.

"Hello?" Bill Pratchett said.

"Hi. Lucy McNeil here. From the library?"

"Yes. Hi. What can I do for you? First of all let me explain that I knew nothing about that stunt Heather was going to pull at your library. I thought we were dropping in for nothing more than a pleasant chat about your festival."

"Not a problem. I understand. I'm wondering if you have time to meet. Maybe a drink somewhere?"

"Why?" A tinge of suspicion crept into his voice.

"I have friends in publishing, and I heard you sent Todd's new book to his publishers, and they love it."

He chuckled and the suspicion disappeared. "Word does get around. Yes, I had a call from the editor earlier. We're good to go. They're preparing a contract now. I'm never adverse to talking about good news over a drink. I'm staying at the Ocean Side Hotel. Do you know where that is?"

"I do. How about half an hour?"

"See you there."

My next call was to Shannon McKinnon. I'd thought it all over once again after Bertie left with her tea, and Shannon, I concluded, was my most likely suspect for Todd's murder, considering the highly personal method of the killing, and that she, of all people, would have had reason to use the arrow as a way of sending him a message.

"It's Lucy from the library here, Shannon. I'm wondering if you heard the news?"

"What news?"

"Todd Harrison's book has been accepted by his publisher. Word is it's going to be given a record-breaking advance and all the publicity to go with it." Okay, I hadn't heard any such thing, but when trying to trap a killer, one should be allowed a degree of literary license.

"I guess I'll be finding myself a lawyer, then." Her tone was icy.

"I have a better idea. The book isn't finished. From what I heard it still needs a substantial amount of work. The publisher will be searching for a suitable writer to finish it. How about you?"

"Me? Why should they consider me?"

"I'm leaving work in a few minutes. How about we meet for a drink at the Ocean Side in about half an hour, and we can talk it over?"

"Sure. I don't see how you can help me, but I don't have anything better to do tonight."

Not exactly the enthusiasm I was hoping for, but it would do. *Would I be able to trick Shannon into confessing to murder?* Probably not, but I was hoping she'd give me something to take to Sam Watson.

I called to Charles that it was time to leave. I called again to Charles that it was time to leave. When suggesting we meet in half an hour, I'd forgotten how long it could sometimes take that cat to get ready. I took out the package of treats I keep in the desk drawer for just such eventualities and shook it.

The little head appeared out of nowhere. He accepted the treat and then allowed me to pick him up and put him in the carrier.

I called goodnight to those of my coworkers still in the library, and we headed to my car. Fortunately, our house is close to Highway 12 leading into Nags Head, so I didn't lose too much time going home, taking Charles into the house, and setting him free before going out again.

It was coming up to six o'clock when I finally arrived at my destination, and the Ocean Side Hotel was a busy place. Family groups returning from the beach: sunburned kids, sandy bathing suits, happy smiles. Adults heading out for dinner or drinks, many of them also sunburned and all of them with happy smiles.

Bill Pratchett was waiting for me in the comfortable lobby bar. He'd taken a chair at a low table in a dark corner of the room, next to the unlit fireplace. He already had a glass of beer and a bowl of mixed nuts in front of him.

"Thanks for seeing me," I said as I sat down. I chose a chair that gave me a view of the lobby and entrance to the bar so I could watch for Shannon.

He lifted his glass. "I have something to celebrate."

"Did you get a good advance?"

"Their initial offer isn't as much as I might have hoped for, but I can hold out for a few days. If they don't up it, I'll take it. I trust you won't be letting anyone know I said that."

"Your secret is safe with me," I said.

"I could have threatened to take the manuscript to another publisher. I could have tried to start a bidding war, but I figured now's not the time to drag this out. We have to get that book into production while Todd's name's still known."

"Heather's okay with that?"

"She is. She needs the money, and she needs as much of it as she can get her sticky hands on right now if she's going to mount a foolish political campaign."

That was a distraction from what I wanted to talk about, but I followed the trail anyway. "Why foolish?"

"She has way, way too much baggage. New York City journalist. Husband famous for writing the sort of fantasy books that some people think's a bad influence on kids, with magic and made-up religions, and all that stuff. When she was in New York, she didn't make the sort of friends she should have. Instead, she managed to make a lot of enemies, politically connected enemies, spreading rumor and insinuation on that podcast of hers in a desperate attempt to get her number of listeners up." He drank his beer. "Not my problem if she wastes Todd's money. I'll still get my cut."

"What can I get you?" the smiling waiter asked me.

"A glass of white wine would be nice, please."

"Ready for another, sir?"

"Why not? I'm celebrating." Bill scooped up a handful of nuts.

Shannon McKinnon crossed the lobby and came into the bar. I lifted my hand, and she noticed me. Then she saw I was with Bill. Her eyes narrowed, but she came over. "Lucy. I see you found someone else to drink with."

"That's okay," I said cheerily. "Please join us."

Shannon sat down.

She and Bill watched each other.

The waiter brought the drinks and a fresh bowl of nuts. He asked Shannon what she wanted and went to get it.

"I've had a great idea." I made an attempt to sound spontaneous. "Bill, you don't want anyone threatening a lawsuit against Todd's literary heirs. Shannon, you don't want to go to the time and trouble, not to mention expense, for a highly unpredictable outcome. So, why not work together?"

"Is this arrangement a setup?" Shannon said.

So much for appearing spontaneous. "If you want to call it that."

"Not on my part," Bill said around another mouthful of nuts. "I fail to see why you think I'd want to work with her on anything at all."

"Todd's book—" I began.

"*My* book," Shannon said. "What he did with my book, anyway."

"The book in question is not finished. Someone has to finish it."

"You want me to do that?" Shannon said.

"You think I'm going to hire any old wanna-be off the street to finish Todd's book?" Bill said.

"Why not? The two of you should be able to at least talk about it." I sipped my wine. They eyed each other warily, thinking over my idea.

Or maybe they were wondering how best to get out of here as fast as politely possible and leave me to pay the bill.

"I'd want full editorial control," Shannon said.

"Not happening," Bill said. "The publisher likes what they've seen. We're sticking to that."

"Then no," Shannon said. "I can't work on a book based on my own ideas and not make my own changes."

"Why not at least consider it?" I said. "Perhaps some good can come out of Todd's death. For you anyway."

"No," Shannon said.

The waiter brought her drink and put it in front of her.

She stood up. "I appreciate you trying to help, Lucy, I do. But nothing good can come out of Todd's death for me. All it's done is eliminate any chance of him recognizing what he owes me. That's all I ever wanted. Contrary to what I said to you earlier, now that he's gone, and I am sorry about that; he was a good writer—I realize there's no point in me pursuing any lawsuit. No one would believe me, and I have no proof of what I'm saying. I've been thinking it all over these past few days. I'm going to take my writing in an entirely new direction: modern American teens wrestling with the real world and real-world problems, not popping through portals in space and time or fighting with dragons. I'm excited about it. I hope to have a sample to read at the festival. Goodbye, Mr. Pratchett. I wish you well with the book."

"When you have something ready to be read," he said, "please contact me."

She smiled. "I will."

She left. Her untouched drink sat on the table.

"You had to know that wasn't going to work out," Bill said to me. "Even if she wanted to do it, no way would she be a fit. It's not easy finishing someone else's book, and the publisher will have a pretty good idea who they want to use."

"I tried," I said.

"You were hoping she'd confess to killing Todd because he stole her idea. I overheard some of Heather's wild theory to the effect that you're some criminal mastermind who manipulates everyone, including the police, because you want to bask in the attention."

I opened my mouth to respond, and he laughed. "Bunch of nonsense, and I told Heather so. She said she's well aware of that.

Not a nice person, our Heather. Never has been. Totally manipulative. As far as Heather's concerned, other people have been put on this earth for her to step on."

"Did that include Todd?"

"Probably. Unlikely he cared. They suited each other. Both ruthlessly ambitious in their own way. Although Todd could be a lot more subtle about it."

Bill was the only person I'd been talking to about this situation who knew both Todd and Heather. He was relaxed and comfortable, enjoying his beer. I decided to probe and learn what I could. If anything. "Do you know Heather well?"

"I've known her for a long time. Since her newspaper days, when they first moved to New York. I met Todd through Heather. She introduced us when he was writing his first book and I was trying to get my agency up and running." He scooped up a handful of nuts.

"Was it a problem for you when they moved to Nags Head from New York City? As his agent, I mean."

He shrugged and tossed the nuts into his mouth. "Not at all. Not many, if any, of my authors live in the Big Apple, and it doesn't matter. Never did, but even less now we do absolutely everything by email. I've never even met many of my authors in person." He chuckled. "Just as well considering how fast some of them turn over."

"Whose idea was it to move here? Todd's or Heather's?"

"Heather. Totally Heather, for all Todd told interviewers he 'wanted to go home.'" Bill made quotation marks in the air with his fingers.

"Heather told the police the opposite. She said Todd suggested the move."

"Heather tells the police what it suits Heather to tell the police. Might not matter—she has a way of believing what she wants to believe regardless of reality. No, it wasn't Todd. He loved living in the big city. He loved everything about it. The noise and the crowds and the traffic not the least. He wouldn't have lasted here much longer."

"You think he wanted to move back?"

"I know he did. And he intended to. With or without her."

"Why did she want to move here?"

"At a guess, I'd say because she wanted to be a big fish in a small pond rather than a small fish in a big pond. Political ambitions. Nothing more. She wouldn't have had a prayer of a chance at getting the nomination in New York State. At least here, in North Carolina, she can call herself a local girl who finally saw the light and moved back home."

"What would have happened to the marriage if Todd left?"

Bill scoffed. "What marriage? Todd stayed married to Heather because divorce is messy, not to mention costly, and outside of his writing life, he was lazy. Divorces are expensive, and they can get nasty and out of control. Heather stayed with Todd because it suits her image to be a faithful wife. Her self-image most of all. If—*when* the Senate run fails, she'll likely go back to NYC."

"Were you good friends with them? You seem to know a lot about their marriage."

"When they lived in the city, Todd and I got together in person occasionally to have a drink or lunch and talk over the business stuff. I ran into Heather now and again through mutual friends. People let things slip over a couple of beers." He lifted his glass in a salute to me. "People sometimes let personal stuff slip when they shouldn't. As for me, you'll notice I'm not telling you anything about me, am I? Todd's dead, so he doesn't care what anyone says. I have his last manuscript, so I won't need to have much more to do with Heather. We didn't part on good terms. I had to remind her I'd go to court to get it if I had to."

"Do you have a case? If she didn't give it to you? Rumor in the publishing world is that Todd was looking for a new agent."

"Todd was always talking about looking for a new agent. Nothing ever came of it. As I might have mentioned, he could be downright lazy when it came to the business part of his career. An agent might have approached him once word of his new book got around. Wouldn't have mattered. I could have talked him out of leaving."

"What do you think of the new book?"

"It's good. Better than that Frighteners junk. And that, young lady, is not to be repeated outside of this glass of beer. I make a hefty chunk of my income from that junk. If you're looking for someone to accuse of killing Todd, it wasn't me. I can be lazy too sometimes, and now I have to start trying to find a promising new client to keep my agency afloat."

"I know I'm prying, but Todd did bring his problems to my door, and he died there, at my house, without telling me what those problems were."

"Go ahead. I'm not the keeper of anyone's secrets. Sometimes not even my own."

"You said Heather liked the image of a faithful wife. Does that mean she wasn't? Faithful, that is?"

"That, Library Lady, I don't know. I never heard any rumors about her, but she knew how to keep her nose clean. If you're asking if she and I ever had anything going, the answer is a definite no. She can be attractive sometimes—most of the time, I guess—but that icy ambition makes for a cold shower."

"Todd came to my house the night he died, saying he wanted to talk to me. Do you have any idea what that might have been about?"

"Not the slightest clue. You're a librarian, not an editor or a publisher. Not even an agent. There are better ways of asking a library to stock your books." He snickered. "Like I said, I know Heather better than I knew Todd, from her early journalism days. If you're thinking Heather might have killed Todd, not on. Not her style, and she had no reason to. Nothing she ever told me at any rate. Although marriages, even the best ones, and theirs wasn't that, have a lot of secrets."

"What about the money earned by the new book? She'll inherit it all, I presume."

"Yeah, and then that's it. The new book'll have a big initial run, and that'll spark some renewed interest in his earlier work, but with no book tour or public appearances by the author, it'll soon drop off the charts. And most importantly, there will be no follow-up. Not worth killing him, by a long shot."

As long as he was chatting comfortably, I asked another question that had been on my mind. "Did Todd or Heather ever mention a local woman by the name of Lorraine? She's a musician."

Bill's brow wrinkled in thought. "Sounds mildly familiar."

"Heather accused Lorraine of stalking her husband. She put the police onto Lorraine, who flatly denied it."

Bill snorted in laughter. "Now I get it. Yeah, I have heard that name. I had a FaceTime call scheduled with Todd one day, couple of weeks ago. When I called, Heather picked up. He'd left his iPad open. She told me he'd gone out for lunch with some woman.

I didn't want to know, but she went on anyway about how Todd had started seeing a girlfriend from the old days."

"They were never boyfriend and girlfriend, but high school acquaintances."

"Details are irrelevant to Heather. It was like two o'clock in the afternoon, on a Friday as I recall, and Heather had clearly gotten a jump on the weekend with a couple of lunchtime drinks. Bad habit in a prospective politician. She started going on about how she was sick and tired of Todd's constant complaining, about the book, about having moved, about her trying to make political connections. She figured he was ripe for falling for the wiles of any woman who'd give him a sympathetic ear."

"She was right about that, but not in the way she thought. Lorraine wanted them to be friends, and Todd did also."

"Heather doesn't believe men and women can be friends."

I didn't take that line of thought to where it might lead. Bill told me he and Heather had been friends when she first moved to New York. How much knowledge of that "icy" ambition he referred to came from personal experience? I decided that question was not relevant now. Judging by the way Bill was talking to me about her, about her and Todd, openly and comfortably, if anything had ever happened between Heather and Bill, it was long over. Even if Bill did still carry some well-suppressed passion for Heather, I could think of no reason for him to kill Todd over it. Not only Bill told me the couple didn't have a loving marriage. Lorraine had said so also.

"Why would Heather turn the cops onto Lorraine?" I asked. "Tell them Lorriane had been stalking Todd?"

"Who knows. Because she wanted to make trouble? Because she wanted to deflect any suspicion that might be turned her way?

Isn't the spouse the police's usual first suspect? She literally might believe it, Lucy. I don't know what happened between them when Todd got home that day. Heather was angry when she spoke to me. Maybe he attempted to calm her down by telling her Lorriane wouldn't take no for an answer. A spurned lover is also a pretty good suspect."

"The police say Heather has a rock-solid alibi."

"I'm glad to hear it. I don't need any more complications with this business." He grinned. "Anything else you want to ask? Other than if I killed my best client?"

"I wasn't going to ask that," I said.

"No, but you're digging. So, I'll answer. I did not. You'll have to look elsewhere. Todd was going to be in for the big bucks with this new book, and I knew he was thinking about going to another agent. I'm pretty confident I could have talked him out of doing any such thing, but it's possible they'd talk a better talk than me and manage to convince him."

The lobby bar was filling up as Bill and I talked. People called for drinks and greeted friends. Waiters took orders and served drinks and bar snacks. A table of six arrived, roaring with laughter, tripping over their own feet, obviously not out for their first drink of the evening. Through the east-facing windows, I could see people enjoying the swimming pool; others, laden with towels and beach bags, returning from the beach along the boardwalk that weaves though the tall grasses and across the dunes.

"Before you go," Bill said. "Full confession time: I'll admit that I might—might, mind you—have considered killing Todd for the entire amount his new book will likely earn, but not for a measly fifteen percent. I don't need to give you an alibi, but I will. I was in Presbyterian Hospital when Todd died."

"Oh. I'm . . . sorry to hear that."

"I had a heart attack a year ago. Bad one. This time it was heartburn, but I went into a panic and called an ambulance. I was resting in the sweet arms of an ER nurse waiting to be seen by a doctor at nine o'clock last Tuesday night. Now, you might be thinking maybe I hired a contract killer." He winked at me. "If I had the funds to hire a hitman, I wouldn't need to kill for my fifteen percent, now would I?"

"I guess not."

He finished his drink and gathered up the last of the second bowl of nuts. "I'll bid you a good night. When's this festival of yours again?"

I told him.

"I might be back. I like this Shannon McKinnon. Didn't at first, thought she considered herself entitled to be published because she once had a good idea. But now I'm interested. I'd like to hear her reading. Good night, Lucy."

"What about Ruth Vivac?" I asked. "I saw you meeting with her the other day."

"I told her I'd consider her, but I won't. Her writing's fine, even good, but it's not for me."

"Thanks for agreeing to meet with me."

He put money on the table. "Drinks are on me. If it pans out with Shannon, I owe you. Truth be told, I don't think Todd's new book is going to hit the heights everyone's expecting. He's got a loyal fan base. Loyal to the point of rabid. Fans like that rarely take it well when their authors make a change. They don't like change."

Chapter Twenty-Four

Wednesday evening, Connor was scheduled to attend a fundraising dinner for an environmental organization, so I would be on my own. I like being married. I love being married to Connor. But I have to confess: I do enjoy doing my own thing on occasion.

I was trying not to remember the last evening I'd been on my own at home, and what happened then, as I left work. I made a quick stop at the drugstore and pulled into the driveway shortly after five. A small, dark car was parked in front of the neighbors to the north of us, and I paid it no attention. Before getting Charles out, I went to check the mailbox. I was pleased to see that no offerings of cheap flowers or stuffed toys graced our steps.

The door of the small car opened, and a woman stepped out, closing the door behind her. She walked toward me. "Mrs. McNeil."

I didn't bother to disguise my groan. Not again! "I don't know what you want, but I'm tired and I've had a long day, and I have to see to my cat. Please go away."

Layla stepped off the sidewalk and put a foot onto my scruffy, sand-choked grass. Large round sunglasses covered her eyes, and her dark hair cascaded in a sleek black river down her back. She wasn't wearing a suit today, but wide-legged pants with thin black and white stripes and a denim jacket over a blue T-shirt.

"You're trespassing," I said. "Please leave. Any more harassment, and I will call the police."

She winced and tried to force out a smile as she took a step backward. "I'm not here with or on behalf of Heather. She doesn't know I've come."

I went to my car and got Charles. He peered out of the carrier at the woman.

"What do you want then?" I asked.

"To apologize."

That caught me by surprise. "What?"

"I want to apologize for Heather's behavior and for my participation in it. I've quit my job. I'm going back to Elizabeth City. I'll be looking for another line of work."

Charles whined and scratched at the netting on the carrier. "I have to take this one in," I said. "If you promise me this isn't some trick of Heather's to get the inside scoop on my nefarious activities, you can come in."

"I promise."

"No cameras. No phones. No filming or recording."

"Like I said, Mrs. McNeil, I've quit my job. I have no one to report this visit to. Nor do I want to."

I led the way into the house via the kitchen door. Layla followed me. I dropped my purse onto the counter and put the cat carrier on the island. Instead of shooting out the moment I opened the door, as he usually did, Charles emerged slowly. He sniffed the air. Layla tentatively held out a hand. He sniffed it.

And then he flipped over onto his back, waved his legs in the air, and stretched his neck. Layla rubbed his tummy while he curled his feet around her arm. When he eventually started to scratch and bite, she pulled her hand away. "This is a nice cat. What's his name?"

"Charles. Named after Mr. Dickens. He's originally the library cat, and he comes to work with me every day. He seems to like you. I take that as a good sign. Have a seat and tell me what's on your mind." I picked Charles up and put him on the floor. Guest welcomed in a suitable fashion, he checked out his food and water bowls. "I have tea in the fridge, or I can make hot tea or coffee, if you'd like."

"A glass of tea would be nice. Thank you." She sat quietly on a stool, hands in lap, not fidgeting while I got the drinks. I put the glass in front of her and then sat down opposite her and waited.

She dipped her eyes, sipped her tea. I let her compose herself. Then she put the glass down, lifted her head. The round, dark eyes looked at me. "I'm going into my senior year of college. I'm taking modern languages at Blacklock College in Elizabeth City. I've been considering a career in public relations or corporate communications."

"Do you know Professor McClanahan?" I asked. "Edward McClanahan?"

Her eyes lit up. "Oh yes. He's one of my favorite teachers. Such a character and so smart. I took his Latin course last year because I needed a filler class and the time suited me. I loved it. I'm going to take the advanced course next year."

Eddie McClanahan was Bertie's gentleman friend. The dictionary definition of an absent-minded professor, he set us on a heck of a wild goose chase the day after my wedding.

"Heather Harrison advertised for a PA. She was clear it was a summer job, just three days a week, while she explored the possibility of going into politics. If she decided to go ahead, and once her real campaign began, she'd be looking for a more permanent assistant, which suited me perfectly. I'm going back to college in the fall. My family has a vacation home in Kill Devil Hills, and I know the area pretty well. I liked the idea of living here all summer, and I could stay at our family's place rent-free."

"It's not even the end of July," I said. "But you've quit already."

She twisted the glass in her hands and studied the countertop. I waited.

When Layla lifted her head, her dark eyes brimmed with moisture. "I . . . don't like Heather. And I don't like what she made me do. Not that I did anything, but I had to stand by and watch her bully people. People like you. She knows you didn't kill Todd for the attention."

"I'm aware of that."

"I don't think I want to go into politics after all. Not if that's what they're all like."

"They're not," I said. "My husband has never dealt in dirty tricks, and all he's ever done for the citizens of Nags Head is what he promised to do and what they elected him to do."

"I've heard that about him. Good to know. Not that I'm likely to change my mind. I'm going back to Elizabeth City. I'm going to see about getting a start on the fall semester, try and finish my degree early. I wanted to face you myself and tell you I'm sorry."

"You don't need to apologize," I said. "All you did was watch Heather do . . . what she did."

"Still. I'm glad I got the chance to say goodbye."

I smiled at her. "I am too. Did you tell Heather you were quitting."

"Yeah. This afternoon. It went about as well as you'd expect. She called me ungrateful and said she'd blackball me." Layla snorted. "As if she has any influence with anyone or anything. And then it was all how sorry she was to see me go, and what could she do to convince me to stay. And then back to saying it was just as well I was quitting as she needed someone more competent and less emotional than me."

"When did you start working for her?"

"End of May. About eight weeks ago."

"So you knew Todd, her husband?"

"Oh yeah. Obviously, being a writer, he worked at home. And as Heather doesn't have a campaign yet, so no office, when I was working with her it was at their house."

"What did you think of him?"

"Hard to say. He seemed nice enough. He was distant but polite. Friendly enough, but not overly friendly. Not the slightest bit interested in her political career. I thought that was odd. You'd think the husband of a senator would have to be involved, wouldn't you?"

"Have you read any of his books?"

"I read one when I first got the job with Heather, thinking I could talk about it with Todd. It was okay, but that type of fantasy's not really my thing. I tried to ask him about the books, about his writing process and all that, but he didn't have much to say. He told me he was finished with that series and starting something new. He didn't really talk to me about anything. He didn't talk to Heather a lot either. To be honest, Lucy, I figured their marriage wasn't anything more than a front. They were polite enough to each other most of the time, but they didn't show any sort of . . . affection. Do you know what I mean?"

I did, and that corresponded with what Bill Pratchett told me about the Harrison marriage. "Did they fight or argue?"

"Not when I was there, but I was only part-time. More like they didn't talk to each other much. Things were okay at first—with the job I mean. I was excited about it, and I started thinking maybe I could consider a career in politics. Like as a campaign manager or staffer or something. But ambition made Heather turn mean. I want no part of that."

Layla had finished her tea, and I offered her another. She accepted, and I got out the jug. She'd come here to apologize to me, which she didn't have to do, but I appreciated it. She'd done what she came for but was making no move to leave. She needed to talk it out, to convince herself she'd done the right thing in quitting the job. I had no plans for this evening, and I was happy to listen. As was Charles, curled up on the top of the cat tree, watching her.

"Turn mean," I said. "You don't think that was her nature all along?"

"Oh, I'm sure she isn't a nice person. Not deep down, where it counts. The leopard doesn't change its spots that fast. She was nice to me when I met her and started working with her. She was excited about the idea of running for the nomination and what might come after. She was pleased with the work I was doing, and said so many times. But then . . . things quickly started not going well. The local party people aren't keen on her running, and she isn't likely to get a great deal of support for the nomination. Someone found a recording of her old podcast where she agreed with a guest saying all politicians are corrupt and the party system needs to be gotten rid of completely, and they shared it with everyone. As the pressure started building, she started cracking. It wasn't pleasant to see. And then, the day before Todd died, she got a phone call that had her really upset. She was almost crying."

That caught my attention. "What was the call about?"

Layla shifted on her stool. She slid her eyes away from me. "Heather and I were working in her office. She left the room to take the call. When she came back, she was obviously bothered by it, like I said. She told me I could leave early, she had something to attend to. I gathered my stuff, but before I left, I had to use the restroom. I guess she thought I'd gone, and she went into Todd's study. She never did that when he was working."

I didn't say what I was thinking. Layla hadn't accidentally overheard what Heather and Todd were discussing. She'd deliberately hung around, listening. Probably hiding behind doors or leaning up against the wall.

Who among us wouldn't? I wondered.

"Do you know what upset her?" I asked.

"This is just hearsay, right? I mean, I didn't hear it all. As I was in the restroom with the door closed. But the guest powder room is right next to Todd's office, and they weren't keeping their voices down.

"Like I said, when things started not going her way, Heather started getting desperate, and her mean side came out. It was only after Todd died that she turned on you. I didn't think that was fair. And then she started making accusations against the police department. That detective who's on Todd's case, the older one. He talked to me about things I'd observed in their house, and I thought he was nice. Thorough too."

"Things you'd observed? Did you have anything to tell him?"

"I told him honestly that Todd and Heather didn't seem to have a close marriage, but nothing was wrong with it either. They didn't fight, at least not when I was there. No one threw things or slammed doors or made threats." She shrugged.

"This conversation you happened to overhear. What was it about?" I was asking out of more than idle curiosity. If something of significance happened the day before Todd died, it might have something to do with his death.

"I didn't hear it all, like. But I caught the word 'blackmail.'"

"Heather was blackmailing someone?"

"Not her. Someone was blackmailing her. Or threatening to do so."

"Over what?"

"Something about her covering up a relationship a congressperson was having with the teenage daughter of a staffer. Heather somehow learned about it, but she didn't tell anyone, in exchange for the congressperson's endorsement for her own campaign."

"I'm not sure I get it," I said. "Heather wasn't the guilty party, was she? She just kept quiet about what she knew. Is that grounds for blackmail?"

"In politics almost everything is grounds for blackmail. The congressperson abruptly resigned, claiming she needed time to care for her seriously ill husband. You might have heard about that?"

"Not that I recall. Is this the state senator whose seat Heather is after?"

"No. If he endorsed Heather, that would be a huge boost to her campaign, but so far he's not announced his support for anyone. Besides, the congressperson in question is a woman, I got that much. A woman having an affair with a teenage girl? That'd be a career ender. In some circles anyway."

"Probably."

"Whoever called Heather has lost his blackmail chance against the congresswoman, so now they're after Heather. Not only did Heather know about the affair, but she was directly asked about it, without naming names, by one of the guests on one of her last podcasts, and she changed the subject. This person who called was threatening to expose Heather for covering it up."

I shook my head. "I still don't see it. Politicians are guilty of a lot more than not wanting to spread gossip about someone else's business."

"Considering Heather's entire campaign was going to be based on eliminating influence and corruption, that could have sunk her before she so much as got out of the gate."

I still didn't necessarily agree, but if Heather thought the revelation would endanger her campaign, that might be all that mattered.

"Todd asked her how much she got from the congressperson. She said not a red cent. I don't know if I believed her."

"That might do it. If Heather was asking for money to keep quiet about what she knew, rather than just this person's support. Even if she wasn't, if it looked like she was paid off—yeah, I can see it being bad. What happened then?"

"Heather didn't deny knowing what had been going on, but she insisted she wasn't paid for her silence, and she didn't ask for an endorsement from the guilty party either. She just thought it wasn't any of the public's business. Todd said something to the effect that he'd never before known her to care about protecting other people's privacy. They must have moved away from the wall at that point, because I couldn't hear any more. I left. The next day, Heather was, like, determined. Focused, getting down to business."

"What did Todd do that day?"

"He spent most of the time in his office, as usual. I saw him for a few minutes when he came into the kitchen to get something for lunch. He said hi, made a sandwich, cleaned up, and took the sandwich back to his office. That was all pretty normal behavior for him. He was, like, super tidy and neat. I liked that about him. When my dad makes a piece of toast, the kitchen looks like a bomb went off."

"Did he seem bothered?"

"Why should he be? Mom or one of my sisters always cleans up after him."

"I mean Todd. The day he died."

"Oh right, him. Hard to tell, as he didn't usually say much to me. He went out about three thirty, and I left not long after. I never saw him again."

"That night Heather went to dinner with the local representatives of her party. Did you go with her?"

"No. No staff."

Had Layla heard correctly? Was someone threatening to blackmail Heather? Or had the young woman misunderstood the conversation she was not party to?

I thought over what happened on the day after this phone call. Todd came to the library at four o'clock for the scheduled meeting. He'd been polite and engaged. I hadn't met him before, and I didn't know him at all, but I didn't think he'd been overly distracted. The meeting ended around five, and he left. Todd then showed up, uninvited and unannounced, at my house at nine.

I'd been late for the meeting, but no one mentioned Todd doing or saying anything startling or unexpected.

I sucked in a breath as a thought occurred to me. Ruth had jokingly told him I was an amateur sleuth. That I'd helped the police solve crimes before. Todd, so the attendees said, seemed interested in that. Todd attempted to speak to me in private after the meeting, but he never had the chance.

Might Todd have intended to ask me to investigate this blackmail attempt? Either to uncover the blackmailer or to find out if the accusations against his wife were true?

Could that be what brought Todd Harrison to my house that night? Possible. But it didn't explain why someone killed him. The blackmailer, if one existed, had nothing against Todd. Nothing I knew about anyway. Although, I had to admit to myself, no reason I should know about it.

"Did you tell the police this? About the blackmail conversation?" I asked now.

Layla dipped her head again. Her black hair fell over her face. "No. It had nothing to do with what happened to Todd right? I didn't want the cops to think . . . to tell Heather . . . I'd been listening to their private conversation."

"Before you leave town, you need to call Detective Watson. It's not up to you to decide what matters or not. Everything matters in a murder investigation."

"Okay. I will." Layla climbed off the stool. "I'd better go. Thanks for listening to me, Lucy. The experience of working for Heather didn't turn out well at the end, but I have something to put on my résumé. If anyone asks why the job only lasted two months, I can say she let me go after the sudden death of her husband."

I walked her to the door. "Do you know if Heather's been bothered by any of Todd's readers?"

She rolled her eyes. "Yes, and she's not at all happy about it. They've come to the house a few times. Some of them asked if they could see Todd's office. Heather wasn't very polite in telling them no, and they had some rude words in return. She caught a girl creeping through the shrubbery at the side of the house one night. I wasn't there, but I heard all about it the following day, and I gather she sent the girl packing. Heather doesn't want any advice from me, but before I left, I suggested she lie low on the political campaigning for a while. Todd's fans will turn against her fast enough, and although they're hardly influential in politics and could probably not care less, in a small community everyone is influential." She laughed. "I had this roommate at college first year. She was such a fan of this sci-fi TV show, when it was canceled she literally had a breakdown. Like the end of the world was nigh. It's absolutely ridiculous the lengths to which some of these fans take their obsession. Particularly when the series or show ends and they're not ready to let it go."

* * *

Layla left. I wished her well, closed the door behind her, and checked it was locked. I picked up my glass and took a sip. The word "fan" lingered in the young woman's wake. *Fan. Fanatic.*

Last night Bill Pratchett had said much the same. Fans could take it personally when a favorite series abruptly ended. Rabid, he called some of those fans.

The death of Todd Harrison. After he announced he would be writing no more Frighteners books.

A highly personal killing with a bow and arrow.

Was it possible?

Might one of Todd's *rabid* fans have killed him? Had someone been so disturbed at the idea of their beloved author abandoning the Frighteners series before it concluded to their personal satisfaction, they killed him?

What sort of person would do that?

A *fanatic*, of the sort who'd make a pest of themselves by visiting the location of the author's death on the schedule laid out in his books.

A *fanatic*, of the sort who'd want to make a big show in front of their friends of how much the Frighteners books meant to them.

I jumped to my feet, snatched up my purse and keys, and ran out of the house.

I knew where the Peterson family lived.

Chapter Twenty-Five

Ralph Harper and his sister Jo, good friends of the library, grew up in the house where Connor and I live now. Their family home had not been lived in for many long years before they sold it to us. Neither of the Harper siblings had ever married, and they now live comfortably together in a small house across the street from the Peterson family. The second youngest Peterson daughter, Phoebe, used to work with Jo to maintain her extensive vegetable garden and help care for their chickens. Ralph was a fisherman from a long line of fishing people, and he still owned and captained a charter fishing boat. Tonight his rattletrap of a truck wasn't on the concrete pad that served as his parking space. Jo was most likely at home. She didn't drive. She rarely left the house. At one time she'd been a total recluse, but since she'd become involved in strange happenings in what was now Connor and my house, she slowly emerged from her shell. Just a tiny bit. Much of that was due to the help of library stalwart Tim Snyder.

All the houses on this road, including the Petersons' and Harpers', had been built on stilts to allow stormwaters to wash underneath. The Petersons' was one of the largest. Multistoried, multi-staircased, painted gray with white trim. It's hard to maintain a lawn and garden in the choking sand that makes up the soil on the narrow strip of land that forms the Outer Banks, but Maureen Peterson had lined her driveway and walkway with terracotta pots overflowing with tall grasses, colorful annuals, and tumbling variegated vines. The house didn't have a garage, and tonight two vehicles were parked side by side in the driveway. I recognized the white van, suitable for transporting a family of seven, often parked outside the library.

Mrs. Peterson answered the door to my ring and looked startled to see me. As she should. Librarians rarely make house calls. The *ping ping* of a badly and unenthusiastically played piano sounded from somewhere in the house.

"I'm sorry to drop in unexpectedly," I said. "I hope I'm not interrupting anything?"

"No. Not at all. We've finished dinner, and the girls are going about . . . whatever they do. Come in, come in." She stood back and I stepped into their home. The entrance was small but nicely furnished, with a chair for sitting in while taking off shoes, a low table for placing hats and scarves, a reproduction pink and pale green Chinese vase containing one large black men's umbrella. A corridor led deeper into the house, a series of doors opening off it. A steep staircase accessed the second floor. Formal school portraits of the five Peterson daughters, taken over the years, lined the staircase.

"Come into the living room, please." Mrs. Peterson bustled me inside. "And tell me what brings you here, Lucy. Never mind the noise—Rosemary's in the music room, practicing for the summer recital." Mrs. Peterson's personality was written all over their house. The color scheme was pink, the decor fluffy. White chairs and sofa piled high with plump pink cushions. White drapes with pink tassels. Paintings of pink sunsets. Pink frames on the numerous family photographs scattered across the side tables. Dainty pink porcelain Dresden shepherdesses next to those photographs.

Ping ping.

"Here on library business?" Mrs. Peterson gestured to an overstuffed pink chair. "Something that can't wait until tomorrow? Would you care for tea?"

"Nothing to drink, thank you. I don't want to keep you. I was hoping to talk to Primrose. Is she in?"

"She is, although she's planning to go out with her friends shortly. Always on the go, those girls of ours. Charity has a soccer game to get to." She rolled her eyes. "Another soccer game. And now she's nagging Al to buy her a car so she can drive herself around." Al was the rarely seen, rarely heard Mr. Peterson. "What do you want to talk to Primrose about?"

"You told me she's a big fan of Todd Harrison's books. Are you aware she's the president of one of his online fan clubs?"

Mrs. Peterson groaned and threw herself onto the sofa. "Not that again. It's been nothing but Todd Harrison this and Todd Harrison that for a week. If the man wasn't dead, I'd kill him myself." She winced. "Sorry. That comment was thoughtless of me. Not his fault the young people like his books so much. Yes, I knew about the fan club. I saw no harm in it, initially. It's only recently she's begun taking her enthusiasm to extremes. I suppose I should be pleased Primrose is devoted to her reading, even if it is *that sort* of book. Better than Charity and her sports nonsense."

I didn't bother to point out that "that sports nonsense" was helping to pay for the girl to go to college.

The piano music stopped.

"Keep practicing," Mrs. Peterson bellowed.

Ping ping! Faster this time. I sensed an air of desperation in the pounding of the keys.

"Is the library organizing some sort of tribute to Todd, and you'd like Primrose and her friends to speak? She was so excited when she heard he was coming to the festival. She was naturally quite disappointed when it turned out that he . . . uh, wouldn't be attending, but she was disappointed again at the new author you found to take Todd Harrison's place. Too juvenile for her, she says. I said—"

"Can I speak to Primrose?" I asked.

The girl herself stepped into the living room, dressed in jeans with rips in the knees, again wearing the T-shirt featuring the warrior woman and her wolf. She'd applied a minimal amount of makeup (probably the most her mother allowed), and her shiny blond hair cascaded loosely down her back. "I'm here."

"Primrose is about to go out," Mrs. Peterson said. "She's going to a movie with her friends, isn't that right, dear?"

Primrose nodded. I studied her face, looking for signs that she and her gang might be planning another raid on my house, although it was not yet three nights since the last one.

"I said I'm sorry," she said. "It won't happen again."

"What are you sorry about?" her mother asked. "What won't happen again?"

"I'm glad to hear it," I said. "But that's not why I'm here. Mrs. Peterson, would it be possible for me to speak to Primrose in private?" This house was an older one, built before fully open plan was all the rage, and it hadn't been updated. The rooms were enclosed with doors leading into the corridor. Nice when wanting to talk to someone with some degree of privacy.

Ping ping.

Mrs. Peterson looked between her daughter and me.

"I'm interested in the Todd Harrison fan club, that's all," I said.

"It's okay, Mom," Primrose said.

"Very well. I'll be in the kitchen." Maureen Peterson slipped away.

I wasn't here to accuse Primrose of anything. I knew the girl and her family moderately well. As I've said, I've been wrong before, but I couldn't see this bright-eyed, intelligent, polite girl being a cold-blooded killer. No matter how much of a *fanatic* she might be about the author.

Whoever followed Todd Harrison to our house that night, with a compound bow and two arrows ready at hand and plans to use them, was very cold-blooded indeed.

The piano music stopped.

I had little doubt Rosemary was perched on the edge of the piano stool, straining to listen. I had little doubt the girls' mother was doing much the same, as were any of the other daughters in the house at the moment.

As for Mr. Peterson, outnumbered and outmatched, he drifted through their lives like a silent shadow.

"Did you know Todd had been researching archery for his new book?" I asked Primrose.

"Yeah, I did. I went to a book signing he did at that little bookstore in Buxton last month. Someone asked a question about how much research he does for his books, and he told us he'd been learning how to shoot a bow and arrow. That's an important part of the world building for the new book. It's going to be a totally different world from the one in the Frighteners, this world after everything's fallen apart, like—"

"Did that make you interested in learning archery?"

Her eyes narrowed. She wasn't a fool. "No, it didn't. I read about lots of interesting things, doesn't mean I want to live them. I didn't go walking in the desert because I liked *Dune* either."

"Did anyone in the online fan club talk about trying it out?"

"No."

"Tell me more about the fan club. Do you know many of those people outside the group?"

She eyed me warily, not sure what I was after. I wasn't entirely sure myself. "Not as in we're close friends, like, no. A couple of girls in the club go to my school. We bonded over our mutual love of Todd and the Frighteners series, but that's about all."

"I understand why you came to our house those nights. You wanted to honor Todd in the way he would have understood."

She nodded.

"I'm wondering if any members of the club seemed more," I didn't say fanatic, "determined than the others. Anyone particularly distraught by his death or wanting to do more than the rest of you were comfortable with?"

"No."

"Whose idea was it to come to our house that first night?"

She shrugged and studied the pattern on the pink rug beneath her feet. "I don't remember."

"Did anyone object to it?"

"No one. They all thought it was a great idea. A couple of the girls couldn't make it. Family stuff and all. I told you we won't come again. My dad would have a fit if I got arrested for trespassing, and as for Mom, I have no idea what Mom would do. She can freak out sometimes."

I was getting nowhere. This was pointless. I couldn't come straight out and ask Primrose if she thought one of her friends had killed Todd, and I didn't know who else to ask if they'd noticed anyone acting suspiciously. Considering, as far as I was concerned, the behavior of all of them was, if not suspicious, downright weird.

"The first night you came to our house, you initially stayed on the public beach. But then some of you came onto the deck, and later into the house itself. Was it you who suggested getting closer, Primrose?"

She continued studying the rug. She shrugged. I took that as an embarrassed yes. I'd suspected she was the ringleader. I guessed she was the one behind the initial expedition, but she was afraid to admit it.

"Todd had a new project underway. He'd dropped the Frighteners series and was writing something new and different. Did you have any feelings about that?"

She lifted her head and looked at me. "I'm sure anything Todd wrote would be wonderful. I hope they can still publish the book. At that signing in Buxton, the one I told you about, he was so excited about the new book, he made everyone else excited too. Everyone except for Noah. He was my boyfriend, like, then."

"Did you and Noah meet in the fan club?"

"Gosh, no." She laughed. "Noah only went to the bookstore with me that night 'cause I needed a ride. We had a big fight after. He thought Todd was a fake, and he called me an idiot for caring about a stupid bunch of books."

Something niggled at the back of my neck. "You said Noah *was* your boyfriend. But he picked you up the other night at my house. He was there on the other occasions. I thought he was with you. Wasn't he?"

Mrs. Peterson told me Noah had mocked Todd, and following that Primrose said she never wanted to speak to him again. But now, after the author's death, Noah was being, in Mrs. Peterson's words, surprisingly understanding. So much so the teens were dating again. He'd taken her hand on the beach as they walked away, and she had not pulled it free.

I remembered how he turned on Jolene, when she innocently invited Primrose to her house. How earlier, Noah pulled Simone away from Primrose when the other girl also suggested they do something together.

The niggle turned into an itch.

The doorbell rang.

Chapter Twenty-Six

"I'll get it," Mrs. Peterson trilled, her voice so close to us she obviously was not in the kitchen. "Rosemary, keep practicing!"

Ping ping.

"That's my ride," Primrose said. "Noah and I are going to see a movie. Do you want to know anything else, Mrs. McNeil?"

"No. Thanks for your time."

"Primrose has a visitor, Noah," said the voice from the hallway. "She'll be with you in a minute. Come in."

"Thank you, ma'am," the boy said politely.

Primrose and I left the living room. Noah stood at the bottom of the stairs, smiling. He was dressed in a sports team T-shirt, jeans, and sneakers, and had a baseball cap on his head. When he saw me, the smile faded, and he looked almost frightened. "What are you doing here? I thought you were going to forget about the other night."

"What night?" Mrs. Peterson said. "What happened that night?"

Once again, the piano stopped. Upstairs, a floorboard creaked, and I heard a ball being dribbled across the floor.

"You've been very kind to Primrose this past week," I said to Noah. "Mrs. Peterson told me about it. It's nice that you and Primrose have gotten back together."

He smiled at the girl standing next to me at the entrance to the living room. He took two steps toward her, coming further into the hall. "She's been upset about that author guy's death. I've been trying to help. After all, that's what friends are for. Isn't it?"

Primrose gave him a dazzling smile. She was a pretty girl in the way that all healthy young women are pretty. But when she looked at Noah, her face lit up, making her truly beautiful.

He smiled back at her. Proud to be with her. Happy to be the object of that dazzling smile. "Ready to go, Prim?"

"Yeah. See you later, Mrs. McNeil. I'll just grab my phone." She ran off.

Upstairs, the soccer ball continued bouncing.

If Primrose had been dating Noah, and she broke off with him because he made fun of her devotion to her favorite author, they'd obviously reconnected as he comforted her over the death of her idol.

Nice how that worked out for him.

"My husband's been talking about taking up archery." I tried to sound oh so casual. "He says it's a fast-growing sport. Do you enjoy it, Noah?"

The boy was watching for Primrose to return, likely thinking about the evening to come, not paying attention to me anymore. "It's okay, I guess."

As soon as the words were out, he realized what he'd said. His head swiveled toward me, and panic filled his eyes. "I mean, I've heard it's fun."

"Archery? You mean like Robin Hood?" Mrs. Peterson said.

"You didn't mean to do it, did you?" I said to the boy. "You were fooling around. Having fun."

"I didn't—"

"Proving yourself worthy of Primrose."

"What are you talking about?" Mrs. Peterson said.

Charity appeared at the top of the stairs, dressed in her soccer uniform, hair tied back in a high ponytail, ball loosely cradled in her arms. "Hey, Noah. What brings you here *again*? Mom, is Dad ready yet? I'm going to be late if we don't leave now. If I had my own car, he wouldn't have to take me everywhere."

No one answered her. "You need to talk to the police," I said to Noah. "Tell them what happened. Tell them it was an accident. You were playing, right? You didn't intend to hit him. You were obviously scared when you saw that you'd hit him, and you didn't know what to do. You saw me come out of the house and find him, and you knew I'd call for help."

"I'm not going to the police," Noah said. "Prim, hurry up. I'm leaving!"

Primrose appeared at the far end of the hallway, phone in hand. "Don't be so impatient. I'm texting Julianne to ask her if she wants to meet us later."

He turned to leave. "Go with Julianne then. I'm outta here."

Mrs. Peterson took a step forward. She stood between the boy and the front door, facing him. "What is Lucy talking about? Has something happened the police need to know about? You weren't in a car accident were you? Primrose, did you know about this?"

Noah grabbed her. He spun her around, throwing one arm across her throat and the other tight across her chest.

The look on Mrs. Peterson's face would have been funny if I wasn't suddenly terrified as to what Noah would do. Her eyes bulged and her mouth opened and closed as she struggled to breathe.

"Noah, what are you doing?" Primrose said.

I held out my hands and tried to keep my voice soft and calm. "Noah, Mrs. Peterson is having trouble breathing. Why don't you let her go, and you and I can talk."

"Primrose, we're going! Come here, now!"

I glanced over my shoulder to see the girl behind me, her face a picture of total shock. Rosemary's dark curly head popped out of what was presumably the music room. "Dad!" she screamed.

"Have you gone nuts?" Primrose yelled at Noah.

"You're coming with me. Now. Let's go."

Mrs. Peterson's arms flapped in the air. Round, frightened eyes stared at me. She gave her head a feeble shake. Noah tightened his grip.

"Let go of my mom," Primrose said.

Noah edged backward, dragging Mrs. Peterson with him. Her hands clawed at the arm across her throat. "I'll let her go when you get yourself over here."

"I don't understand," the girl said.

"Dad!" Rosemary began to cry.

"She's lying," Noah said, presumably referring to me. "She knows it wasn't an accident, and she's going to tell the cops."

"What wasn't an accident?" Primrose asked.

"Noah killed Todd," I said. "Deliberately or by accident doesn't matter right now. What do you think you're going to do, Noah? Drive off into the sunset with Primrose? Steal a boat and make for Mexico? The Coast Guard will be onto you in minutes."

Primrose stood beside me. "Let go of my mom and we'll talk about it."

Noah relaxed the hold on Mrs. Peterson's neck. She gasped and sucked in lungfuls of air. She looked at her daughter and shook her head again, telling Primrose to stay where she was.

"It's okay, Mom. Noah and I are going to go for a short drive, right?"

"That's right," Noah said. He took another step back. Mrs. Peterson stumbled along with him. He was now standing at the bottom of the staircase.

I put my right arm firmly in front of Primrose, blocking her way. I couldn't let her go with Noah. Who knows what he might do when he realized they were not going to get away, and even if they did, Primrose was no longer likely to be favorably inclined toward him.

Would he try to go out in a blaze of glory, like the confused, frightened, mixed-up teenager he was? And take Primrose with him?

"That's not going to happen." I struggled to keep my voice calm, a woman in control. My librarian voice.

"It's okay, Mrs. McNeil," Primrose said. "Noah would never hurt me. Would you, Noah?"

"I love you Primrose," he said softly. "I've always loved you."

She pushed my arm out of the way.

"No," Mrs. Peterson squawked.

"Dad!" Rosemary yelled.

"Hey, Noah! Catch!"

Startled, Noah started to turn. At the top of the steps Charity tossed her ball into the air, lifted her right leg, and kicked the ball as hard as she could. Encumbered by Mrs. Peterson, who tried to pull away from him at the sound of her eldest daughter's voice, Noah couldn't raise his hands in time to knock the ball away. It struck him solidly in the face. He yelled in pain, let go of Mrs. Peterson, and staggered backward, blood streaming from his nose. He hit the wall, and his head flew back, stunning him. Primrose ran forward, and I was right behind her.

Charity flew down the stairs almost as fast as her ball had.

Primrose reached him first. She grabbed the still-stunned Noah and shoved him onto the floor. She leaped on top of him before he could move, and Charity and I piled on. "Rosemary, call the police," I said.

"My phone's on the floor, Rosie," Primrose yelled. "Get it. Use the emergency button."

The boy buckled and swore and tried to throw the three of us off.

"Stop that!" Charity ordered.

"Help, help!" Rosemary shouted. "He tried to kill my mom!"

"Prim," Noah cried. "I only want to be with you."

"Stand aside, girls. I've got this," Mrs. Peterson ordered in a loud, commanding voice.

I dared take a glance up and behind me. Maureen Peterson wielded the black umbrella like a baseball bat. Judging by the expression on her face, she would have no hesitation in using it.

One at a time, first me, then Charity, and last of all Primrose got to our feet. Noah lay on the floor, face up, hands held protectively above his blood-streaked face, breathing heavily, alternatively crying and swearing.

"Don't you dare move." Mrs. Peterson's glasses were askew, her hair had come out of its clip, her eyes were wild, her lips tight, her face determined.

The front door opened. Al Peterson strolled in. He held a hammer in one hand and a bag of nails in the other. He wore overalls, and a streak of dirt crossed his right cheek. "That's the picnic table leg fixed. Anything else need doing, Maureen?"

He froze in his tracks. He looked from one of us to another. The cowering, weeping boy on the floor, bleeding copiously from his nose. His eldest daughter, triumphant in her soccer gear; his second daughter, crying; his fourth daughter, also crying on the phone with the 911 dispatcher. At his wife, changed into something out of one of Todd Harrison's fantasy novels, holding her weapon high above her adversary, ready to use it.

He looked at me.

"Hi," I said.

"My dad's here now," Rosemary said into the phone.

In the distance, the sound of sirens heading our way.

Chapter Twenty-Seven

"At first," I said, "I thought one of his fans killed Todd, angry because Todd announced he wasn't going to write any more of the Frighteners books."

"Isn't that a bit extreme?" Connor said.

"Extreme, yes," I replied, "but not totally beyond the bounds of possibility. Remember when we were talking about the death of John Lennon? Murdered by a Beatles fan for his own twisted reasons. The word 'fan' is derived from 'fanatic.'"

"Which is why big stars have security around their houses and bodyguards when they go out," Sam Watson said. "Although novel writers don't usually have to go to such extremes."

"What have you taught me to ask, Sam? *Qui Bono.*"

"Who benefits," Connor said.

"Yes. The first question to ask is, who benefits from this crime. Only when I remembered that, did it become clear to me that Noah Carpenter benefited. Not only did his plan work, and Primrose fell into his arms, seeking consolation in her grief after Todd's death, but he killed the man who, in his mind, caused the breakup in the first place. Not a fan, but a rival."

It was very late and at last I was back in my own house, huddled over a cup of hot tea and a warm cat in my own living room. Earlier, I'd stayed with the Peterson family while the police spread throughout and around the house and the investigation began. Noah was hustled away, still proclaiming his devotion to Primrose.

The girl herself, when all the excitement was over, collapsed into her mother's arms, crying. Alerted by the sudden police activity outside their windows, Ralph and Jo Harper ran over to ask if they could be of help. The police agreed that Primrose's statement could wait until morning, and she'd been taken to the Harper house to be put to bed.

"Mom was a total rock star!" Charity exclaimed to her father. "She should take up fencing. Mom, have you ever thought about fencing?" Charity extended her right arm, waved it about, dipped and dogged until her father snapped that this wasn't a joke.

She picked up her ball, tossed it into the air, and caught it as she asked Holly Rankin, "Can I go now? I have a game to get to."

"'Fraid you're going to miss your game," Holly said. "The detectives will have questions. Hey, is that blood on that ball?"

"Yup. Bam! Got him right in the nose!" Charity tossed it from hand to hand. "Game-winning goal."

"In that case, please put that thing down. It's evidence."

Charity gulped and quickly did so. It rolled harmlessly across the floor and came to rest against the staircase.

Mrs. Peterson groaned.

We were sent to the kitchen to cool our heels while the police cordoned off the front hall pending the arrival of the forensics team. Mr. Peterson put the kettle on and got cold drinks out of the fridge for Rosemary and Charity. He added a plate of huge homemade cookies, bursting with chocolate chips. I picked one up and took a bite. My stomach rolled over, and I put it down again, trying not to gag too obviously. Mrs. Peterson noticed but she said nothing.

We cradled our drinks and didn't say much while we waited, listening to the sounds of the police doing what they needed to do at the front of the house.

"I hope," Mrs. Peterson said at last, "they don't leave too much of a mess."

"Is that all you can think of at a time like this, Maureen?" Al said. "Our daughter was in serious danger."

"Nothing came of it, did it? But housework still has to be done."

"I figured that Noah Carpenter was a slimeball all along." Charity's thumbs flew across her phone, alerting all her friends to the developments. "But would Primrose listen to me? No."

"I'll thank you," Al said, "not to go around saying 'I told you so.'"

We didn't have to wait long for Sam Watson to arrive. After taking our initial statements, he said we could leave; he'd speak to us again in the morning. The front hall and the staircase were blocked off, so the family had to go elsewhere for the night. Calls were placed to the other two daughters, Phoebe and Dallas, to ask if they could spend the night at their friends' houses. The rest of the family would go to the home of Mrs. Peterson's parents, who lived not far away. Last of all, I was allowed to leave, and an officer was summoned to drive me home in case I suffered from some residual shock. Sam Watson told me he'd check on me later and take a detailed statement.

When I bid good night to my escort and went into my own kitchen, I found Connor rummaging in the fridge for a snack.

"The food was dreadful at that thing. And even worse, not enough of it." He turned to me with a big smile on his face, a loaf of bread in one hand, and a package of cooked ham in the other. The smile died. "What's happened?"

"Better put the coffee on. It's going to be a long night," I said.

Chapter Twenty-Eight

I slept surprisingly well and woke to sunlight streaming through the ocean-facing windows. I blinked and looked at the clock on the side table.

Eleven o'clock.

I threw off the covers and rolled out of bed. My stomach rolled over separately from the rest of my body.

"I called Bertie and told her you'd be in late," Connor said from the doorway. "Coffee's on. Can I get you one?"

"I don't feel like coffee for some reason. Cup of tea?"

"Coming right up."

I went into the bathroom and studied my haggard face in the mirror. The item I'd bought yesterday at the drug store was still in my purse. I decided to worry about that later.

By the time I'd showered, washed my hair, and dressed for work, I was feeling considerably better. Connor was sitting at the dining room table, phone and mug of coffee beside him, typing on his work laptop. He gave me a smile when I came in. "You okay? Ready for breakfast? Muesli and yogurt do?"

I kissed him. "I'm okay, but just toast please. I'll get it myself."

"Sam Watson told me to call him when you were up. He'll be here soon."

As I nibbled cautiously on the edges of my toast and sipped at my tea I called Maureen Peterson. I wanted to check on the family, make sure they were recovered from the ordeal, and that the girls, Primrose in particular, were getting any help they might need.

Al Peterson answered his wife's phone. "Thanks for calling, Lucy. We've been allowed back into the house. Maureen's resting."

"How's Primrose?"

"Shook up, but she'll be fine. To my surprise, Charity's been heaping praise on her, telling her she obviously has good instincts because she broke up with Noah initially. Dallas and Phoebe are heartbroken at having missed the action and thus having nothing to tell their friends except secondhand. Rosemary is acting out all the drama for anyone who will listen. According to Rosemary, she single-handedly saved us all."

I laughed to hear it. "You have good daughters, Al."

"I do. We have good neighbors too. Jo Harper is here making lunch, and Ralph's offered to run any errands we need. I've taken the rest of the week off work. Detective Watson came by earlier, and took detailed statements from us all. Hard to deal with, sometimes. We invited that boy into our home. Let him make friends with our daughter."

"Try not to dwell on that," I said. "All's well that ends well."

Of course, it hadn't ended well for Todd Harrison. Noah told us he killed Todd; he even said it hadn't been an accident, but if he denied it to the police, our statements wouldn't be enough.

Charles heard a car in the driveway before I did. I opened the door to see Detective Watson climbing the steps, followed by Butch.

"I'm pleased to see you up and about, Lucy," Watson said as Butch gave me a quick, and highly unprofessional, hug.

Connor came in from the dining room. "Coffee?"

"Sure," the police officers said.

"Go on through and grab a seat," Connor said. "Lucy too, and I'll bring the coffee. More tea, honey?"

"No, thanks. I've had enough."

We made ourselves comfortable in the living room. The big windows showed a blue sky and a blue ocean, white-tipped waves rushing to shore. The beach was busy today.

A seagull perched on the deck railing. Charles sat on the window seat, watching it.

"This time," Watson said, as he accepted a steaming mug from Connor, "we can't blame Lucy for putting herself in danger. You had no idea Noah Carpenter would show up at the Peterson house at the exactly the right or, I should say, wrong time."

"True. At first, I wasn't even thinking of him. I thought Todd's killer was one of those overly keen fans. A true fanatic, which obviously Noah was not. He didn't come to our house those nights to grieve or even to play at being a Frightener, but to show Primrose how kind and sympathetic he was. I totally failed to notice the significance of that. A couple of times he showed some possessiveness toward her, trying to separate her from her friends, but I thought nothing of it. I suppose I assumed he just wanted some alone time with her. Which, of course, he did, but it went deeper than I'd imagined. A lesson for me for the next time."

Connor groaned at the words "next time," and I gave him a smile before continuing. "I went to the Petersons' house, hoping that once she thought it over, Primrose might be able to give me an idea of who among her crowd would have been so upset or angry at Todd they'd kill him. I would have taken that name to you. Promise."

"Walk me though what happened, Lucy," Watson asked. "Step by step."

I did so. No one interrupted except for a few startled gasps when I described Charity's skill with a soccer ball and Mrs. Peterson's talents with an umbrella. When I finished, Connor asked, "Has the boy confessed, Sam?"

"Yeah, he has. In the car taking him to the station he was raving about how Primrose threw him over for that old guy—his words, not mine—who she didn't even know. He, Noah, needed to give Todd Harrison a taste of his own medicine. Noah is a minor, and he said all of that without benefit of council and without a parent present. His parents are arranging a lawyer for him now, and I'll be speaking to Noah when the lawyer arrives. It's my experience that when a man, no matter what age he is, commits a crime to either impress a woman or with the intention of getting her to favor him again, he can't keep quiet about it."

"We men are fools for love." Connor put his hand on mine, and I gave it a squeeze.

Butch chuckled. I guessed he was remembering the first time he met Steph. They'd hated each other on sight.

"Whatever he says," Watson said, "we'll get him. I had officers making calls this morning. Noah and his family moved to Nags Head about two years ago. Before that they lived near Greensboro. The high school Noah went to has an archery club, and Noah was a member of that club."

"That is worth knowing," I said.

"I've been to the Carpenter home. His parents are being polite and cooperative, although they're deeply shocked. His mother told me Noah brought his archery things with him when they moved, but he didn't take up the sport again. She thought everything had been thrown out, sold, or stuffed into the back of a closet. But . . ."

"But . . ." I prompted.

"Their house backs onto a wooded area. We're searching those woods now, and I got a call a short while ago to say evidence has been found indicating arrows have recently been fired at the trees. The evidence, I must point out, is not conclusive—not yet—and nothing but circumstantial. But . . ."

"But," I said, "it's all part of putting together the puzzle."

Watson finished his coffee. He stood up. He cleared his throat. "While we're here," he said. "I have some personal news I want to share."

"Go ahead," Connor said.

"I don't like the sound of that," I said.

"I won't say the chief paying any attention to what that fool Heather Harrison had to say, and ordering me away from Lucy, was the cause, but it might have been the impetus I needed. CeeCee's making not very subtle suggestions it's time I retired, and I've been mulling it over for some time. I handed in my notice of intention to retire yesterday afternoon. Not long before I got the call summoning me to the Petersons' residence."

I leaped to my feet and wrapped him in a hug. "I am going to miss you so much."

He gave me a hesitant squeeze back. "I'm not going anywhere, Lucy. CeeCee and I are staying right here. I might do some fishing, though. Interested in joining me, Connor?"

"For sure." Connor held out his hand, and Watson shook it.

Butch was smiling. "We'll all miss him, but it's a mighty well-deserved retirement."

"Does the chief have any thoughts about a replacement?" Connor asked.

"He has a candidate in mind. A good one. I think you'll approve, Your Honor."

I glanced at Butch. "Not me," my friend said. "I'm not ready yet, and not entirely sure I want the job. I like being on the road."

Connor's phone rang. He glanced at it. "It's my office. I'm going to take this. I told her not to call if it wasn't important."

"Obviously, I'll be following the Carpenter case to the end," Watson said as we headed for the door. "I'll keep you posted."

"Hold up." Connor put his phone away. He was grinning. "Heather Harrison has put out a statement on social media. She's withdrawing from the race for the party nomination. Something about being so deep in grief she's unable to give the campaign the focus and attention it needs."

"I totally forgot to tell you what I learned yesterday," I said. "I'm pretty sure I know why Todd came to see me that night." I filled the men in quickly on what Layla had told me.

"Someone was threatening to blackmail Heather?" Connor said.

"Either that or for some reason she wanted her husband to think so. I suspect the former. Her PA, Layla, gave me all the dirt. Everything Layla heard was from the other side of a closed door, when Heather thought she'd left for the day, so take it with a grain of salt. But essentially, what Layla heard was Heather telling Todd someone was threatening to reveal that when Heather had her podcast, she was on the verge of exposing a congresswoman's career-ending misdeeds. Instead, she took a bribe to keep quiet."

"Is that true?" Connor asked.

"She denied it to Todd."

"Why would someone blackmail Heather over it? Rather than the congresswoman?"

"The congresswoman resigned shortly after. Making the blackmail material worthless. So, if it is true, the blackmailer likely turned to a secondary, shall we say, victim."

"Sounds like a hard thing to prove," Butch said. "And not all that serious in the scheme of things. Unless the original act was illegal. Was it? It is a crime to cover up an illegal activity."

"Not illegal, but unethical," I said.

"Probably enough to scupper Heather's political ambitions," Connor said. "The info doesn't even have to be made public to do its damage. Heather is not her party's preferred candidate for the seat; they'll be more than happy to have a reason to order her to withdraw. Which appears to be what happened. Either they got the info, or she realized she was about to be toast in any event, so she took the high road and quit."

"Can't say I'm sorry to hear that," Watson said.

"We'll never know, not for sure, but I believe that's what Todd wanted to talk to me about the night he died. At the library meeting, before I arrived, someone told him I'm a part-time PI—"

Connor choked.

Watson said, "What?"

"Yeah, right. Me, Samantha Spade. Todd likely didn't know whether or not to believe Heather's claim of innocence, so he wanted to look further into it. If she had taken money in exchange for her silence, that puts a whole new spin on what might otherwise be brushed off as not a big deal. Enter local gumshoe, who has some peripheral relationship with regional-area politics."

"That," Connor said firmly, "is not a rumor I ever want to hear again."

Chapter Twenty-Nine

Once the police left, Connor and I (and Charles) headed for work. Because he was a juvenile, Noah's name was not being publicized for the killing of Todd, but word was out that an arrest had been made.

When I got to the library, I told my coworkers, in confidence, what happened last night. That done, when I finally settled down to work, I didn't get much done. I spent what remained of the day in a bit of a daze.

Sam Watson phoned me late in the afternoon with an update. In the presence of his father and his lawyer, Noah Carpenter admitted he'd been following Todd Harrison for some time, waiting for an opportunity to—in his words—confront the author. Noah's mother rarely, to the point of almost never, drove her car, and Noah had tossed his long-forgotten archery equipment into the trunk. He said he'd been inspired by Todd's mention of learning archery to try the sport out again. He didn't say what he wanted to try it out on.

The night in question, Noah drove to Todd's house. Todd's car was in the driveway, but Mrs. Harrison's was not, so he assumed the author was at home alone. He was working up his courage to confront Todd, to accuse him of turning young people's minds against their friends through his books, when the author left the house, got into his car, and drove away. Noah followed Todd to South Old Oregon Inlet Trail Road and saw him park and be admitted to a house. Noah crept around the back, hoping to catch Todd doing . . . something. When Detective Watson asked him why he'd gone to the trouble of taking the bow and arrows out of the trunk, Noah calmly said, "I figured it was up to me to give the guy a taste of his own medicine. What's that saying? 'Live by the sword, die by the sword.' Too bad for him." At that point the lawyer finally managed to get Noah to stop talking, and the interview concluded.

"Creepy," I said.

"Yes," Watson said. "Creepy indeed. I suspect you did more good than you realize in this case, Lucy. If Noah Carpenter had been allowed to get away with believing he could kill someone who, in his mind, had stopped him from getting what he wanted, even inadvertently, I hate to think where that might have led."

"Did we stop a serial killer in the making?"

"Perhaps. From what you've told us, Lucy, if not a serial killer, he was heading for a future of domestic abuse. It all starts with separating the object of your affection, meaning the one you want under your control, from friends and family. Todd was beginning to do that to Primrose. I'll keep you posted on any fresh developments."

At closing time, Bertie called us all to the main area of the library. While waiting for the others to arrive, I glanced around the room. The crowded shelves, the silent computers, the comfortable chairs. Row upon row of books. At quiet times like this, I often like to imagine my favorite literary characters kicking back and chatting after a long tiring day of being read.

What would they make of us? I wondered. Elizabeth Bennet, Jane Eyre. Captain Ahab. Even Sherlock Holmes. They would be amazed at our technology, our dress, some of our freedoms, perhaps our longevity. But I doubted very much they'd be at all surprised at our daily lives. For good and for bad, life goes on relatively unchanged.

Louise Jane clattered down the stairs, interrupting my contemplation, and the rest of the staff soon gathered.

Charles settled on the computer table in order to take part in the meeting.

"I wanted to take advantage of us all being in the building at the same time," Bertie said. "I've been thinking over the events of the past few days, as I'm sure you all have."

We nodded.

"Here at the Bodie Island Lighthouse Library, we believe, above all else, that literature has the power to change lives. Unfortunately, it would seem as though on occasion that power can be turned to the dark side."

"As can love," Denise said. "But love remains good."

"Nicely said."

"Group hug!" Ronald said.

And Charles agreed.

Chapter Thirty

At last the day of our Young Adult Literary Festival arrived. It was a gorgeous day, sunny and warm, but not too hot. The wind was light and fresh, blowing away any trace of humidity.

Louise Jane had done a great job of organizing all the physical and technical details. A stage had been set up on the lawn, rows of chairs lined up in front of it. Sound equipment had been checked and rechecked. Josie's bakery and the bookstore had erected tents, and they were already doing a brisk business. The clown and the face painter entertained the little kids while excited teens greeted their friends and found themselves seats.

The entire Peterson clan had come and brought Jo and Ralph Harper with them.

I'd taken a few moments to stand by myself, nervously going over in my mind what I hoped to talk about as the moderator of the dystopian fiction panel. On the program it was listed as "Brave New World? Attempting to Find Utopia in Fiction." Over the previous few days, Louise Jane, Theodore and I had decided to broaden our discussion to include books such as *1984*, *The Hunger Games*, and *Station Eleven*, along with the great classic *Brave New World*.

"Got a moment, Mrs. McNeil?"

I looked up to see Primrose Peterson standing in front of me. She looked good, I thought. Eyes bright, color in her cheeks, dressed in denim shorts and one of her Todd Harrison T-shirts. I hadn't spoken to her since the night of Noah's attack.

"Of course," I said. "How are you doing?"

"Good. Real good. I wanted you to know Mom's got me seeing a therapist. About Noah, I mean."

"That's . . . good."

"The funny thing is, I was never that keen on him. I didn't stop seeing him because he mocked Todd that night at the library. That was just an excuse to do what I wanted to do in the first place. Dump him, I mean. And then, after Todd's death, he was all supportive-like, giving me a ride to the . . . uh . . . your house, and all. Listening to me talk about how much I loved Todd's books. But it would never have gone beyond that, and I figured he'd soon realize it. I never for a minute thought he'd . . . kill someone for me." Her eyes filled with tears.

I was glad Primrose was getting professional help. It must be a heavy burden indeed to know someone died because of you, even though you bore no responsibility whatsoever.

"Noah's asked to see me. My therapist says absolutely not." She wiped at her eyes and then gave me a weak smile. "As though Mom or Dad would even consider letting me go."

"That's for the best," I said.

"The therapist talks a lot about obsession and how to recognize when someone—a boy, I mean—is being more than just jealous or wanting to spend time alone with you. But to know when . . . it's not right. She tells me to trust my instincts in those cases. If it doesn't seem right, it's not."

I put my hand lightly on her arm. "Wise words." I was sorry Primrose had been forced to learn such a difficult lesson at her young age. "I hope you're coming to our panel on dystopian fiction. Even in matters that have nothing to do with love or romantic relationships, we need to learn that when something doesn't seem right, it probably isn't."

"Cool. Oh gosh. Is that Jacob Rose over there?"

I turned to see her pointing at a tall, thin man with a neatly trimmed goatee, dressed in a blue-and-white-checked shirt and jeans, talking to Ronald.

"Yes, it is."

"I'd love to meet him. Can you introduce me, Lucy? Wait—let me buy a book first, so he can sign it." She turned and ran away, hair streaming behind her. Jolene, a girl I recognized from the Todd Harris fan club, joined her, and they skipped together to the bookstore booth.

I smiled to myself.

Primrose Peterson would be okay.

* * *

I spotted Heather Harrison picking her way across the grass. She was alone, dressed plainly in white capris, a polka-dotted linen shirt, and huge sunglasses. She took a seat in the back row, folded her hands together, and sat quietly. Ronald approached her, and they spoke briefly. She shook her head, and he left her.

"Looks like it's going to be a nice day," Bill Pratchett said to me.

"Good weather always helps at an outdoor event," I replied.

"I have news. The publisher has taken Todd's manuscript and found a top-notch writer to finish it off. They agreed to an advance far more than even I was expecting, so the promotion budget is going to be huge. You'll want to stock it in your library."

"I can only hope it doesn't mean a revival of his fan clubs," I said.

He laughed. "I see Heather's here. I'll go and say hi."

Bertie climbed onto the stage, tapped the mic, and said "Can everyone hear me?"

Those seated yelled, "Yes," while everyone else rushed to find a chair. Bertie acknowledged Todd's absence and paid tribute to him. She introduced Heather, who stood up and thanked Bertie for her kind words and sat down again. Connor welcomed everyone on behalf of the town and left the stage.

"He keeps it short," a woman behind me said. "I like that in a politician."

And the program began.

The day was a huge success, and we were absolutely thrilled.

Both Ruth and Shannon were well received, Jacob Rose was a big hit, and Lorraine and her band had people up and dancing in the aisles. The audience seemed to enjoy our panel discussion. I shouldn't have had to worry about getting Louise Jane and Theodore Kowalski to talk about books. The problem was bringing the discussion to an end. Louise Jane managed to keep her focus entirely on the topic at hand, but as soon as it was over and she left the stage, she made a break for the parking lot and leapt into a waiting car. Off to her vacation rental, I assumed. Notably the driver of the car didn't get out to join the festivities. That, I thought, might have something to do with the presence of Sam Watson.

Finally it was over, books read from, talks given, stories told, music played. Festivalgoers were streaming toward their cars while others bought yet more books and treats to take home. I was at Josie's bakery booth, trying to snatch one of the last of the day's offerings, when Sam Watson joined me. A woman was with him. She was around my age, mid-thirties, a good six feet tall, racehorse thin, dark skinned, short haired, with large, piercing dark eyes.

"Lucy McNeil, I'd like you to meet Rhonda Thomas." He didn't need to say anything more for me to know who this must be. "Detective Thomas is joining us from New Orleans. She's working alongside of me for the next while, and she will take over fully when I leave. Rhonda, Lucy works here, at the library."

I held out my hand. "Pleased to meet you."

She shook my hand in return. Her grip, I thought, was stronger than it needed to be.

"Great day, Lucy," Sam said. "One of the things I'm most looking forward to about my retirement is having time to finally settle into a serious book. I'm going to start with *1984*. CeeCee's waving to me. I'm sure I'll see you around."

He left us. I smiled at the new detective. She did not smile in return. "I've heard you've helped Detective Watson on some of his cases."

"I've tried to do what little I've been able to," I said modestly.

"Don't let that habit continue. I do not take orders, advice, or assistance from civilians." The dark eyes bored into mine. "Do you understand?"

"Uh . . ." I gulped. "Yes. I understand."

"Glad to hear it." She walked away without another word.

Chapter Thirty-One

Connor and I drove separately to the library because he'd been asked to pop around to his parents' house on the way home. Something about a leaking tap.

All day, as well as trying to enjoy the festival, I'd been gathering my courage around me. On the way home, I stopped at the store for two items. For the next hour I paced nervously, while Charles watched. A few weeks ago, I'd tried my hand at making my Aunt Ellen's recipe for beef stew and put it in the freezer. It waited on the counter for Connor to get home, when I'd pop it into the oven. I'd managed to score two coconut cupcakes from Josie's bakery booth for our dessert.

Eventually, I heard his car in the driveway, his footsteps on the stairs, his key in the lock.

My husband, my handsome, kind, charming, adorable husband, came into the house. He gathered me into his arms and kissed me.

When we separated, he said, "Leak fixed. Dad's back's been acting up, so Mom wouldn't let him crawl under the sink, fearing he'd get stuck. Thus the call to me. It was a great day, Lucy. You and the library outdid yourselves. I was pleased Heather Harrison came and equally pleased she didn't try to grandstand. Everyone in the political world is speculating about her withdrawing from the race. No one thinks it's because of her husband's death, but I haven't heard word of the real reason. If she can bide her time, wait it out, I suspect we'll see her back on the scene someday."

"Would you like a drink?" I asked.

"Thanks. Beer'd be good."

"I have something better than beer."

"Better than beer? Yeah, okay, that'll be good."

I took the two bottles I bought earlier out of the fridge, and two of the crystal champagne flutes we'd been given as wedding gifts down from a top shelf. I opened the first bottle and poured a glass of clear, bubbling liquid. I tossed a dish cloth over the top of the other bottle and twisted and turned until the cork popped. I then poured the clear, bubbling liquid from the second bottle into the second glass, which I handed to Connor.

I took the first glass and lifted it in the air.

He looked at the bottle. Sparkling water.

He looked at the other bottle. Champagne.

His mouth fell open. He struggled for words. Eventually he croaked, "Lucy?"

"Congratulations." I drank my water.

Author's Note

The Bodie Island Lighthouse is a real historic lighthouse, located in the Cape Hatteras National Seashore on the Outer Banks of North Carolina. It is still a working lighthouse, protecting ships from the Graveyard of the Atlantic, and the public is invited to tour it and climb the 214 steps to the top. The view from up there is well worth the trip. But the lighthouse does not contain a library, nor is it large enough to house a collection of books, offices, staff rooms, two staircases, and even an apartment.

Within these books, the interior of the lighthouse is the product of my imagination. I like to think of it as my version of the TARDIS, from the TV show *Doctor Who*, or Hermione Granger's beaded handbag: far larger inside than it appears from the outside.

I hope it is large enough for your imagination also.

Author's Note

Acknowledgments

I loved learning about modern archery for this book. Thanks to Janice from XQuest Archery in Ottawa, Ontario, for sharing her boundless enthusiasm for the sport, for patiently answering my questions, helping set the scene, and making recommendations for the type of equipment the characters used.

Thanks to my agent, Kim Lionetti, for continuing to love this series and to all the marvelous people at Crooked Lane (especially Rebecca Nelson and Matt Martz) for keeping it going. Big thanks in particular to Sandy Harding for all her suggestions as to how to make the book better, and for fixing all my errors and missteps.

To my online buddies at Mystery Lovers Kitchen and Cozy Mystery Crew. The strongest support networks an author can have.

Most of all, my thanks to all the readers who continue to love this series and support it. It's that love and encouragement that gets me sitting (or standing rather) at my desk (or countertop) every day. Cozy readers really are the best!

Changes are afoot for Lucy and Connor and the gang. Here's hoping you'll tune in to find out what's up next for them all.